HELL IS COMIN' TO CALL

After a few moments, Leach expressed what they were all thinking. "Don't look like there's nobody home but the little lady and the young'un. We'd best wait a few minutes more to make sure her old man ain't settin' by the fire."

"Maybe he's off ridin' with that posse, lookin' for us," Snake said, amused by the thought.

"Yeah," Roach said, grinning, "that'd be somethin', wouldn't it?" Turning to Leach, he urged, "Ain't nobody else around. Let's go on down and pay our respects."

"Now don't go off half-cocked till we see for sure there ain't no rifle pointed at us," Leach said. "We'll just ride up nice and neighborly till we see what's what."

Even as he spoke, h̶e̶ ̶k̶n̶e̶w̶ was probably wasted. B̶ ̶ his nostrils caught the v̶aged an old woma̶ her husband and th̶ ̶ ̶ ̶ ̶ ̶ ̶beside her . . .

DEVIL'S KIN

Charles G. West

A SIGNET BOOK

SIGNET
Published by New American Library, a division of
Penguin Group (USA) Inc., 375 Hudson Street,
New York, New York 10014, USA
Penguin Group (Canada), 10 Alcorn Avenue, Toronto,
Ontario M4V 3B2, Canada (a division of Pearson Penguin Canada Inc.)
Penguin Books Ltd., 80 Strand, London WC2R 0RL, England
Penguin Ireland, 25 St. Stephen's Green, Dublin 2,
Ireland (a division of Penguin Books Ltd.)
Penguin Group (Australia), 250 Camberwell Road, Camberwell, Victoria 3124,
Australia (a division of Pearson Australia Group Pty. Ltd.)
Penguin Books India Pvt. Ltd., 11 Community Centre, Panchsheel Park,
New Delhi - 110 017, India
Penguin Group (NZ), cnr Airborne and Rosedale Roads, Albany,
Auckland 1310, New Zealand (a division of Pearson New Zealand Ltd.)
Penguin Books (South Africa) (Pty.) Ltd., 24 Sturdee Avenue,
Rosebank, Johannesburg 2196, South Africa

Penguin Books Ltd., Registered Offices:
80 Strand, London WC2R 0RL, England

First published by Signet, an imprint of New American Library,
a division of Penguin Group (USA) Inc.

First Printing, January 2005
10 9 8 7 6 5 4 3 2 1

For Ronda

Chapter 1

"Lookee yonder, Leach." Ernest Roach waited for his two companions to catch up. When Leach and Snake pulled up on either side of him, Roach pointed, directing their gaze toward the modest cabin at the foot of the hill.

Leach didn't say anything for a moment or two while he looked the tiny homestead over. The cabin looked to be two or three years old. There was a small barn built off to one side, open on both ends, with a corral attached. "One horse and one mule," he commented to himself.

"Damn! Look at that!" Roach broke into his thoughts, and Leach turned to follow the direction of Roach's gaze. He immediately saw the cause of his companion's excitement. A young woman emerged from the barn, walking briskly toward the cabin. A toddler trailed along behind, holding onto his mother's skirt as she stepped around the larger puddles, trying to hurry to get out of the rain.

"One horse and one mule," Leach repeated, this time loud enough for the others to hear.

"And one cow," Snake interjected dryly, having noticed the animal's head appear at the barn entrance.

All three were silent then, waiting to see if the man of the house would then appear. After a few moments, Leach expressed what they were all thinking. "Don't look like there's nobody home but the little lady and the young'un." He removed his wide-brim hat and flung some of the water from it before replacing it on his head. "We'd best watch for a few minutes more to make sure her old man ain't settin' by the fire."

"Hellfire," Roach replied, anxious to get a closer look at the woman. "What if he is? We can take care of him right quick."

"Maybe he's off ridin' with that posse, lookin' for us," Snake said, amused by the thought.

"Yeah," Roach said, grinning at the half-breed, "that'd be somethin', wouldn't it?" Turning to Leach, he urged, "Ain't nobody else around. Let's go on down and pay our respects."

Leach didn't reply, having come to the same conclusion. He gave his horse a kick and started off through the poplars toward the foot of the hill. He didn't speak until halfway down, when he reined up momentarily to issue some words of restraint. "Now don't go off half cocked till we see for sure there ain't no rifle pointed at us," he said. "We'll just ride up nice and neighborly till we see what's what." Even as he spoke, he knew his warning was probably wasted. Roach went crazy anytime his nostrils caught the scent of a woman. He had even ravaged an old woman a couple of days before—with her husband and three young'uns lying dead beside her.

Inside the cabin, Sarah removed her woolen shawl, and shook some of the water from it before draping it across the back of a chair near the fireplace. Using her skirt for a towel, she dried her son's hair and face. Holding the child at arm's length, she smiled at him. "You'd just as soon stay out there in the rain and splash around in the mud, wouldn't you?" The child giggled as she playfully ruffled his hair. "You're just like your father." The comment caused her to pause and think of her husband. Jordan had only been gone for two days, but it seemed like a week. She tried never to let him know how frightened she was when he was away from the cabin. When she was growing up on her father's farm, there had always been a lot of people around: her family, the hired hands, her mother's maid. Now there were only the three of them, and sometimes she would not see anyone else for weeks at a time. The isolation never seemed to bother her husband. In fact, he thrived on it.

Her thoughts were interrupted when she heard the horse nicker. Thinking that maybe Jordan was returning, she went to the door and looked out. What she saw immediately troubled her. Three men were filing down the slope, their yellow slickers glistening in the rain. She didn't recognize any of them, and alarming thoughts sprang to mind at once. Just two days before, the Thompson family had been massacred. Sheriff Winston Moffett had sent his young deputy to fetch Jordan to join a posse to search for the murderers. Jordan had been reluctant to leave Sarah and Jonah alone, but felt he had an obligation to the community.

She didn't like it when Jordan was away, fearing the possibility of incidents like the one facing her now. Feeling her heart pounding in her chest, she went to the cupboard and took a single-action revolver from the top shelf. With the pistol in her skirt pocket, she returned to the door, little Jonah clinging to her leg.

"Mind your manners, boys," Leach warned as the three men approached the house. Although the cabin door was opened only a crack, he could see the woman standing there watching them. *With a gun in her hand if she's got any sense,* he thought. Slow walking their horses, the three rode up before the cabin, halting a few yards from the door. "Hello the cabin," Leach called out. "Anybody home?" He glanced over at Roach and shot him a warning frown. Roach was fairly fidgeting with anticipation. "We're ridin' with the posse, lookin' for them outlaws. We could sure use a cup of coffee if there's any to spare."

His words were far from reassuring to Sarah. She was tempted to simply make no reply, hoping they would then ride away. But she knew they had seen her peering out the crack of the door. Finally she responded, her voice trembling with fright, "I'm afraid we can't ask you inside." She hesitated, searching her mind for something that might persuade them to leave. "We're sick. I think it may be the pox."

Certain now that there was no one else inside but the woman and her child, Leach dismounted. Snake and Roach followed suit. "Ain't no need for you to be concerned, ma'am. We're just checkin' on folks in this part of the valley, makin' sure you're all right."

"We're all right," Sarah quickly replied. Then remembering what she had just said, she added, "We're just sick is all. I'm sorry I can't invite you in for coffee."

"Is that a fact?" Leach responded. "Well, this looks like your lucky day. Roach here is a doctor. He'll be glad to take a look atcha." With a nod of his head, he motioned toward the cabin wall.

Roach understood. Grinning widely, he moved to a position to the right of the door and inched his way closer, while Leach continued to engage Sarah in conversation. With another silent motion, Leach directed Snake to move around to the back of the cabin. Then he took a couple of steps toward the door.

Certain now that the strangers meant to do her harm, Sarah took the pistol from her skirt pocket and cocked it. Her hand trembling, she held it before her. "I'm afraid I must ask you to leave," she said as bravely as she could manage, but unable to keep her voice from quaking. "My husband should be here at any minute," she added.

Seeing the barrel of the pistol now protruding a few inches through the partially opened door, Leach stopped. He gave Roach a nod. "Now look here, lady. There ain't no call to point a gun at me. We just wanna get out of the rain for a while."

"Please leave," Sarah pleaded, her voice without all pretense of bravado, the hand holding the revolver trembling perceptively.

She had no sooner uttered the words than Roach suddenly grabbed the barrel of the weapon and wrenched it from her hand. Following Roach's move, Leach quickly stepped forward and grabbed Sarah's arm before she could slam the door. "Come on out here, missy, and let's have a look atcha," he crowed as he kicked the door open and hauled her violently out into the rain. With little Jonah clinging to her skirt and screaming with fright, she fell to her knees in the mud, reaching instinctively for her son. She drew the terrified child up close to her in a vain effort to protect him, knowing their fate was in the hands of God.

"Damn!" Roach exclaimed, fairly salivating in his anticipation and delighted with his prize. "She's a real looker, ain't she?" Without hesitating, he reached down and, grabbing her by the bodice of her dress, pulled the struggling woman to her feet. "I'm claiming the first ride on this little filly." With a sharp rap across Jonah's face to quiet the bawling youngster, he started to drag Sarah inside the cabin.

"The hell you say," Leach said, catching him by the arm. After seeing Sarah up close, his desire was as fervent as that of the lustful Roach. "Who the hell said you had the right to have her first?"

Roach, his passion already overheating, tried to jerk his arm free of Leach's grasp. But Leach held him firm. When Roach released his grip on Sarah's bodice in an attempt to shove Leach away, Sarah saw her chance. She grabbed Jonah by the hand and ran for the corral. Locked in a shoving match, Leach and Roach didn't realize she had taken flight before she had scrambled between the rails of the corral.

Having heard the commotion at the front door, Snake turned the corner of the cabin in time to see

Sarah and the child running for the barn. Without hesitation, he raised his rifle and fired, putting two bullets in the fleeing woman's back. Knocked down immediately, Sarah fell sprawling in the muddy slime of the soggy corral and lay still.

Roach was devastated. Arriving beside the body a moment or two behind the half-breed, he bemoaned the lost opportunity. "What the hell did you do that for?" Roach demanded.

Snake shrugged as he stared down at the woman's body, her young son crying at her side as he vainly begged his mother to wake up. "She was trying to run" was Snake's simple explanation.

The absolute senselessness of the killing infuriated Roach. "Why, you dumb son-of-a-bitchin' half-breed, you ain't got no more sense than that. . . ."

"Maybe I shoot you," the stoic half-breed said in reply, gazing at his partner with steady lifeless eyes.

"Well, that would just about fix things up proper, wouldn't it?" Leach stood gazing down at the dead woman, her son now wailing in terror. "Somebody shut that young'un up."

Without a moment's hesitation, Snake swung his rifle, catching the unsuspecting child beside his temple with the barrel. The force of the blow knocked Jonah several feet away, where he then lay as still as his mother.

"Well, I reckon you shut him up all right," Roach said sarcastically, still frustrated by the somber half-breed's lack of constraint.

"What was you aimin' to do?" Snake replied coldly. "Take him to raise?"

"It's done now," Leach said, stepping between the two. "Let's see what we can find and get the hell outta here."

Snake turned and went into the barn while Roach remained standing over the body. "That's just a damn shame," he complained. "That damn Injun just ruined all our fun." He squatted on his heels and pulled Sarah's skirt up.

"You aimin' to jump on a dead woman?" Leach wanted to know.

"Hell no," Roach at once retorted. "I'm just lookin' at what I missed. Damn"—he sighed in frustration—"she was a pretty thing."

Leach shrugged, figuring they had wasted enough time. "They all look pretty much alike with their clothes off. Let's get going."

Just then, Snake came out of the barn, carrying a shotgun. Holding it up, he said, "This is what she was runnin' for—found it hid in the hay rack." He walked over to the horse to get a closer look. "Pretty good horse," he decided. "Wanna take it with us?"

Leach hesitated for a moment before answering, "Nah, I reckon not. If we happen to run into that posse, we don't wanna be riding with this feller's horse." He turned and started for the cabin. Behind him, Snake removed a couple of rails from the fence and chased the livestock out. Leach didn't bother to ask the half-breed why. Snake just did whimsical things.

They found little of real value in the tiny cabin. They took what food they could find, as well as Sarah's pistol and a box of cartridges. Snake strapped the shotgun on his horse. "I reckon that's about it,"

Leach commented as he stepped up in the saddle. Snake took a piece of wood from the fireplace and, using it as a torch, touched off a fire in the middle of the cabin, piling on curtains and furniture to give it fuel.

Already mounted, Roach shook his head. "Now what the hell is he doing that for?"

Leach shrugged. "I don't know. It's the Injun in him, I reckon."

Jordan Gray stood transfixed, staring vacantly at the lifeless bodies of his wife and son. Oblivious to the cold, steady rain that beat down upon his face, he felt as helpless as he ever had in his entire life. Stunned, his brain refused to function for what seemed an eternity, until finally, drained of all energy, he dropped to his knees in the muddy corral. Tears streamed down his rough cheeks as he gently lifted his wife's face from the wet mud and held her head with one hand while he struggled out of his coat. Laying her head carefully upon the coat, he paused a moment to wipe the filth away from her cheek before moving several yards away to gather up the body of his son.

Jordan had never been one to waste time wondering about the why of things. Unlike her husband, Sarah Gray had always held a certain fascination for why things happened the way they did. She had often sat out under the stars at night, trying to imagine what part she and her little family had to play in God's great plan for all the creatures of his universe. In contrast, Jordan never gave things like that much thought. He seriously doubted that a grand plan even existed. All his life, since being orphaned at age ten, he had known only one religion that produced any definable results, and that was hard work. And to feed and clothe his family required practicing that religion from sunup to past dark in the fields he had cleared. He never let his mind dwell upon whether or not his lot in life was fair. It was all he had ever known, and if he thought about it at all, it was just to be grateful that he had a strong back to do the work.

For the past four years, he had had a reason to work even harder. The only miracle he had ever known in his life was when Sarah accepted his proposal of marriage, and never a day passed that he had not marveled at the wonder of it. One year to the day after they exchanged vows, Jonah was born. Sarah had wanted to name their son after her father in hopes of appeasing the old man somewhat for going against his wishes and marrying one of his hired hands. At least, that was what Jordan supposed. Jonah Wheeler had begrudgingly offered forty acres of his farm as a wedding present, but Jordan had politely refused, preferring to start a new life with indebtedness to no man. Sarah cheerfully supported her husband's pride, and bade her mother and father goodbye as she and Jordan rode off to find land of their own. It had been a hard four years, but they had been the only happy years of Jordan Gray's life. Hardly a day had passed during that time when he did not marvel at his good fortune. Sarah was his life.

Now, kneeling in the muddy quagmire of his corral, created by six days of steady rain, and holding the bodies of his wife and son wrapped in his coat and pressed close to him, he felt the fatal results of his pride. He clenched his eyes tightly closed, grimacing with the pain he felt when he pictured Sarah's final moments. From the marks left in the mud, he could see that she had attempted to make a run for the barn and was shot down halfway across the small corral. Her murderers didn't waste a bullet on little Jonah, simply knocking him in the head as he must have cried out for his mother. Unable to contain his grief as these horrible images flooded his brain, Jordan looked up to the leaden skies and cried out his pain. He had not been there when they needed him most. The irony of the situation increased his agony tenfold. He had been away with a posse, looking for outlaws who had raided another isolated farm two days before, leaving a family of five dead. If he had stayed at home, Sarah and Jonah might still be alive.

As he looked around him now, his world seemed dead, gray as the dingy clouds hanging low overhead. The smoldering ashes of the cabin he had built were in the final stages of life as the steady rain patiently extinguished each lonely spark. The barn was still standing, but the livestock were gone. The only things left to him were his rifle and his horse. There was some money he had been saving to purchase another fifty acres near the river—if the raiders had not discovered his hiding place and dug it up. Everything else was gone. Suddenly the thought struck him that he hated the sight of this place, and he wanted to be away from it. All meaning to his life would be buried with his wife and son.

It was almost sunup by the time he finished digging

the grave on the little hill behind the cabin. This was Sarah's favorite spot to gaze at the stars, out from under the huge poplars that shaded the little cabin in summer. *She'll always be able to look up at the stars,* he thought as he gently lowered the tiny body of his son to rest beside her. He stood back to look up into the dark sky, which was already melting into lighter shades of gray in anticipation of the sunrise. It had stopped raining sometime during the night. He had not taken notice of the exact moment as he had steadily worked at his grim task. Parting clouds overhead held promise of a clear day, suggesting that the long rainy spell might be over. The signs were lost on him. It no longer mattered that he was late in the spring plowing.

His tears exhausted, he was forced to choke back a dry sob as he began to shovel the saturated earth into the open grave. "I'm sorry, honey," he blurted, unable to contain his grief when the first wet shovelful fell heavily upon her feet. Even though he knew she was no longer there, he could not bear to cover her with dirt. Vivid images of her radiant face raced through his mind, and he backed away from the grave, trying to control his emotions. Knowing it had to be done, he took hold of the shovel again and set to his grim chore.

The dismal task finished, only then did he give thought to the immediate demands of the living. His mind already overburdened with the guilt of not having been there to protect his family, he felt another stab of guilt when he realized that he had not unsaddled his horse. The poor beast had stood uncomplaining all night. Jordan quickly pulled the saddle off and led the chestnut gelding to the barn. He left it there with a portion of oats while he returned to look through the ashes of the house.

The fire had pretty much destroyed everything, but Jordan continued to search for anything that might have come through unscathed. Lifting a charred timber that had been the cabin's ridge pole, he caught a glimpse of something shiny in the ashes beneath it. Brushing away the ashes, he reached down to retrieve a broken length of silver chain. Standing up again, he carefully wiped the chain on his shirt. It had held a small heart-shaped locket. The locket had been his wedding present to Sarah. He dropped the chain into his pocket and began sifting through the ashes in hopes of finding the locket. After half an hour with no luck, he gave up. It was useless to continue searching the ruins of his life. Everything was gone. Suddenly feeling totally exhausted, it occurred to him that he had not slept in two days. He walked back to the barn, sat down against the side of it, and closed his eyes for a few minutes. A few minutes turned into several hours, as he drifted off into a deep sleep.

He was awakened by the sun shining through the open end of the barn. A new day, it would go unappreciated by the man as he set his mind for what he had to do. He had no notion as to whom or how many he must hunt—only that hunt them he would, if it took the rest of his life.

Sheriff Winston Moffett was not in a good mood. He was late for breakfast, and that always served to put him in a foul mood. His deputy, young Johnny Spratte, had failed to show up for work that morning, and

Winston didn't like to leave the jail unattended when there was a prisoner in one of the two cells. When seven thirty came and passed, and Johnny had still not shown up, Moffett opened up the cell and roused Ned Tucker from the bunk. Ned hadn't had time to sleep off his drunk, and protested his eviction before the usual time, but Moffett would not relent. His belly was already growling like a catfight about to commence.

Hell, I made it to work on time, he said to himself, thinking about his tardy deputy. *If I can make it, he by God can.* Speculating that Johnny felt justified in coming to work late because he had ridden with the posse, Moffett would be sure to remind his wild young deputy that riding a posse was part of the job. The sheriff had led the posse, and in spite of returning late in the night—and having to lock Ned up—he was at work on time this morning.

Still grumbling to himself, he was about to step up on the wooden walkway that fronted the hotel when he caught sight of a rider approaching from the far end of the street. He paused long enough to identify Jordan Gray, mildly surprised to see the quiet young settler in town after having ridden with the posse for two days. His interest tuned more toward a plate of potatoes and eggs than Jordan Gray's reasons for being in town, the sheriff stepped up on the boardwalk and ambled into the hotel dining room.

Having spotted the sheriff at about the same time Moffett had seen him, Jordan guided his horse directly to the hotel. Still somewhat dazed, he went through the process of dismounting and tying his horse, his motions trancelike, before following the sheriff into the dining room.

"Well, Jordan," Moffett greeted him when he walked in, "I'm surprised to see you here this mornin'. I thought you'd wanna be with that pretty little wife of yours after riding around in the rain for two days."

"Sarah's dead," Jordan answered bluntly. "Jonah, too."

Moffett dropped his fork. "What? Dead? How?" he stammered.

"Murdered," Jordan replied, his words devoid of emotion. "By the same bunch we've been chasin', I reckon."

"Damn!" Moffett muttered, unable to think of an appropriate reply. "Damn," he repeated. "We were lookin' in the wrong end of the valley. They musta doubled back on us." Seeing the blank look on Jordan's face, the sheriff wasn't sure what action the bereaved young man expected of him. "I reckon we could get up another posse," he volunteered, glancing at his breakfast rapidly cooling off. In fact, Moffett had been satisfied that he had done all that was required of him in regard to the raid on the Thompson place. He had assumed that the raiders had left the territory, and were consequently out of his jurisdiction. He felt badly for the Thompson family, all five murdered, but he was relieved that he did not have to go up against a gang of ruthless killers. Now this with Jordan Gray, and his eggs were getting stone cold. Feeling a tiny stab of guilt for thinking of his stomach in the face of such tragic news, Moffett realized he must answer the call of his responsibilities.

"How long ago you figure it was?" the sheriff asked, reluctantly pushing his plate away.

Jordan hesitated. "A day or two—I don't know." It occurred to him then that he had not taken the time to look for signs that would even tell him which way the raiders had left when they finished their evil business. He promised himself that he would tuck his emotions away from that point on.

Moffett placed his hand on Jordan's arm, reassuring him. "Don't you worry, son. We'll go after them, soon as I can round up another posse." The implications of Jordan's tragedy began to take hold in the sheriff's mind. Maybe this band of raiders had not left the valley after all. Who might be the next to be hit? His own house was over a half mile from town. "Yes, sir," he decided, "we'd best not waste any more time." Grabbing a biscuit from his plate, he got to his feet.

Outside the hotel, Moffett paused, looking up and down the empty street as if searching for candidates for his posse. "I wonder where the hell Johnny is," he complained. He pulled his watch from a vest pocket and stared at it for a few seconds. It was already half past eight, and still no sign of his deputy. He looked into the expressionless eyes of the man stoically watching him, waiting for some show of action. "It's gonna take me some time to round up some of the boys who rode with us out to the Thompsons'. Why don't you go on back to your place and scout around? And we'll meet you out there."

Jordan didn't react at once as he studied Moffett's face. He was thinking that maybe it had been a waste of time coming to the sheriff for help. He should have scouted around, picked up the raiders' trail, and gone after them while it was still fresh. After a moment, he nodded his head and turned to leave, just as Rufus Bailey unlocked the door of the saloon next door to the hotel. Jordan paused when Rufus walked over to greet them.

"Damn, I'm right sorry to hear that," Rufus said when Moffett related Jordan's tragedy. "I'd volunteer to ride with you, Sheriff, if I wasn't by myself in the saloon until this afternoon when my help comes in."

"I'm lookin' for Johnny," Moffett said. "Was he in the saloon last night?"

Bailey nodded. "Yeah, he came in after you came back, stayed around for about an hour, then lit out for somewhere. He didn't say where."

Moffett shook his head slowly, thinking about his young deputy. "I swear, I mighta made a mistake when I hired that boy," he speculated aloud.

Rufus hesitated for a moment, as if not sure he should say what he was thinking. "It ain't none of my affair, but I'd say Johnny Spratte picks a pretty rough bunch for drinkin' partners. I mean, with him supposed to be a lawman."

This piqued Moffett's interest. "Whaddaya mean?" he asked.

"I mean there was three pretty rough-lookin' fellers passed through here a couple of days ago. You probably saw 'em."

The sheriff nodded. "Johnny said they was with a cattle drive north of town."

"Well, I don't know about that," Rufus replied, shaking his head. "They didn't look like no ranch hands to me. One of 'em looked like a half-breed. I probably shouldn't have even served him any whiskey. I was kinda glad they moved on. Johnny sure seemed to enjoy their company, though."

Moffett, feeling Jordan Gray's eyes on him, spoke in his deputy's defense. "What with the Thompson murders and all, I naturally was curious about any strangers in town, but Johnny said they was all right." He shifted his gaze, avoiding Jordan's eyes. "I'll have a talk with Johnny when he comes in."

Jordan had heard enough, a clear picture already forming in his mind. He remembered that it had been primarily Johnny Spratte directing the posse at the Thompson place. He had been so sure of the direction to search that Moffett had let him lead. The rest of the posse, Jordan included, followed along blindly until it became obvious that there was no trail to follow. Thinking back now, he felt sure it was also Johnny who had insisted that the raiders were long gone from this valley. The thought also occurred to him that there had been no sign of any cattle drive anywhere near Crooked Creek.

Jordan untied his horse and stepped up in the saddle. "I wouldn't wait too long for Johnny." He stared hard at the sheriff. "I don't think he'll be coming to work." That said, he turned the chestnut away from the rail, and rode away.

With his sorrow tucked carefully away in his mind now, Jordan set about his task with a clear head. After a brief visit to the new grave to say a final farewell to the two souls who had completed his world, he turned his thoughts to concentrate on their killers. There was no doubt in his mind that his search was for the three strangers Rufus had talked about. They might be four now. Johnny Spratte was somehow involved. Maybe he had joined them.

Jordan didn't consider himself much of a tracker. He had never had reason to be. But he studied all the tracks and signs he could find around the corral and the ruins of the cabin. He soon found that there were too many tracks, which resulted in telling him nothing beyond the fact that the raiders had ridden their horses back and forth, and all around the cabin. There may have been three horses; there may have been thirty. There was no way he could be sure from the churned-up mud that had been his yard. Feeling the frustration that fueled his anger even more, he walked away from the barn to a distance of about forty yards. Keeping that distance between him and his home, he then began a slow walk in a circle around the barn and the charred remains of his house, his eyes focused on the ground before him. He crossed a fresh set of hoofprints that his horse had left just minutes before as he returned from town. A few yards farther on, he saw the sharp imprint of a deer track. *Heading for what's left of the garden,* he unconsciously observed. Halfway around the circle, he found what he was looking for.

He felt a numbness that shot up the length of his spine as he stood motionless for a few seconds, gazing at the hoofprints in the soft, wet sand of the creek. Looking back toward his cabin, he saw that the tracks were mixed together, telling him that the raiders had ridden single file until coming to the small creek that wound around behind his barn. They had fanned out to cross the creek, leaving three clear sets of tracks. His earlier feelings were strengthened. The murderers of his wife and son were the same three strangers in Rufus Bailey's saloon. This was the only reasonable conclusion.

He knelt down to examine the tracks carefully, looking for any distinguishing markings of the shoes. Prepared to follow the prints into the bowels of hell if necessary, he studied the impressions in the sand intensely. There was nothing he could discover that made any of the tracks remarkable. One of the horses might have a nick in one shoe. He couldn't even be sure of that. Feeling a need to somehow put his hand on the men he hunted, he placed his fingers on one of the prints and gently traced the outline. A surge like lightning shot up his arm; the immense pain he had been struggling to contain would no longer be denied. With clenched teeth and every muscle in his body taunt, he lifted his head toward the heavens and roared out his frustration. It would be the last time he would give in to such an emotional display of his anger. From that point on, he would lock his emotions away, replacing them with a cold, hard determination to hunt down the men who had killed his wife and son.

He rose to his feet again and followed the direction of the hoofprints with his eyes. They were heading for the northwest corner of the wide river valley, away from town, probably to cross the wagon trace to Fort Smith. With a controlled urgency, Jordan returned to the barn. He filled a sack of oats for his horse and dug up the money he had buried under a cornerstone of the cabin. There was nothing else to pack. A change of clothes and his rifle and cartridges were already on his saddle, having been there since he was riding with the posse. He would need to spend some of the money for cartridges. His rifle, an 1866-model Henry, was the only remembrance he had of his father. The old man had bought the rifle in 1868, when he had paid fifty dollars for it. He had bought it from a returning war veteran who had purchased it at a government sale for fourteen dollars and fifty cents. His father had not begrudged the young man for the excessive profit of the sale. A good, dependable rifle, though not an unusually powerful one, it held sixteen shots in its magazine. Jordan had killed many a deer with that rifle.

He paused for a moment to think about his father. Jordan had always supposed his father was a good man. He didn't know for sure, since he was only ten years old when his father was crushed under a giant oak tree while clearing some land for Jonah Wheeler. Since his mother had left them two years prior to that to return to her parents' home in Virginia, Jordan was left an orphan. Jordan felt a begrudging respect for Jonah Wheeler. The man had felt a responsibility toward him, and Jordan owed him for it. After all, he had given the boy a place to live, but after all the years Jordan lived and worked on Jonah's farm, he was never elevated above the status of hired hand. Jordan had never been content to work on a farm. He would have left to seek his fortune in the mountains of the Rockies as soon as he was full grown, but there was one overpowering force that held him there: Jonah Wheeler's daughter, Sarah.

Sarah—a ray of golden sunshine whose smile would always lighten his darkest days. It was Sarah who befriended the orphaned boy when there was no one else for him to turn to. Although her father discouraged it, she and Jordan became close friends, spending a great deal of time together after Jordan's work was done. Thinking about her now, Jordan was forced to smile when he remembered the times she would sneak a piece of cake, or a slice of pie, from the kitchen for him. It was only natural that childhood friendship developed into love as they grew older. In Jordan's case, it was more aptly described as adoration, for he never dreamed Sarah could ever become his wife.

When they went together to tell her father of their intention to marry, the old man at first ordered Jordan off the farm and forbade the union of his only daughter to a hired hand. Had it not been for the intervention of her mother, the young couple might have been forced to elope. As it was, Myra Wheeler was able to persuade her husband to allow a marriage there at the farm, hoping she could at least keep her daughter close to her. When the prideful young man insisted that he would seek land of his own, she persuaded Jonah to offer him part of the farm. Like her daughter, Myra saw a sincere quality that showed a genuine strength of character in the young man. Suddenly shaking his head to rid his mind of thoughts of the past, he looked around him at the sorrowful ending of his marriage. How, he wondered, could he ever be forgiven for this?

He thought about the last time he saw her. She had walked arm in arm with him to his horse, cheerfully going on about the shirt she was going to sew for little Jonah. Smiling warmly, she had kissed Jordan and stood back while he stepped up in the saddle. "I'm going to make you a pie with the last of those apples," she had said. Knowing her well enough to see through her casual facade, he knew she was afraid to be left alone. He didn't want to leave her, but Winston Moffett had sent Johnny Spratte with word that he needed Jordan and his rifle.

Bringing his mind back to Winston Moffett, he felt no necessity to wait for the sheriff to assemble another posse. It would be a waste of time. Without a backward glance, not even a final look at his wife's grave, he stepped up in the saddle and gave the chestnut his heels, guiding the willing gelding toward the road to Fort Smith.

Chapter 2

"Well, I'll be damned," Leach uttered, his words trailing off as he spotted the young man pausing at the swinging doors of the saloon.

Following the direction of Leach's gaze, Roach grinned. "He said he would meet up with us here. I swear, though, I thought it was just the whiskey talkin'. Johnny somethin'—what was it?"

"Spratte," Leach replied, a smirk forming upon his face. "Johnny Spratte—*Deputy Sheriff* Johnny Spratte." The irony of it amused him.

Always the stoic realist, Snake commented dryly, "Maybe he ain't come to join up with us. Maybe he's got that posse right behind him." He set his half-finished glass of beer on the table and rested his hand on the handle of his knife.

Leach gave the half-breed's concerns no credence. He fancied himself a fair judge of a man's character, and he was pretty sure of Johnny's. "He ain't with no posse." He glanced over at Snake. "He's just tired of tryin' to make an honest livin' in a flea-bitten little

24

town, same as you or me—just like he said. Hell, he led that posse off on a wild-goose chase, didn't he?"

"He did at that," Roach chimed in and raised his hand to catch Johnny's attention.

Johnny's face lit up when he spotted the raised hand on the far side of the crowded saloon. He immediately pushed through the doors and made his way across the noisy room.

"Well, now, lookee here," Roach greeted him, a broad smile plastered across his face, "if it ain't the deputy sheriff."

Johnny grinned back. "I told you I'd be comin' to join up with you fellers. This is the third saloon I looked in. I knew you'd be in one saloon or another."

Leach studied the ex-deputy as he pulled up an empty chair, smiling like a kid at Christmastime. When Johnny had seated himself, and signaled the barkeep for a glass of beer, Leach asked, "You think you got sand enough to ride with us?" His eyes now cold and searching, he didn't pause to wait for an answer. "This ain't no Sunday picnic. A man's gotta have a belly full of guts to ride with us."

The smile remained on Johnny's face, although it had lost a considerable amount of its original shine. He realized that all three were now staring at him, sizing him up. Looking from the steady, lifeless eyes of the half-breed to the frozen smile of Roach, he realized that they all questioned his commitment to ride on the other side of the law. Returning his gaze to lock onto Leach's, he said, "I reckon I've got as much sand as it takes."

"You ride with us, and you'll damn sure find out

how much sand you've got. Ain't that right, Snake?" Not waiting for an answer from the somber half-breed, Leach continued to stare the young man down. Shifting his eyes momentarily to the Colt .45 in Johnny's holster, he asked, "You ever use that gun on anything bigger than a snake or a rat?"

Johnny hesitated. He considered lying about it, but Leach's penetrating gaze seemed capable of seeing through a lie. No longer able to match Leach's stone-cold gaze, he shifted his eyes down to the glass of beer before him. "I ain't never had to," he finally answered. "But I reckon I damn sure can."

Leach made no comment for a long moment, his eyes still locked on Johnny's. Then his stone countenance was finally broken by the hint of a grin. "Well, I reckon you'll damn sure get a chance to prove it." The hazing over, he drained the last swallow of beer from his glass. "Won't he, boys?"

"Wouldn't be surprised," Roach commented, his grin back in place. "You might get like ol' chief here"— he nodded toward Snake—"and go outta your way to shoot somebody." Not amused by the comment, the half-breed only grunted in response.

"We take what we want," Leach said. "Sometimes folks get in the way, but that's just their hard luck."

Feeling as if he had been accepted, Johnny relaxed. "That don't bother me none. I'm done with hiring my ass out for twenty dollars a month."

"That's good," Leach said, "'cause you know a little too much about us to back out now." It was a serious threat, even though he was smiling when he said it. That bit of business concluded, Leach proceeded to the next subject on his mind. "It's a good thing you caught up with us when you did 'cause we ain't gonna be here very long. You notice that bank across the street when you walked in here?" Johnny nodded, although he had really paid no attention to what was across the street. Leach continued. "That's the First Mercantile Bank of Fort Smith. When they open in the mornin', we're gonna make a withdrawal."

Johnny's pulse quickened; he was excited by the immediate promise of wealth. He assumed he would be given an equal share of the money, and whatever the amount, it would be a hell of a lot more than his previous twenty-dollar wage. In truth, the only one of his new partners who begrudged a new split in the spoils would be the somber half-breed.

"We was through here last month," Roach said. "They got one old man that opens up ever' morning and two women that come in about thirty minutes later." He chuckled as he added, "They might as well set the money outside the door and let anybody who wants it just pick it up."

"We best keep a sharp eye, though," Leach was quick to warn, lest their new recruit think the bank robbery a virtual cakewalk. "This town's got a mean son of a bitch for a deputy marshal. His name's Jed Ramey, and he's got a reputation for runnin' off all the outlaws that ever set foot in Fort Smith." That said, he added, "That's the reason there ain't no guard at the bank. But we'll have to do our business quick and get the hell outta town." He paused to gauge Johnny's reaction. "How's that sound to you?"

"Sounds just right to me," Johnny answered with a cocky grin. "Count me in."

Leach nodded, then glanced at his other partners briefly before reminding the newest member of his little gang. "In for a penny, in for a pound—if the goin' gets rough, you'd best be willin' to use that gun you're wearin'. If you don't, Snake here might cut out your gizzard." Leach's face was dead serious for a few long moments before breaking into a smile, as if he were joking.

The half-breed did not smile, looking at Johnny with a cold stare. "Maybe I cut it out, anyway," he said.

"Maybe you ought to try," Johnny responded, his hand dropping to rest on the handle of his pistol. He was unsure of the belligerent attitude exhibited by the sullen half-breed, but he knew better than to let Snake intimidate him.

Snake simply grunted, unimpressed by the ex-deputy's show of bravado. Leach and Roach both laughed, accustomed to the sour disposition of their half-Choctaw partner. "Don't let ol' Snake buffalo you," Roach said. "He's always got briars in his britches."

The brief tension of the moment over, Johnny relaxed, relieved that he had not been challenged in earnest. "Why, sure," he blustered, "no hard feelin's." He managed a grin, but Snake never changed his stoic expression. Already bored with the game, Snake ignored Johnny's outstretched hand, pushing his chair back to fetch another glass of beer. Left red-faced with his hand stuck out, Johnny looked at Roach, bewildered. "What the hell did I do to rile him?"

"It don't take nothin' to rile Snake," Roach said with a chuckle. "He stays riled all the time. I ain't ever seen him crack a smile." The thought nudged his curiosity, and he looked over at Leach. "You ever see Snake smile, Leach?"

"Come to think of it, I ain't," Leach replied, grinning as he scratched his chin thoughtfully. "He came close the other day when he carved that woman up that tried to scratch his eyes out."

Roach shook his head, picturing the scene. "He sure cut her up good and proper. I kinda felt sorry for the poor woman." His brief flicker of compassion went out as quickly as it had sparked, and he got to his feet. "She was a fair-lookin' woman for her age," he said, nodding agreement with his own statement. "I got to go to the outhouse. All this beer is about to bust out."

Johnny didn't ask—he could easily assume the woman in question was probably Frances Thompson. She had been viciously slashed about the face and neck when they found her lying near the front steps of the cabin. He remembered Sheriff Moffett's remark as they picked up the body. *Now what kind of animal would do a thing like that to a woman?* It was not a pleasant thought. And at the time, it had caused him to question his intention to join the men the posse searched for. The incident had quickly left his mind, however, crowded out by the prospect of easy money and high adventure. Sitting at the table now with Leach as Roach made his way toward the back door, he told himself that he had made the right decision. Lost in his thoughts momentarily, he glanced up to find Leach studying him intensely.

"You ain't lettin' Snake bother you, are you?" Leach asked.

"Hell no," Johnny quickly responded. "I ain't bothered by no man."

Leach smiled. "Good. Just don't get crossways with Snake unless you're ready to fight. He ain't got no sense of humor, and it don't take a helluva lot to touch him off." He got up from his chair. "I reckon it's about time to call it a night. We got to go to work in the mornin'." He winked at Johnny, then left to follow Roach out the back door. "Tell Snake we're leavin'."

Johnny followed him with his eyes until he disappeared out the door. Then he shifted his gaze to the bar, where the scowling half-breed stood drinking his beer. It was a motley bunch he had chosen to ride with. He wondered again if he had made a mistake. If he had doubts, now was the time to change his mind and walk out. The Indian was absorbed with his beer, and Leach and Roach were out back. His indecision dwelt for only a moment, replaced by the thought of a pocketful of money, courtesy of the First Mercantile Bank.

Wilson Barnett glanced up at the clock over the teller's cage and checked it against the time on his pocket watch. One minute to nine—even though Ethel and Polly were waiting outside, he would not unlock the front door until the minute hand stood precisely on twelve. The bank opened at nine, not one minute to nine, and not one minute after nine. It had been that way for fourteen years. Wilson felt it of utmost importance that the people of Fort Smith could depend upon the bank to be consistent in its hours as well as in all other services.

"Good morning, ladies," Wilson said as he unlocked the door and held it for Ethel and Polly to enter.

"Good morning, Mr. Barnett," both women returned, a ritual repeated every day of the workweek. This day would prove to be a departure from the routine of hundreds of days before, however. "Good morning, Mr. Barnett," a gruff voice echoed right behind the women.

Startled, Wilson almost closed the door on Leach, but Leach pushed his way through, causing one of the women to stumble. Leach was quick to catch her arm and prevent her fall. "Easy, there, little lady. You don't wanna fall and bump your head." He flashed a wide friendly smile to Wilson.

"I beg your pardon, sir," Wilson immediately began to apologize. "I didn't even see you in the door." Accustomed to seeing many strangers pass through the busy little settlement, Wilson was not surprised that he didn't recognize the man. He had to admit that this one looked a good deal rougher than most who visited his bank. "Can I help you? We're just opening up," he started.

Before Leach could answer, Roach stepped inside the door behind him. Without glancing toward his partner, Leach said, "Yes, sir, me and my friend here wanna make a withdrawal, and we're kinda in a hurry."

"A withdrawal?" Wilson asked, certain the man was confused. "What kind of withdrawal are you thinking of? Do you have a note from another bank? A check?" He was beginning to fear his day was going to start with a troublesome problem with a saddle tramp hoping to get a loan. His irritation turned to concern when Roach, still smiling at him like he was a rabbit in a trap, moved over to position himself beside the two ladies. A movement near the front window caught his eye, and he glanced up to discover the back of another man outside. The realization of what was about to occur struck him with a numbing paralysis.

Noting the sudden fear in the banker's eyes, Leach drew his pistol. "Yes, sir—a note, that's what we've got. Take a look at it," he said, enjoying the look of cold terror it caused in the banker's face.

The sudden appearance of a weapon caused an immediate squeal of horror from both women. Roach quickly stepped between them and placed a restraining arm around the shoulders of each. "Just keep quiet and do what I tell you," he commanded. Then softening his tone, he told them, "We ain't lookin' to hurt you pretty things. You just behave yourselves, and you'll be all right."

Leach took one quick glance to satisfy himself that Roach had the women under control; then he shifted his gaze back to lock onto the quivering eyes of Wilson Barnett. "Now, then, I expect it's time to open that safe, unless you want a couple of holes in that fancy vest you're wearin'."

Wilson's knees sagged perceptibly as his legs threatened to fail him. Still, he tried to make an appeal to the bank robber's sense of decency. "The money in that safe belongs to the hardworking people of this community. I don't have the authority to open the safe."

The front door opened, and Snake's voice insisted, "We ain't got all day."

"That's a fact," Leach said and cocked the hammer back on his forty-five. Holding the muzzle only inches from Wilson's face, he threatened, "This here's your authority. I'm tired of pussy-footin' around with you. Start workin' the combination on that safe."

Wilson took a frightened step backward. Grabbing him roughly by the shoulder, Leach spun him around and gave him a shove toward the safe behind the counter. The terrified banker stumbled to his knees before the safe. With the muzzle of Leach's pistol against the back of his head, he fumbled with the combination. In his nervousness, he missed one of the stops, and the safe failed to open on the first try.

"I swear, I'll blow a hole in your head if you don't get that damn thing open, and I mean right now," Leach threatened. He took a quick glance over his shoulder toward the front door, then another at Roach, still with a frightened woman under each arm. Showing no urgency, Roach smiled at him, but Leach was impatient. "Damn you!" he spat at the fumbling banker and was about to administer a rap on the head with his pistol when the safe opened, revealing two cashier's drawers resting upon a stack of paper money.

The sudden sight of all that money captured Roach's attention. He released the women and stepped forward to get a better look. Hysterical with fear, one of the women bolted for the door. "Snake!" Roach yelled.

The warning was unnecessary for the stolid half-breed met her as she pulled the door open. With one hand, he grabbed her by the throat and backed her into the bank. She attempted to scream, but the force of the steel grip was crushing her windpipe, preventing her from breathing. With cold, dispassionate eyes, he watched her as he clamped down harder and harder until her eyelids began to flutter and her body went limp. Still he held her for several long moments before releasing his grip and letting her fall lifeless to the floor. "She ain't gonna make no more noise," he commented dryly.

The horrifying sight of her fellow employee being strangled by the half-breed before her eyes—as casually as if he were wringing a chicken's neck—was too much for Polly's already terrified brain. She crumpled to the floor in a dead faint. Roach looked from one woman to the other, then back to the expressionless countenance of the half-breed. "Damn, Snake," he said, "you sure are hard on women."

Leach, his mind never straying from the business at hand, was occupied with stuffing several canvas bank sacks as full of money as he could get them. He tossed the full bags toward Roach while he swept up the remaining bank notes, all the while keeping one eye on the stunned banker crouching against the wall. "I thought there'd be more in here," he complained to no one in particular. "But I reckon it'll do for a good while." Without turning his head, he asked, "Is Snake watchin' that street?"

"Yeah," Roach replied, "nobody's comin'."

His task almost completed, Leach tied off the last sack. "Where're the horses?"

"He's already bringin' 'em around," Roach answered, seeing Johnny rounding the corner of the building, leading the horses. He watched Leach pack away the last of the money, then glanced at Barnett cringing against the wall. "What about him?"

Leach hesitated for a moment before answering, "Call Johnny in here. Snake can hold the horses."

Roach shrugged and did as he was instructed. Johnny walked in the door, eyes wide with excitement as he witnessed the scene inside the bank. Gazing from the sacks of money to the bodies of the women—one stone still, the other showing signs of motion—to the frightened banker cowering against the teller's cage, he felt a sense of surrealism. It was like a scene from a play, not real somehow. His momentary paralysis was interrupted by Leach's simple command.

"Shoot him," he said, nodding his head toward Barnett. Johnny hesitated, not sure he had heard right. "Shoot him," Leach repeated, this time more emphatically. "He's seen faces and heard names. Dead men make poor witnesses. Shoot him."

Johnny suddenly felt numb throughout his entire body. Knowing that both Leach and Roach were watching his reactions closely, he tried to keep his emotions concealed. But he knew without doubt that he was being given no choice in the matter, and the consequences were certain to be fatal if he showed a reluctance to kill. He drew his pistol and pointed it at the terrified banker. The sudden discharge of the forty-five revolver surprised him. In his nervousness, he had not realized that he was slowly squeezing his trigger finger. Barnett jerked violently, then slumped forward, killed instantly by the bullet in his brain, his chin resting on his chest. Johnny stood motionless, staring at the small hole in Barnett's temple. In the two years that he had worked for Winston Moffett as a deputy, he had never shot at anyone. In fact, the only man he had seen with a gunshot wound, before the scene at Thompson's, was a drunken cowhand who had accidentally shot himself. The feeling of numbness was rapidly being replaced by one of slight nausea, and he quickly sought to control it by blustering, "What about her?"

Leach and Roach turned to consider Polly Price, who now seemed to sink back into a dazed stupor, a result of the added trauma of seeing her employer wantonly shot in the head. Leach spent but a moment to decide. "Hell, she's gone loco. Leave her." There was an urgency about their situation now that a shot had been fired. "We've got to get the hell outta here. That shot'll bring the whole damn town down here." That thought replaced all others for the moment, and the three outlaws quickly grabbed the sacks of money and filed out the door.

Though now late in the morning, there were only two people in the dusty street, and they were standing outside the saloon across the street. Casting curious glances at the stoic half-breed holding the horses, the two men prudently moved their conversation farther away toward the corner of the building when their glances were met with Snake's menacing leer. At the sound of the gunshot, both men jerked their heads around in surprise, then realized what was happening when the outlaws emerged from the bank. With no further hesitation, they disappeared around the corner of the saloon.

Chapter 3

"Gawdammit, not in my town!" Jed Ramey roared, his eyes flashing angry sparks as he surveyed the scene at the bank. "Nobody walks into my town, robs the bank, and murders two of my citizens." He whipped around to the traumatized girl now being administered to by the town doctor. "Who was it, Polly? Have you seen 'em before?"

Still shaking violently, Polly was in no condition to testify. The only witness to the two brutal murders, she had trouble speaking coherently about what had taken place there. "Ethel," she muttered, "he just killed her with his bare hands."

"Who, Polly?" Jed pressed. "Who killed Ethel?"

"I don't know," she wailed. "He just killed her with his bare hands."

Ramey continued to press in spite of Doc Peters' insistence that the young woman needed rest before the marshal questioned her further. "How many were there?" He would not relent until he got some useful information from her. The daring robbery and murders were a direct assault upon his reputation as a lawman, a personal insult to his pride. He took the heinous crime as an attack upon him personally. At the moment, he cared less about Polly Price's mental state than the fact that the outlaws were getting away. At this point, he didn't know how many were in the band that had hit the bank, any description of the outlaws, or which way they would likely be heading. His anger was growing by the second. If he thought he could get away with it, he was tempted to force the shaken young woman to remember. It was all he could do to wait her out a few minutes longer until she finally began to take control of her emotions.

Gradually, she was able to tell him there were at least four men involved. She could not be sure how many were outside the bank. Her description of the outlaws inside the bank was sketchy at best, with the exception of the man who strangled Ethel. His features would remain to haunt her dreams for days to come. She described him to the U.S. deputy marshal as accurately as she could, but the picture in her mind was impossible to convey. The vivid image of the snarling savage was seared into her brain. Ramey was about to question her further when his deputy, Lem Deacon, came in from the street.

"Pete Crowder and Jake Spooner seen 'em when they come outta the bank," he said. "There was four of 'em, all right—three inside the bank, like Polly said, and one holdin' the horses outside."

Two of the town's drunks, Ramey thought, *waiting for the saloon to open*. "Are they sober enough to know what they saw?"

"They're sober," Lem answered.

"All right," Ramey declared. "We're wastin' time." He took one last look at the shaken girl. Feeling he should say something, he mumbled, "Much obliged, Polly. Doc here will take care of you." To Lem he said, "Four of 'em, huh? We'd best round up a half dozen men and go after 'em." Ramey hoped for six quick volunteers to put the odds in his favor, but he knew two men whom he wanted for sure. As they walked out the door, he instructed Lem, "Hustle down to the livery stable and tell Bates I need him on this one. Then go by the blacksmith shop and fetch Alvarez. And anyone else that's got a horse," he called after his deputy, who was already on his way. When Ramey turned to go to his horse, he was confronted by Pete and Jake.

"We seen 'em, Jed," Jake blurted, glancing at his friend for confirmation. "They was toting sacks of money. Wasn't they, Pete? Four of 'em—they jumped on their horses and hightailed it past the hotel."

Ramey studied the two town drunks for a moment before deciding he could rely on their testimony. "Toward the river?" he asked.

"Nope," Pete replied. "They was headed straight south, past the hotel."

Ramey was mildly surprised to hear this. He would have assumed the outlaws would head for the river in an attempt to lose anybody who was tracking them before making straight for the vast lawless frontier simply known as Indian Territory. "You sure about that?" Ramey asked. "You and Jake ain't had a few snorts this mornin', have you?" It was hard to tell. The pair reeked of stale whiskey all the time.

Pete looked genuinely hurt. "Ah, Jed, you know Sweeney don't open up till almost ten."

"All right, then," Ramey said. "Much obliged. You tell Sweeney to give you one drink apiece and put it on my bill."

This lit up both faces. "Why, thanks, Jed," Jake beamed. "That's mighty sportin' of you." His face turned dead serious then. "You know I'd ride with you, but my back's been kinda stove up lately."

"Yeah, I know," Ramey replied as he stepped up in the saddle. Time was getting away from him, and it would take more time to get a posse under way. "You and Pete done a good job." He backed his horse away from the rail and turned its head toward the other end of the street, thinking he wouldn't want those two on a posse if they were the only volunteers.

Within minutes after Ramey reached the marshal's office, Alvarez showed up. Bates appeared shortly after. Ramey knew he could count on those two. Both men had ridden with him on every posse he had assembled since being appointed deputy marshal. Rough, no-nonsense men, they didn't scare easily, even with prospects of facing desperate outlaws. There was no better tracker around than Alvarez. The burly blacksmith knew horses and could tell you everything about a particular horse but the color, just by looking at its tracks.

"How many days, you reckon?" Alvarez wanted to know as soon as he dismounted. "I brought grub for three days."

"That oughta be enough," Ramey replied, then turned to greet Bates. "Figurin' on about three days," he advised Bates.

Bates nodded. "Lem said they killed Barnett and Ethel Bowden. Is that a fact?"

"Yeah," Ramey replied. "And left Polly scared half outta her mind. I don't know why they didn't kill her, too. Figured she'd gone crazy, I reckon."

"That's a sorry piece of work," Bates said, shaking his head thoughtfully. "We need to hang them bastards proper. When are we gonna get started? I reckon they headed for Indian Territory."

"Accordin' to what Jake and Pete said, they didn't head for Injun country right off—rode out to the south of town. Lem's rounding up a couple more men. Then we'll get outta here as soon as everybody's ready to ride."

It was close to noon before a posse of Ramey, his deputy, and four volunteers assembled before the marshal's office to receive their instructions. In addition to Bates and Alvarez, Lem had found Eldridge Thornton, a carpenter, and Franklin Morris, Wilson Barnett's cousin who ran the general store.

When they rode out the south road, there were too many tracks to be able to distinguish between the everyday traffic and the trail left by the four outlaws. For that reason, Alvarez and Ramey scouted the western side of the road, searching for the place where the outlaws cut back toward the river. Lem and the others scouted the other side of the road, just in case Ramey's guess was wrong. It was a foregone conclusion in everybody's mind that the outlaws would head for Indian country, a territory that had become home to robbers, murderers, rapists, and every other fugitive from justice. The question was where they had cut off the wagon track.

About four miles south of town, Alvarez signaled with a wave of his hand. "Here they are," he stated when Ramey joined him. "Plain as day. They didn't make no effort to hide 'em."

"I ain't never run into no outlaw yet with the brains God give a grasshopper," Ramey stated dryly. "I didn't expect these four would be any brighter."

They waited for the others to catch up, then followed the tracks of the four horses, which led west and north again, toward a grove of trees, apparently heading back in a general direction that would strike the river. Riding into the trees, the posse discovered a small stream and, from the tracks around it, decided the outlaws had paused there to water their horses. Pushing on, they came to a barbed-wire fence bordering the edge of the trees with a large expanse of grassland beyond.

"Everett Sloan's place," Bates observed, looking out across the rolling pasture. Small groups of cattle, scattered about the grassy hills, paused in their grazing to stare at the six riders.

"Ain't too hard to trail 'em, is it?" Alvarez commented dryly when Ramey rode up to where the blacksmith was gazing down at a section of wire lying flat on the ground. Obviously having no wire cutters, the outlaws had simply roped a couple of fence posts and pulled them out of the ground. Alvarez's simple statement would prove to be wrong, for as soon as the posse crossed over the wire, the tracks they followed split off in four different directions, scattering across the grass.

"Dammit to hell," Ramey cursed, knowing he might have underestimated the four. The grass, already thick from the heavy spring rains, made tracking difficult, especially when hoofprints were mixed with those of the cattle. With no other choice that he could see, Ramey split the posse up to try to follow individual sets of tracks. After an hour of what amounted to nothing more than time spent riding around in circles, he called in his posse. "I reckon they bamboozled us all right. Might as well ride on down to the river. Maybe we can pick up their trail on the other side." Frustrated, the marshal was becoming more and more irritable. He didn't cotton to being outsmarted by outlaws. He kicked his horse hard and started toward the trees that bordered the river.

They found that their luck was no better on the other side of the river. Scouring the riverbank up- and downstream, they found no tracks. "Now how the hell can four horses ford a river and not leave one set of tracks coming out on the bank?" Thornton expressed the disbelief everyone felt.

Thoroughly irritated, Ramey replied, "They can't. They either swum their horses downriver, or up-, or they doubled back and came out on the same side they went in. These boys are goin' to a heap of trouble to hide their trail, instead of just hightailing it to Injun Territory." He looked over toward the sun, now lying low on the hills. "We've wasted the afternoon riding up and down this riverbank. I expect we night as well make camp here and figure on searching both sides of the river again in the mornin'."

Morning brought a steady drizzle that further dampened the spirits of the small posse. "This ain't gonna make it any easier," complained Thornton, the only member of the group who had neglected to bring a slicker. He pulled his hat down low on his forehead and draped his blanket over his shoulders as he fanned a fire into life.

Ramey had no sympathy for him. *Anybody ought to have enough sense to bring a slicker on a posse*, he thought. *Now the damn fool is going to have a wet blanket, too.*

After a quick breakfast of bacon and coffee, the posse began their search once more. As each hour passed, with no positive results, Ramey became more and more frustrated. It was becoming painfully clear that they had no earthly idea which way the outlaws headed, and the thought of being outsmarted riled Ramey to the point of almost becoming livid. It was Morris who first expressed what the entire posse was thinking.

"Hell, we might as well admit it. They whipped us. We might as well head on back."

The others looked at him, somewhat surprised that he would be the first to admit defeat, since he was a cousin of the murdered banker.

"I reckon Morris is right, Ramey," Bates said. "There ain't no use in ridin' around in circles."

Ramey was not a man to take defeat gracefully, especially in the face of such an openly brazen crime. Four outlaws had ridden into his town, robbed and murdered, and were getting away free as a flock of vultures. Though maintaining a stone-cold exterior, Ramey was fuming inside. If they didn't find the four, it would be the first violent crime to go unpunished since Judge Isaac C. Parker came to town. Already, Parker had earned the nickname of the Hanging Judge, doling out sentences that served notice on the lawless breed that had taken refuge in Indian Territory. Fort Smith was the last outpost of civilization before the vast plains of the Oklahoma Territory, and Jed Ramey prided himself on his part in filling Judge Parker's jail—a jail rightfully called Hell on the Border by those lucky enough to escape the gallows. With this in mind, Ramey held the posse to its task, still searching for some sign that would reveal the direction taken by the outlaws. Finally, even he admitted that it was impossible to follow someone who left no trail. At half past four, he gave up the search.

Wet and discouraged, the posse of six crossed back over the river, just as the sun broke through the clouds, making its first appearance of the day. The men peeled off their slickers, and Thornton draped his soggy blanket loosely across his horse's rump to let the air help dry it. It was Morris who happened to spot movement in the trees some two hundred yards downstream. Thinking it a deer at first, he casually pointed it out to Alvarez. The blacksmith stared hard at the spot Morris indicated before suddenly declaring, "That ain't no deer. That's a horse." He turned at once to signal the marshal. "Ramey!"

Ramey turned his horse and rode back to where Alvarez now sat motionless, his eyes trained on a section of young willows near a bend in the river. "Morris thinks it's a deer, but if it is, it's the first one I've ever seen wearin' a saddle."

Ramey stared at the spot for a long moment, trying to get a better look. "Might be Everett Sloan, lookin' for strays," he finally said. "We'll ride on down there to take a look." With the rest of his posse gathered around, he cautioned, "Might not be Everett, too, so keep your eyes peeled and stay behind me."

Jordan Gray stretched his legs and back, trying to ease the stiffness caused by spending so much time in the saddle. He was not accustomed to such long hours on a horse. The last few years had mostly been spent walking behind a mule. *Reckon I'll get used to it*, he thought as he watched the chestnut drink from the river. An hour's ride, at most, should put him in Fort Smith. It would have been no more than a long day's ride from his cabin to the bustling town. But he had lost a day's ride when he turned off the road to follow tracks that turned out to be nothing more than a farmer and his two sons returning from the settlement. The delay added to the urgency already driving him to catch up to the four outlaws. He had ridden the chestnut hard for the last four hours, so he had decided to rest the poor horse before he found himself on foot. Absorbed in these thoughts, he was unaware that he had company until the chestnut acknowledged the presence of other horses.

Turning to discover a half dozen riders approaching, he unhurriedly walked over and pulled his rifle from the saddle sling. Then, moving away from his horse, he positioned himself next to a sizable tree trunk. Until he could determine the nature of his visitors, he wanted to have quick cover convenient. A man couldn't be too cautious this close to Indian Territory. That was one reason he had moved away from his horse. If, for some reason, bullets started flying, he didn't want his transportation hit by a stray.

"Howdy," Jed Ramey called out when within a couple dozen yards of the stranger.

"Howdy," Jordan returned, carefully watching the man leading the file of riders.

Ramey continued to approach. "What are you aimin' to do with that rifle?" he asked.

"Depends on what you're aimin' to do, I reckon," Jordan replied matter-of-factly.

Seeing the man was dead serious, Ramey pulled his jacket aside, revealing his badge. "I'm Federal Marshal Jed Ramey," he announced, "and I'm lookin' for some fellers that held up the bank and murdered some folks."

Seeing the lawman's badge, Jordan relaxed and walked over to replace his rifle in the sling while the other members of the posse dismounted. "I reckon I'm lookin' for some outlaws myself," he said.

"Is that a fact?" Ramey replied, studying the young man intently. "I don't believe I've ever seen you around here before. What's your name, young feller?"

"Jordan Gray."

Ramey glanced at the lathered chestnut. "Looks like you've been ridin' that horse pretty hard."

"That's the reason I stopped to let him rest," Jordan answered somewhat curtly, suddenly uncomfortable with the marshal's manner. He supposed that the law-man, by virtue of his profession, was suspicious, but he didn't appreciate the way all six stared at him. "Like I said, I'm lookin' for some outlaws. They murdered my family."

"Murdered your family?" Ramey echoed with an obvious smirk in his voice. "Well, Mr. Jordan Gray, I'm afraid I'm gonna have to find out a little bit more about you." Without shifting his gaze from Jordan, he said, "Lem! Take a look in them saddlebags there." With the hint of a smile on his lips, he added, "You don't mind, do ya, Mr. Gray?"

"Matter of fact, I do," Jordan replied. "You've got no reason to search me. Just what do you think you're lookin' for?"

"Maybe this," Lem called out. He had wasted no time going through Jordan's saddlebags. He held up a small bundle wrapped in oil cloth as if displaying a trophy.

Ramey shifted his eyes briefly to look at the package, then back to lock on Jordan again. "What is it, Lem?"

"Money," Lem replied excitedly. "He's got a nice little bundle of money here."

"Is that a fact?" Ramey responded. "Lathered-up horse and a bundle of cash money—that don't look too good for you, does it?" Ramey sensed that the day was not going to be a total loss after all.

"That money's what I've saved up for three years. It's all I've got after they burned my cabin down. If you'll send somebody over to see Sheriff Moffett at Crooked Creek, he'll vouch for me." He glanced around him, searching among the faces surrounding him for one that believed him. There was none. Instead, he was met with accusing stares and rifles at the ready. The enormity of his mistake in trusting a badge struck him soundly. He was being railroaded. Of that, there could be no doubt. Lawmen or no lawmen, he rued the decision to put his rifle away.

"Where's the rest of your friends?" Ramey asked. "Judge Parker might go easier on you if I told him you cooperated. Where are you supposed to meet up?"

"Damn you," Jordan spat back, his patience at an end. "I told you the truth of the matter. You're barkin' up the wrong tree. While we're standin' here jawin', the men I'm lookin' for—maybe the ones you're lookin' for—are gettin' away."

Without warning, Ramey backhanded Jordan sharply across the face. "Don't get testy with me, sonny." Jordan tried to lunge at the marshal, but was immediately stopped, restrained by Alvarez and Bates. Ramey thrust his face up close to Jordan's, almost touching his nose. The marshal had run more than a few outlaws to ground, and they all had a fairy tale ready to tell. This one was a little different, but he still recognized it as just another version. "Now I want some straight answers outta you, or I might save Judge Parker the trouble of trying your sorry ass."

Staggered with disbelief that this could actually be happening, Jordan burned with white-hot frustration inside. "You dumb son of a bitch. Anybody with a spoonful of brains could see I'm not one of the men you're chasin'." His remark earned him another backhand.

"Is that a fact? Well, lemme tell you what I see. Four men come into my town, rob the bank and kill two people. We follow them downriver before we lose their trail, but lo and behold, we run up on a stranger with a lathered-up horse and a saddlebag full of money. That right there sorta paints the picture, don't it?" His tone softened a bit as he took a different approach. "Kinda looks like your friends are gonna leave you to take their medicine while they ride away fat and sassy. Now we followed your trail to the spot where you all split up when you hit the pasture. Where was you supposed to meet up again?"

"In hell, I reckon," Jordan replied, his anger and frustration having gotten the best of him. "I can't tell you somethin' I don't know."

"All right, then." Ramey threw his hands up in surrender. "Have it your way. Somebody's gonna pay for what you and your friends did. You mighta got off easier if you told us where the rest of your bunch headed. Judge Parker likes to have all debts paid in full, so I reckon you've got an appointment with the gallows."

"Why don't we just hang him right here and be done with it?" This was Morris, the banker's cousin, who spoke up, anxious to extract justice for his cousin's murder.

Jordan glared at the man petitioning for his execution. "I told you, you've got the wrong man. While you jackasses are standin' around here talkin' about lynchin' me, the men you're after are gettin' away."

Ramey didn't say anything for a few minutes. He listened to the men discussing Morris' suggestion, watching Jordan's face to see if the immediate threat might serve to loosen his tongue. He had no intention of permitting a hanging, but it wouldn't hurt to let his prisoner think about it.

Jordan became suddenly calm, no longer straining against Bates and Alvarez, who still held his arms securely. There was a doleful look in his eye as he glanced around him, his gaze darting from one face to the next. Ramey had seen that look before. It was the look of a man who had nothing to lose. The deputy marshal had apprehended countless dozens of fugitives from justice in his ten years as a lawman, and he could recognize the warning signs in a man's eyes. This one was getting ready to fight. While a lively discussion ensued among the members of his posse over whether or not to hang the stranger on the spot, Ramey nodded to his deputy. Lem Deacon acknowledged the marshal's signal with a return nod, then stepped up close behind the prisoner, his rifle ready.

"Well, son, looks like you're gonna be the only one standin' trial while the rest of your friends are spending all that money. Climb on your horse. We've wasted too much time here already." He took a step back to give Alvarez and Bates room to turn Jordan toward his horse.

With never a thought of going peacefully, Jordan did not resist when the two turned him toward the chestnut. His concentration was now locked securely upon the rifle still riding in his saddle sling. When he felt a slight decrease in the pressure in Bates' grip on his arm, he did not hesitate. In one violent motion, he wrenched his arm free, flinging Bates several feet away and making him stumble awkwardly to keep from falling. The beefy Alvarez was not so easily over-powered. He clamped down hard on Jordan's left arm, not even releasing his grip when Jordan planted a solid right hand that flattened his nose and caused his knees to buckle momentarily. Anticipating the sudden eruption, Lem was ready with his rifle, bringing the barrel down hard against Jordan's skull. Lem was a big man, with arms almost as stout as Alvarez's. The force he applied to the blow was sufficient to lay Jordan out cold. Unmoved by the sudden violence, Ramey instructed Lem and Alvarez to put the prisoner on his horse.

"Tie his hands to the saddle horn, Lem, and we'll get back in time for supper." Ramey was not satisfied with the results of his posse, but at least he wasn't going back empty-handed. Three might have gotten away, but the one he caught *would by God pay the price for all four.* He watched dispassionately as Lem, with Thornton's and Alvarez's help, hefted the unconscious prisoner up in the saddle. Alvarez in particular was none too gentle in the effort, still smarting from a broken nose. When Jordan threatened to roll off onto the ground, Ramey said, "Let him lay on the horse's neck. Tie his hands together around the neck." He watched them follow out his instructions. "Better tie his feet together under the horse's belly, too. That oughta keep him in the saddle." He was a little surprised that Jordan was still out cold. *Lem must have cracked his skull*, he thought, not really concerned.

Chapter 4

"He ain't moved since we put him on his horse," Bates commented when the posse paused to let the horses drink from a small stream just south of town. This caused the others to take a long look at their prisoner, still lying motionless on the chestnut's neck.

"Lem, you mighta tapped him a little too hard," Morris said, a wide grin spread across his face. "I believe you kilt him."

"Yeah, Lem," Thornton chimed in, "you better check your rifle. You mighta bent the barrel."

Lem grinned, enjoying the banter. "I might have at that, but that's all right. Maybe now I can shoot around corners."

Lem's response brought a round of chuckles from the rest of the posse. Even the usually dour Ramey grinned. The mood of the six men was considerably lighter, now that the brick building that housed the jail and the district court was in sight. In spite of capturing one of the outlaws, Ramey could not feel totally justified in his mind. Three had gotten away. He had recovered only a small portion of the stolen money. But, he asked himself realistically, what else could he have done? There was no trail to follow. His posse could have ridden around in Indian Territory for a month without finding a trace of the other three. It would take a regiment of soldiers to run to ground all the outlaws hiding out in Indian Territory.

"Seems to me the district court oughta show its gratitude to this posse with a round of drinks at Sweeney's." This from Bates. It was followed by another wave of chuckles and comments of agreement. "Alvarez might need somethin' for medicinal purposes."

Alvarez managed a grin and laid a finger gently alongside his swollen nose. "I've had worse than this from a mule kick," he said.

It might have appeared otherwise to the returning posse, but the motionless figure draped across the chestnut gelding's neck was aware of the meaningless banter going back and forth around him. Jordan could not really remember the blow that had cast him into sudden darkness, he only knew that the throbbing in his brain when he emerged felt as if his skull had been split. Consciousness had come slowly, a few degrees at a time, until he had finally become aware of his surroundings. Upon finding himself on his horse, he had at first attempted to sit up, only to find that his arms were tied around the horse's neck. When he realized that none of the men had noticed his efforts, he decided to feign unconsciousness a while longer until he had a clearer picture of his situation.

By the time the posse had stopped on the edge of

town to water their horses, Jordan's mind had cleared to the point where the ground no longer spun around whenever he risked opening his eyes. When the horses started again, leaving the little stream behind, his mind began to race with thoughts of escape. Under different conditions, he would not have considered such thoughts, but it was painfully clear that, at best, there was going to be a great loss of time before his innocence could be confirmed. And he didn't have that time to lose. The men who murdered his family were already two days ahead of him. He could also not ignore the possibility that he was already tried and found guilty. Remembering how the deputy marshal had ignored his suggestion to contact Sheriff Moffett, he realized that Ramey was determined to hang somebody, guilty or not. Jordan had no fear of dying. With the loss of his beloved Sarah and his son, death might bring a release from the terrible grief he felt. If he had fear, it would be the fear of being prevented from finding the men who had taken his family. In the end, there was no decision to be made, for he knew he could not permit himself to be locked in a cell—even if he died trying to escape.

"You fellers go on over to Sweeney's and tell him the court owes you a drink. We'll take the prisoner on over to the jail." Ramey pulled up momentarily, then added, "Much obliged," in way of thanks.

Alvarez, who had been studying the dazed man sprawled across the chestnut's neck, alerted the marshal, "Looks like your prisoner's come to." He had noticed that Jordan's eyes were now open. "I reckon Lem ain't kilt him after all."

Unconcerned, Ramey gazed at Jordan but a moment before commenting, "Looks that way, don't it? I figured we were gonna have a burial or a hangin'. I reckon it's gonna be a hangin'."

With the prospect of a drink of whiskey at Sweeney's, and the opportunity of recounting their heroic capture of a dangerous outlaw to the patrons of the saloon, the other members of the posse had already turned to depart. Alvarez hesitated for a few seconds. "Want me to ride with you? He might still have some fight in him."

Ramey took a long look at the prisoner, still sprawled lifeless, although his eyes were open and seemed to be shifting from side to side in a dazed stupor. "Nah, you go on over and get a drink. Lem and I can handle this one."

Alvarez wheeled his horse and rode after the others, who, by this time, had been discovered by a few people in the street. Before they had reached the hitching rail at Sweeney's, the posse had attracted a modest crowd of the curious. A couple of bystanders fell in step with Ramey and Lem, following the two lawmen down to the jail, gawking at the man tied in the saddle. Jordan, fully alert now, although still pretending to be in a stupor, tried to decide upon his best chance to escape. "Looks like you caught one of 'em, Jed," he heard a man who was walking just out of his line of vision say. "He don't look too spry," he heard another man say. "Looks like you had to crack his head for him," the first voice said, apparently noticing the crusting trail of blood that had dried upon Jordan's face and neck.

"Yeah," Ramey replied, "he had a little fit there for a minute, but Lem took the fight right outta him." A man never made a statement that was farther from the fact. In a matter of moments Ramey would find this out.

Pulling the horses up before a stately brick building that housed the jail as well as the federal district courthouse, Ramey remained in the saddle while Lem dismounted. A couple of off-duty guards, who had been taking the evening air on the wide front porch of the building, got up from their rocking chairs to watch. One of them took a few steps to the edge of the porch to knock the ashes from his pipe. "Well, I see you got one of 'em, Jed. What about the rest of 'em?"

"Scattered all over Indian Territory, I reckon," Ramey answered. "There weren't no way we could cut their trail."

While Ramey talked to the guard, Lem untied the rope holding Jordan's hands. As soon as they were free, he stood back for a moment to make sure there was no violent reaction from the prisoner. Satisfied that Jordan would offer no resistance, Lem untied the rope under the horse's belly, freeing Jordan's feet, and reached up to pull him off the horse. In the next second, Lem found out what it was like to pull a panther off a tree limb. Fists flying and legs driving, Jordan exploded upon the startled deputy. With his shoulders lowered, he drove Lem off-balance, slamming him up against his horse. Before Lem could react, Jordan's hand found the rifle butt protruding from the saddle sling. In the confusion of the moment, the guard talking to Ramey dropped his pipe and pulled his pistol.

Trying to act quickly, he fired, but in his haste, he missed his target, hitting Lem high in the shoulder. The deputy howled in pain and dropped to his knees. Jordan immediately showered the porch with rifle balls, firing and cocking as rapidly as he could. With bullets snapping all around them, the two guards ran for their lives, jumping off the end of the porch to escape the storm of lead.

Ramey, taken completely by surprise, tried to draw his pistol, but his horse, startled by the sudden eruption, reared up, causing the marshal to grab the saddle horn to keep from being thrown. By the time he was able to bring his weapon to bear, he found himself staring at the business end of a Henry rifle, as Jordan stood deadly calm, waiting.

"Put the rifle down," Ramey ordered. "You're already in enough trouble. Don't make it any worse."

"I don't wanna kill you unless I have to," Jordan said. "You have two choices—makes no difference to me which one you pick. You can drop that pistol, and I'll ride out of here. But if you pull that trigger, I'm takin' you with me. What's it gonna be?"

"You're makin' a big mistake, mister," Ramey replied. "You'll never get out of town alive. Now drop the rifle."

"Then I reckon we can finish this conversation in hell," Jordan responded, his tone calm and final.

"Shoot him, Jed," Lem pleaded, still on his knees, his shirt soaked with blood.

The two men remained frozen for what seemed an eternity, their weapons aimed at each other before one was forced to waver. Ramey had faced many a desperate man before. But this time, there was a cool glint in this man's eyes, a gaze as hard and unyielding as cold steel. It was the same gaze he had seen in Jordan's eyes before, and he knew without question that, if he pulled the trigger, he was a dead man. They stood staring into each other's eyes for several long seconds more, fingers on the trigger, until Ramey's hand relaxed and the pistol dropped to the ground. Lem was stupefied. He never thought he would see the day Ramey backed down from any man. In one last attempt, he suddenly reached for the pistol still in his holster. Anticipating just such a move, Jordan caught him with a solid blow with the rifle barrel that knocked the wounded deputy senseless. "I reckon that makes us even," Jordan said. Then turning back to Ramey, he ordered, "Get down off that horse and walk over to the rail."

"You know I'll be comin' after you," Ramey said, forcing as much bluster as a man who had just backed down to an adversary could.

Keeping the rifle trained on the marshal, Jordan stepped up in the saddle after picking up Ramey's pistol. "I hope for your sake you don't catch up with me," Jordan said. "I haven't killed anyone, and I haven't stolen any money." That stated, he picked up the reins of the two lawmen's horses. "I ain't a horse thief, either. I'll let 'em go after I get outta town." Then he was off at a gallop. As he turned the corner at Sweeney's, he could hear the boisterous sounds of the crowd inside listening to the posse's recounting of the day's action. Behind him, a mortified deputy marshal helped his wounded deputy to his feet—with the aid of a few people who had heard the barrage of rifle shots—and two off-duty jail guards, who reappeared from behind the courthouse.

With the town of Fort Smith approximately two miles behind him, Jordan led the horses to a large oak whose branches spread like a giant fan over the wagon track. Confident that the two lawmen's horses would be readily seen from the road, he dismounted and looped their reins over a low-hanging limb. Wasting no time, for he figured a posse was being rounded up as quickly as the marshal could manage, he searched the saddlebags until he found the oil cloth that held his money. Content to settle for the recovery of his property, he replaced everything he had removed from the saddlebags—with the exception of a box of forty-four cartridges. He hesitated for only a moment before dropping it inside his own saddlebags. Without spending a lot of thought on his actions, he tucked a couple of bills under the flap of the marshal's saddlebags. Satisfied that his ledger was balanced, as far as the law at Fort Smith was concerned, he climbed aboard the chestnut. Bending low in the saddle to avoid the low-sweeping limbs of the giant oak, he left the well-traveled wagon track and rode down through a heavily wooded hillside. Letting the chestnut find his own way through the trees, he headed for the river and Indian Territory beyond.

Chapter 5

The old man was close enough now to smell the coffee. The aroma of the boiling black liquid wafted by his nostrils on the gentle evening breeze, luring him like the song of a sultry siren. It must have been nearly a month since Perley had run out of coffee beans, and the prospect of a friendly cup was too much to pass up.

Ordinarily, Perley would have taken a wide pass around a lone campfire this deep in Indian Territory, but this one had aroused his curiosity. Although apparently from a small fire, the thin trail of smoke had been obvious to his trained eye from a couple of miles away. He had first spotted it just before sundown and decided right away that it was not an Indian campfire. His guess had been that it was most likely that of a white man, which, in most cases in this part of the territory, would have given him reason to avoid it even more. White men in this part of the wilderness were usually outlaws on the run, and Perley avoided them whenever possible. About the only time he came into

contact with the lawless breed who hid out in the endless rolling hills was when he rode into Bannerman's
to trade some hides to supplement his meager supplies. He didn't require much: coffee, flour, occasionally a tin of oysters to celebrate Christmas. There was
little left over after his basic requirements were met,
namely, cartridges for his rifle.

Just like I figured, he thought as he watched the
lonely camp by the stream below him. It was a white
man all right. And from his position lying in the tall
grass atop the hill, Perley took his time to look the situation over. The stranger appeared to be a young fellow, and from the look of his gear, he didn't appear to
be a miner or a trapper. *Somebody running*, Perley decided. *Might be best to leave him be*. There were ever-
increasing numbers of settlers moving into the territory,
ignoring the fact that it was designated as Indian Territory, but this young fellow was most likely a fugitive
from the law. He might be quick to use the rifle
propped near his knee. Even as Perley decided it best
to avoid contact with a stranger riding alone across the
Choctaw Nation, the aroma of coffee floated by his
nose on the evening breeze. "What the hell?" he mumbled. "There are some things worth riskin' your neck
for."

"Hello the camp."

Startled by the sudden greeting from the hill above
him, Jordan reacted at once. Without taking time to
think about it, he grabbed his rifle by the barrel and
rolled over behind a cottonwood log. Peering out into
the fading light, he looked quickly to his sides and be-

hind him to make sure he wasn't surrounded. Making no reply to the greeting, he scanned back and forth across the ridge above him, trying to locate the spot from which the voice had come. There was nothing he could see among the scattering of oaks that dotted the ridge as his gaze moved from one tree to the next.

"Ain't no reason to get excited," the voice called out. "It's just ol' Perley." This time the voice seemed to come from farther down the hill to Jordan's right. Jordan immediately shifted his rifle to bear toward the base of the hill.

"Show yourself," Jordan called out. "If you're a peaceful man, you've got nothin' to worry about."

"All right," Perley answered, "but don't go gettin' excited with that rifle. I'm just lookin' for a cup of that coffee I've been smellin' for half a mile."

"Come on, then. I ain't gonna shoot." Peering hard along the base of the hill, Jordan kept the rifle aimed in the direction from which the sound had come. In a few seconds, a form emerged from the heavy shadows, walking slowly toward him. As his visitor approached, Jordan could see that he was leading two horses, one heavily loaded with packs. Whether he was Indian or white, Jordan could not tell in the fading light, but the man could have been either. Dressed in animal skins and wearing a floppy wide-brimmed hat, he walked with a rolling gate, as if his feet hurt. Still cautious, Jordan rolled over on his back and peered out behind him in the near darkness. Seeing no sign of anyone at his back, he rolled over again to keep an eye on his guest.

Perley had not survived the past five years, rambling on his own through Indian Territory, by trusting every stranger he met. Although the young man, now on one knee and watching him approach, appeared to be harmless enough, Perley kept one hand close to the handle of his pistol just in case. In motions slow and deliberate, so as to be obvious, he replaced his rifle in his saddle sling. "Good evenin' to you, young man," he offered.

"Evenin' to you," Jordan returned somewhat cautiously. Now that the old man was close enough to be seen a little better, Jordan decided he posed no threat. Scraggly strands of white hair protruded from around his hatband like the fringe on a buggy, so long that they intertwined with his full face of whiskers, making the old man appear to be peeking out from a mass of vines. Still with his eye on his guest, he nodded toward the pot resting in the coals of his fire. "You're welcome to coffee, but I don't have but one cup."

His eye on the young man as well, Perley grinned. "Oh, I've got a cup, all right." Under Jordan's watchful eye, he looped his horses' reins over a tree limb and rummaged through a pack until he produced a tin coffee cup. "I've been smellin' that coffee for half a mile." He went straight for the pot. When his cup was filled, and he had cautiously sipped a taste of the hot liquid, he smacked his lips and settled himself by the fire. He waited while Jordan propped his rifle against the log he had taken cover behind and moved back to join him at the fire. "It's been at least a month since I've had a cup of coffee," Perley went on. He took another cautious sip, since the metal cup was now hotter than the coffee it held. "The good Lord ain't never invented nothin' to take the place of coffee. I've drunk ever' kind of concoction you can think of to replace it. There ain't nothin'. The Injuns can brew up all kinds of nasty-tastin' medicine outta bark and berries and ever' thin' else, but it's a long sight from genuine coffee."

Jordan made no reply, so Perley rambled on in an attempt to be sociable. Finally he paused, then dispensing with meaningless conversation, he asked, "You don't say a helluva lot, do you?"

Jordan shrugged. "You didn't seem to need any help," he replied.

Perley laughed. "I reckon I do tend to run off at the mouth sometimes." Trusting his instincts, he suddenly extended his hand to Jordan. "My name's Perley Gates," he said. "And I reckon I've been away from folks too long. You're the first white man I've seed for a while." He nodded his head in the direction of his packhorse. "I'm on my way to Bannerman's to trade them skins for supplies. Ten years ago, I coulda loaded that horse up like that in two weeks. Nowadays it takes most of two months, and the pelts ain't near as prime as they was then. Hell, it used to be a man had to spread his bedroll in a tree to keep from gettin' run over by a herd of antelope. And buffalo—hell, I've shot and skinned buffalo right on this spot, but not no more. It's gettin' so's a man can hardly scratch out enough to keep his belly from rubbin' his backbone."

Jordan listened with mild interest. "Why do you stay on in Indian Territory?" The question seemed obvious to him, if there was as little game left as the old man claimed.

"I don't know," Perley replied. "'Cause I was born

here, I reckon. It warn't Injun Territory then. When I was just a young'un, the government moved all them Injuns from back east out here and called it Injun Territory. The game got scarce right quick after that. A few years back, I decided to go on out to have a look at the Rockies. Stayed for most part of two years. I'm thinkin' more and more about goin' back. Trouble is, the damn Injuns out there is still wild. I'm thinkin' about goin', anyway." He paused for a moment. "If you don't mind me askin', what are you doin' out here?"

"Lookin' for somebody," Jordan answered. He let it go at that at first, but the longer he listened to Perley talk, the more convinced he became that the old man was harmless and no threat to him. In fact, he began to believe that it was a stroke of luck that he had run across Perley. The old man might be able to help him, for Jordan had no clue as to where he was searching. This was a fact that he had not allowed to come to the forefront of his mind: he was just wandering, hoping for a stroke of luck. He had not permitted himself to even consider the probability that he might never find the four men he hunted. He wasn't even sure just how vast an area Indian Territory was. And what was beyond? According to his new acquaintance, the high plains and the Rockies were a world apart from the rolling hills of the Oklahoma country. Jordan would have to take his word, for this spot he was camped upon was as far west as he had ever been. Finally deciding that Perley was a friend, Jordan told him who he was looking for and why.

"Well, I swear . . ." Perley uttered after learning of the events that brought Jordan to this little stream in

Indian Territory. "Wife and child!" he exclaimed, shaking his head in sympathy. "No wonder you was lookin' like you didn't trust nobody." He squatted by the fire to refill his coffee cup, then settled himself against a tree trunk to enjoy it. "So you had a little run-in with the deputy marshal over in Fort Smith, didja? I expect ol' Ramey will be comin' lookin' for you."

"You know him?" Jordan asked.

"Know of him," Perley replied. "I've seed him. I was over to Skullyville one time when he come ridin' in, lookin' for some feller that broke outta jail." He paused to cast a sideways glance at Jordan. "I expect that's the first place he'll look for you. It ain't even a day's ride from Fort Smith."

"Where's . . . what did you call it?" Jordan asked,

"Skullyville," Perley said. "South of here, not too far from Swallow Rock boat landin' on the Arkansas. It used to be a right thrivin' little town before the war back east, but it's kinda slid downhill ever since. It's where the Injuns went to git their money from the government. I reckon that's where Skullyville got its name. The Choctaw word for money is *iskuli*, so I reckon they called it Moneytown. Anyway, there was a time when ever' outlaw runnin' from the federal marshal passed through Skullyville. But not so much any-more—they know that's the first place ol' Ramey is likely to look fer 'em."

"Where would you look for the four I'm after?"

"Bannerman's is as good a place as any to start. That's where I'm headin'. I can show you the way. Bannerman's run a tradin' post on Bitter Creek for about twenty years. The Injuns don't bother him because a lot of 'em trade with him. And he sells 'em whiskey. The government would probably close him down, but they ain't ever been able to catch him at it. I'd say there's a good chance the skunks you're after passed through that way. 'Course it's just a guess. Who the hell knows where they're headed? Might be they're just layin' around somewhere, or they've gone on through. But if they came this way, they most likely know about Bannerman's."

With no better option, Jordan decided to follow the old man's advice and accompany him to Bannerman's. Perley took care of his horses, then settled himself by the fire again. Jordan couldn't help but wonder at the almost constant chatter from his new traveling companion. Maybe, he speculated, it was as he had said: he hadn't seen a white man in a couple of months and he was starved for conversation. Jordan had never been one to make small talk, but it didn't matter. Perley didn't seem to notice, leaving little room for Jordan to comment beyond a grunt or nod. In the course of the evening, Jordan came to know almost everything about Perley Gates.

"Yep, my pap was a preacher. Used his life up tryin' to put the Choctaws and the Creeks on the road to heaven. It plum wore him out. My ma had a brother named Perley. She thought a lot of, so she wanted to name me after him. Pap thought that was a fine idea and might help me stay on the straight and narrow if I was always reminded of the Pearly Gates that only opened wide for the Lord's children. When I was a young'un, it started more fights than anything else. But I reckon it toughened me up in the long run."

Perley's talk went on and on until it was time to re-
tire to the bedrolls. As they were arranging their blankets to take best advantage of the warmth offered by
the fire, Perley offered one last observation. "I ain't
tryin' to tell you how to take care of your business. But
if I was you, next time I'd make my camp on the other
side of the stream, so's you had it between you and the
hill right behind you. Ain't as easy for somebody to
sneak up on you. Nothing but open country on the
other side—see somebody comin' for a mile." Jordan
nodded but did not speak in reply. Perley turned his
back to the fire and pulled his blanket up over his
shoulders. "Might not be a bad idea to look for a little
dryer wood to burn, neither—less smoke."

Again, Jordan made no reply, but he made a mental
note to remember to be a little more thoughtful when
selecting a campsite from that point on. It was the first
of many lessons Jordan was to learn about staying
alive in the wilderness. Had he known Perley a little
better, he would have realized that the old man had
seen something of value in Jordan Gray. Had he not,
his many comments and advice would have been
withheld.

The sun had not fully crested the low hills to the
east when Perley led his packhorse across the stream
and set a course toward the northwest. Jordan followed on the chestnut, but not too close. "Don't follow
up too close to ol' Sweet Pea there," Perley had cautioned. "She'll give your horse a kick if you come up
too close behind her. If you ride up beside her, she'll
try to take a nip outta you. I ain't never figured out

why she's got that mean streak—the female in 'er, I guess. She'll tolerate me, but she ain't got much patience for nobody else. I reckon I coulda rightly named her Hell on the Hoof, but I thought if I called her Sweet Pea, she might git to thinkin' she was a lady."

"It ain't workin', is it?"

Perley laughed. "Not so far, it ain't—she's about the most cantankerous beast I've ever seed. But she's a helluva packhorse. If you can load it, she can tote it. It don't make no difference what it is. She'll haul it and still be ready to go when this horse is plum wore out just totin' my old bones."

"Sweet Pea, huh?" Jordan grunted, giving the mottled gray animal a curious eye. His curiosity aroused only slightly, he asked, "What's your saddle horse's name?"

"Frank," Perley replied.

"Frank?" Jordan echoed, somewhat surprised, expecting something of a symbolic nature. "Why Frank?"

Perley shrugged. "I just like it."

If Jordan remembered correctly, he had not smiled since before finding his wife and child in the ruins of his cabin. He could not resist a faint smile now, however, as he followed an old man called Perley Gates on a horse named Frank, leading a pack animal called Sweet Pea, across the Choctaw Nation.

John Bannerman had constructed a small stockade around his trading post back in 1830 when the first news reached the territory that the government was relocating five Indian nations from the East. Before that, he had enjoyed a cordial relationship with the tribes native to that area, primarily the Osage, for over fifteen years. Not certain what to expect with the influx of these displaced bands, he speculated that he might have to defend his store on the banks of Bitter Creek. With help only from his wife, Rose, and his ten-year-old son he built his little fort during a bitter-cold winter, snaking logs in from the hills beyond the creek. The labor proved to be too much for poor Rose, who succumbed to a bout of pneumonia and passed away just weeks after the fort was finished. Bannerman, never a sensitive man, was philosophical about her passing, saying that she had at least held on until the fort was finished.

For the next fifteen years, father and son worked the trading post together. The stockade, it turned out, was unnecessary. After the first year, the gate was never closed, even at night, for the newly arrived tribes offered no threat to the small store near the northern boundary of the Choctaw Nation. The labor that had caused the early death of Bannerman's wife would have been regretted by most men, but Bannerman showed no remorse. His only comment when referring to his late wife was usually to point out that he had been deprived of a damn good cook and he had had to raise a young'un by himself.

Young John Jr., known by everyone as Little John, had grown to be a strapping young man. A shade over six feet tall, with wide shoulders and arms like tree trunks, Little John soon took over the operation of the store from his father. Not content with the meager bartering with the Indians that had been the basis of his father's survival, he hauled a wagon load of whiskey in from Fort Smith. His father had objected to it, and they fought over the issue, resulting in Little John strangling the old man. He buried him behind the stockade wall. When people asked after the old man, Little John told them that he had contracted a sudden case of pneumonia.

Over the years since his father's untimely death, Little John found a new source of business. The territory became a refuge for outlaws, and outlaws paid for their whiskey and supplies with cash. Every two months, Bannerman sent a wagon to Fort Smith to purchase supplies for his store. In effect, he was returning cash money to recirculate in civilization. The fact that it was money originally stolen from the civilized folk never bothered him. The authorities in Fort Smith suspected as much, but there was no way they could prove it.

Now at age fifty-five, Bannerman had seen few changes in the territory over the years, at least in his remote corner of the Choctaw Nation. Towns had sprung up in other parts of Indian Territory, and white settlers had infringed upon the land set aside for the five nations. But things were pretty much the same as far as Bannerman was concerned. Although his hair, once jet-black, was now frosted with white, turning it to a shade of slate gray—and his face was etched with lines like the crevices in the bluffs on the western side of the creek—he was still every bit the formidable brute he had been in his youth. On this day, in late summer of 1875, when his old friend Perley Gates showed up with a young stranger, Bannerman was in a foul mood.

"It's a damn good thing I ain't no Comanche lookin' for a scalp," Perley announced from the doorway.

Bannerman paused, leaning on the broom he had been using. "Hell, Perley, I seen you comin' a mile away. I heard you before that," he lied. In fact, he had been distracted by irritating thoughts of an incident that occurred the night before. His mood improving a bit at the sight of the old man, he added, "Besides, if you was a Comanche, you'd damn sure be lost."

Perley laughed. "I reckon." He walked over to shake hands with Bannerman. "How the hell are you, you old bear?"

"Tolerable, I reckon, for a man my age."

"Hell, wait till you get as long in the tooth as I am," Perley replied. He stepped aside and nodded back toward Jordan, who entered the store after him. "Say howdy to Jordan Gray."

"Jordan," Bannerman acknowledged, along with a nod of his head. When Jordan nodded in return, Bannerman turned back to Perley. "He ain't particular who he rides with, is he?"

Perley grunted, taking mock offense. Unable to think of a clever comeback for the insult, he changed the subject. "What were you lookin' so grouchy about when we come in?"

Bannerman shrugged, as if to indicate it was nothing. "Ah, nuthin' much. That damn half-breed they call Snake was in here last night with some fellers I ain't ever seen around here before." Perley shot a quick look in Jordan's direction to see if he had picked up on the comment. He had. Bannerman went on. "He had a little too much to drink. He never could hold his liquor, anyway. He got to stumblin' around here till he broke a lantern and knocked over a barrel of flour. I had to throw the sorry son of a bitch out."

"I know the coyote you're talkin' about," Perley said. "He's a mean one, all right. You say he was with some strangers?"

"Two I never seen before," Bannerman replied while he finished sweeping up the flour from the plank floor. Picking up the pile in a dustpan, he dumped it back into the flour barrel, then turned it under so the dirt from the floor would not be noticeable. "That feller they call Roach was with 'em. He's been here a few times before, lookin' for whiskey." Oblivious to the solid effect his words had upon Perley and his friend, Bannerman propped the broom in a corner and went to the short bar at the opposite end of the room. "Reckon you fellers want somethin' to cut the dust," he said. "I know damn well Perley does. How 'bout you, young feller?"

"Are they still around here?" Jordan blurted. Unable to control his impatience, he demanded, "Was one of 'em called Johnny Spratte?"

Bannerman paused, shot glasses in his hand, to give Jordan a long, hard look. In this part of the territory, especially in view of Bannerman's clientele, a man didn't ask a lot of questions. Perley quickly stepped in. "Hold your horses, there, Jordan," he said. Then turning to Bannerman, he explained, "Jordan here ain't long off the farm. You'll have to excuse his rough edges. Fact is, he's lookin' for four men that just come from Fort

Smith. They robbed the bank over there a couple of days back."

Bannerman cocked a suspicious eye in Jordan's direction. "You a lawman?"

"Nah, he ain't no lawman," Perley replied before Jordan could answer for himself. He then went on to explain Jordan's reasons for trailing the four.

"Why those low-down sons of bitches," Bannerman exclaimed, upon hearing of the ruthless murders. "Sorry, young feller," he offered in a show of sympathy. "Don't surprise me none. That damn half-breed never has been one to turn your back on. You sure these are the same fellers that hit your place?"

"I'm sure," Jordan replied.

"Well, I'll help you all I can, but I didn't pay much attention to their names. One of 'em mighta been called Johnny. I can't say for sure. I was too busy keepin' an eye on that damn Snake. The more he drinks, the meaner he gets, and they didn't seem to have no shortage of cash. The one they called Roach wasn't sayin' much, just keepin' up with the others, and I kept pourin' as long as they put money on the bar. The other two fellers was as opposite as night and day. The young one whooped and hollered a lot until he passed out. When I finally had to run 'em outta here close to midnight, they had to drag him out and throw him across his saddle. The other feller didn't talk a lot. He just sat there on that chair in the corner and watched the others. He was the one I kinda kept my eye on, too. I figured I'd have trouble with him when the time came to throw 'em out. But he didn't say a word. Just got up and walked out."

"Any idea where they were headed when they left here?" Jordan asked.

"I didn't pay no attention," Bannerman replied. "They did ride out across the creek, but I don't know whether they went north or south when they got across."

"That oughtn't to be hard to figure out," Perley said. "We can pick up their trail on the other side."

His comment surprised Jordan. Perley had given no indication that he was going to accompany him beyond Bannerman's. "I didn't think you were goin' any farther," he said.

"I warn't," Perley replied without emotion. "But you sure as hell ain't much of a tracker, and you'd probably get lost wanderin' around in this territory. I'll ride a piece further with you, if you'll wait till Bannerman here gets through cheatin' me outta my hides."

Jordan couldn't suppress a smile. "Much obliged," he said, "and much obliged to you, Mr. Bannerman."

"Wish I could help you more," Bannerman replied.

Although impatient to take up the trail again, Jordan was more than willing to wait while Perley and Bannerman came to an agreement over the value of Perley's furs. Jordan was never one to need companionship, but he was not too hardheaded to admit that he was not especially skilled in tracking. And he sure as hell wasn't familiar with the territory. Besides, he found that he had taken a liking to the crusty old trapper.

"All right, then," he heard Bannerman say as he totaled up the count. "Looks like you got yourself thirty-seven dollars' worth of credit." He raised his eyebrows slightly as he gave the old man an accusing glance. "And that includes that damn coyote hide in the middle of the pile."

Perley recoiled in mock astonishment. "Coyote?" he exclaimed. "Them was all prime antelope and deer. How in the world did a coyote hide get in there?"

"I wonder," Bannerman replied, amused by the old man's theatrics. He gave Jordan a wink. "I need me a door mat. Maybe I'll use it for that."

Still playing the part, Perley mumbled a few words of disbelief that the lowly pelt had somehow found its way into his pile of prime skins. While Bannerman and Jordan grinned at each other, he selected a few possibles from the shelves. Jordan got the feeling that Bannerman had been exceedingly generous in his evaluation of Perley's pelts in what might even be considered outright charity. Maybe, he thought, the gruff exterior of huge man enclosed a few tender spots in his heart, and in truth, Bannerman had mellowed over the years—a far cry from the callous young man who had strangled his own father.

Jordan lent a hand when Perley and Bannerman carried the skins to the back room. As he looked around the storeroom, it was easy to conclude that Bannerman derived very little of his income from the trading of hides. The walls of the room were lined with barrels. Some contained molasses, a few, dried apples, but most were unmarked, leading Jordan to suspect that whiskey was Bannerman's major commodity.

The trading done, Jordan and Perley got on their horses. With a final tip of the hat to Bannerman, they turned their mounts toward the creek, and Perley led them out. Something triggered a memory in Bannerman's mind, and he called after them, "Johnny Spratte! That *was* the name they called that young feller." Jordan acknowledged him with a wave of his hand. "Johnny Spratte," Bannerman mumbled to himself again, certain of his recollection.

So it was as Jordan had believed. Winston Moffett's deputy had thrown in with the three men who had killed his wife and son. In Jordan's mind, the fact that Johnny had obviously joined the outlaws after the slaughter of his family, as well as that of the Thompson family, made him no less guilty than the other three. He had been with them when the banker and his employee were killed. Consumed by his desire for vengeance, Jordan wanted to cleanse the earth of these men and anything they touched. In his present state of grief, he wanted to kill each one of them, anyone associated with them, and their horses. He would not be satisfied until all traces of their existence were removed from the earth. Even when that was accomplished, he was not sure he could deal with a life without Sarah and Jonah.

Chapter 6

It didn't take long to pick up the outlaws' tracks on the other side of the creek. The four riders had started out toward the west, riding only a quarter of a mile before striking a commonly used trail and following it north. "This trail leads to John Eagle Claw's village," Perley said. "He's the chief. It ain't a very big village, and now that I think on it, I believe that's where Snake's mama lives. I'm surprised he'd even be welcome there. From what I've heard, he caused a lot of trouble there a few years back—killed a man in an argument over somethin'—I don't know what, but I think ol' Eagle Claw run him off. If they're figurin' on holing up there for a spell, they might be in for a surprise. They probably figured his mama's village just might be the closest place to sleep off a hangover."

This made sense to Jordan. According to what they had just learned from Bannerman, it was after midnight when the outlaws left his store, and they were in no shape to ride very far. They no doubt would have been looking for the closest place to recover from a night of drinking. The thought of the four lying around a tipi only a few hours away served to stimulate Jordan's impatience even more.

There was no time wasted as Jordan and Perley started out at a fast walk, following the distinct trail over the grassy hills. Jordan would occasionally push the chestnut into a faster pace, causing the horse to break into a lope. Each time, Perley would caution him not to tire the horse out. "We don't know if we're gonna have to run these horses or not when we get to the Choctaw village."

"Hey, there's a bunch of them damn Injuns snoopin' around our horses!" Johnny Spratte suddenly exclaimed over the steady drone of Roach's snoring. He had spent the balance of the night where his friends had dropped him, with his head halfway out of the open door of the mud hut. His outburst awakened Snake, and while Johnny tried to sit up, in a painful effort to figure out just where in hell he was, the halfbreed crawled over to the door.

"Eagle Claw," Snake hissed, at once annoyed to see the chief nosing around the horses. "He'll be sticking his nose in here before long." Then, as if just remembering he didn't particularly like the young ex-deputy—or most anybody else for that matter—he scowled at Johnny. "Go wake the old woman. Tell her to rustle up some food."

Johnny turned to look at the woman huddled in a corner of the hut. One glance at the wide-eyed expression told him that she had probably not closed her eyes ever since her son and his friends had dropped in for an unexpected visit. Painfully aware then of a pounding in his skull, Johnny attempted to stand up, only to fall helplessly to his hands and knees. Sick, as only an overdose of rotgut whiskey can incapacitate a man, he remained in that position with his head hanging down like an abused yard dog, the earthen floor spinning beneath him. The old woman watched in frightened confusion while the young white man remained on all fours, half in and half out of the doorway, rocking slightly from side to side.

Disgusted with Johnny's apparent weakness, Snake glowered at his mother. "I'm hungry, old woman. Get your fire started before I have to whip you," he scolded, talking to her in the Choctaw tongue.

Speaking for the first time since her son and his three white companions fell in on her in the wee hours of the morning, she nodded toward Johnny. "That white man is crazy. He looks like he's having a fit. How can I start my cook fire with him blocking the door?"

The brief exchange between mother and son served to awaken Leach, who was sleeping closest to the old woman. "What's goin' on?" Leach asked, feeling none too well himself after a night of drinking.

"That damn lawman you picked up is about to puke in the door," Snake shot back in angry disgust. "If he does, I'm gonna shoot the son of a bitch."

Leach knew the belligerent half-breed made a great many threats, some idle, some not. At this point, he didn't care whether Snake intended to shoot Spratte or not. He had more immediate concerns. His bladder threatened to burst if not given relief in the next minute or two. So he struggled out of his blanket and rose to his feet, pausing only a moment to steady himself. A brief glance at the woman to his left startled him for a moment until he remembered the hut belonged to Snake's mother. "Ugh," he grunted for lack of words, and pushed past Snake, who was now on his feet. "I gotta piss," he said. Stopping before the doorway, he planted his boot on Johnny's backside and shoved the stricken man out the door.

Johnny landed face-first in the sandy gravel in front of the hut. The sudden assault served to break the grip he had been desperately struggling to maintain on his insides, and the entire contents of his stomach and bowels immediately moved to exit his body. "Damn!" Leach exclaimed as he stepped aside to avoid walking through the contents of Johnny's stomach. Showing no sympathy for the stricken man, he went around to the back of the hut to relieve himself.

Having the same urgency as Leach, Snake left the hut to join him. He was stopped at once by the sight of Johnny Spratte, lying in his own filth, his stomach continuing to convulse in repeated efforts to empty itself. Snake was already disgusted, and the sight of the helpless man served to infuriate him. Without a moment's hesitation, he pulled his pistol and shot Johnny in the head. Grabbing the corpse by one ankle, he dragged it a few feet out of the way. Then he walked behind the hut to join Leach, who had been abruptly interrupted in midstream by the sound of the gunshot.

"He ain't gonna be no trouble no more," Snake offered nonchalantly and proceeded to untie his britches.

"Reckon not," Leach replied, his own pistol in hand now. Keeping a wary eye on his half-breed partner, he put the gun away and resumed the evacuation of his bladder.

Seeing the guarded look in Leach's eye, Snake shrugged. "I told you I'd shoot the son of a bitch."

Leach was about to reply when they were suddenly joined by Roach, who had been awakened by the pistol shot. Never one to rush headlong into trouble, Roach had grabbed his pistol and crawled up to the door. Seeing Johnny's body sprawled a few yards away, he then spotted the group of Indians standing by the horses, all of them staring in his direction. With neither Leach nor Snake in sight, he prepared to return fire. Drawing down on the nearest Choctaw, he was about to pull the trigger when he heard his partners talking behind the hut. Hesitating then, mainly because the group of Indians showed no signs of advancing toward the hut, he decided to find out what was what before taking any action. He had then made a dash around the hut to join his partners. "Damn!" Roach exclaimed upon turning the corner and finding Snake and Leach completing their morning bladder call. He stood, staring for a moment, before informing them, "Somebody shot Johnny."

"That was Snake," Leach replied without emotion.

"What for?" Roach asked, directing his question toward the stoic half-breed.

"I didn't like the son of a bitch," Snake said, already bored with the subject. "I'm hungry. Is that old woman fixin' some food yet?" Not waiting for an answer, he left them to find out for himself. As he disappeared around the corner of the hut, they heard him mumble, "If she ain't, I might whip her lazy ass."

Roach and Leach exchanged glances. Leach just shook his head. Roach said, "There ain't nothin' sweeter than the love between a mother and son." His comment brought a chuckle, but both men were thinking that the time might soon come when something would have to be done about the belligerent half-Choctaw. Although the men had ridden together for the better part of three years, there was no guarantee that either Leach or Roach wouldn't at any time become a victim of Snake's uncontrollable violence, and he was getting worse with each passing day.

"Uh-oh," Roach uttered as he and Leach walked back around to the front of the hut to discover a gathering of fifteen or more Choctaw men coming their way. All but a few of them carried weapons, either rifles or bows. "That don't look like no welcoming committee."

"Looks like somethin' else we can thank Snake for," Leach replied quietly. He had hoped to hole up in the Choctaw village for a couple of days before moving on. That now seemed unlikely, since a couple of the delegation were leading the white men's horses. "Don't appear we're even gonna get breakfast," he commented. Then under his breath, he added, "That damn half-breed."

Led by Chief Eagle Claw, the delegation approached the hut to be met by Snake standing defiantly before the door, his rifle in hand. For Leach and Roach, however, there was no thought of defiance. The odds were far too great to risk a gunfight. They both hurried inside to collect their rifles, then reappeared to stand with Snake, although not too close.

"So," Snake slurred sarcastically, speaking in the Choctaw tongue, "my people have come to welcome me home."

Eagle Claw stood glaring at the unwelcome prodigal son for a few moments, then glanced at his two companions before speaking. "Thomas Kicking Horse, you have no home here. Each time you return, there is trouble. Now you have killed this white man in our village. There will be lawmen coming to look for you. Maybe the soldiers will come. You bring nothing but shame to our people and your mother's lodge. You and your white friends are not welcome here. Leave this village at once, and never come back here. I speak for all the elders of the village."

"Oh, you speak for all the elders of the village, do you?" Snake mocked, his eyes flashing contempt as he surveyed the committee. "You're all a bunch of women huddled together for protection." Concentrating his gaze upon the chief then, he stated, "I go when and where I want to go. Maybe I do not choose to leave."

"Then we will turn you over to the white lawman in Fort Smith," Eagle Claw responded without hesitation.

"The hell you will," Snake shot back in anger, reverting to the white man's tongue. He made a motion as if to bring his rifle up to a ready position. Before he could raise it, there were at least a dozen rifles pointed at his chest. Both Leach and Roach quickly withdrew a couple of more steps away from their beleaguered partner.

"The fool is gonna get us kilt," Roach whispered aside.

"Hold on, Snake," Leach pleaded anxiously. "The odds are too damn much. Let's just get the hell outta here."

"I ain't lettin' no damn bunch of women—" Snake started before Leach cut him off.

"I ain't about to commit suicide for your damn pride," Leach shot back angrily. "Get on that damn horse or I'll shoot you myself." Turning to address Eagle Claw, Leach said, "We're goin'. We ain't lookin' to cause no trouble in your village."

Snake fixed his white partner with a gaze that would have blistered most men. Leach recognized the hatred in that gaze, but he was prepared to carry out his threat to shoot the belligerent half-breed on the spot. The two locked eyes for a long moment before Snake gave in and walked toward his horse. Leach and Roach both knew it was something that would have to be dealt with later.

"Take this dead man with you," Eagle Claw ordered.

Leach nodded and, with Roach's help, lifted the late Johnny Spratte to lie across his saddle. With Choctaw rifles still trained upon them, the three outlaws mounted and rode out of the village. In parting, Snake growled, "I'll be seein' you," as he brushed past the Choctaw chief.

"Don't come back here," Eagle Claw warned.

"Well, that was some visit, weren't it?" Leach commented sarcastically when the three stopped at a small stream to let the horses drink. Some three miles from the village at this point, those were the first words spoken among them since their impromptu sendoff.

"Yeah," Roach replied. "I was lookin' to lay around there for a while. There was some fair-lookin' little squaws standing around watchin' the chief kick our asses outta there."

Still seething, Snake didn't comment for a few minutes. He reined his horse back even with Johnny's and, grabbing one of Johnny's boots, dumped the corpse on the ground. "I shot him, so I'm claimin' his horse." He looked from one face to the other, daring protest from either man. There was none, both men being wise enough to know this was not the time.

Seeking to change the subject, Leach said, "Dammit, I'm hungry. We might as well fix us some breakfast." That suggestion was one that all agreed upon, so they dismounted, and Roach got busy making a fire. There wasn't much to prepare beyond some bacon and coffee. Since money was not a concern after robbing the bank in Fort Smith, they had planned to stock up on provisions at Bannerman's. That plan had been altered when they had gotten drunk and Bannerman kicked them out before such basic needs as provisions could be taken care of.

It was a quiet trio of outlaws who sat around the tiny fire, chewing on the tough bacon and washing it down with bitter black coffee. Roach broke the silence once when he complained that he regretted the fact that they had not bought some sugar at Bannerman's. Leach thoughtfully sipped the hot liquid from a tin cup, keeping a watchful eye upon the sulking Snake. The brooding savage was deep in his own thoughts, paying little attention to his two partners. Leach knew that he was working something over in his mind, and he was wary that it might be in retaliation for threatening to shoot Snake back in Eagle Claw's village. In fact, Snake had revenge on his mind, but it was directed at Eagle Claw and the men of the village.

After they kicked out the fire and got under way once more, they rode off to the northeast. With each mile they rode, Snake thought more and more about the people who had thrown him out. Finally it took total control of his mind, and he pulled up short. Roach and Leach pulled up to see why he had stopped. "I got a score to settle," he announced. "I'm goin' back to take care of them bastards."

Leach and Roach exchanged glances. They had just been allowed to leave the village unharmed, and it seemed the best thing to do was to simply leave the trouble behind. "I ain't goin' back to that village," Leach said.

"Ain't nobody asked you to," Snake snarled. "I don't need no help. I'll catch up with you after I'm done."

Seeing an opportunity, Leach quickly nodded, and with a frown toward Roach to caution him to hold his tongue, he said, "All right. Me and Roach are gonna hold to a line toward the edge of them hills yonder." He pointed out a range northeast of the spot they stood on. "If you don't catch up right away, we'll be headin' for Kansas City."

Snake acknowledged him with a simple nod of his head and, without another word, turned back toward the Choctaw village. Roach stared after him for several long seconds before speaking. "What in hell do we wanna go to Kansas City for? We go back to that town, and they'll hang us for sure."

"They might at that," Leach replied, a sly smile creeping across his unshaven face. It was unnecessary to say more.

Roach grinned when he realized they had been given the opportunity to rid themselves of the unpredictable half-breed. Kansas City was an unhealthy place for the three outlaws since they had shot a young deputy sheriff and a woman who got in the way of a bank robbery that went bad. Snake should have known at once that Kansas City was the last place Leach intended to visit at this point. Leach was surprised that Snake had not questioned it. But then, the half-breed didn't think much farther than the length of his nose. "I reckon one of us would have had to shoot him before long," Roach said. "It was gettin' so I didn't wanna turn my back on him." In complete accord with Leach's sudden decision to lose their volatile partner, he asked, "Where you think we should head?"

"I'm thinkin' west, maybe north, someplace we ain't been before—find some new pickin's. We could cut back and follow the river to Fort Gibson. I ain't never been there, but I've heard tell it's a thrivin' little town. Might be a good place to light for a spell. Whaddayou think?"

"Hell, sounds all right to me." It didn't really matter to Roach where they went as long as there were whiskey and women.

Chapter 7

John Eagle Claw walked outside when he heard some of the women down by the creek calling out that riders were approaching. Thinking that Thomas Kicking Horse and his friends might be returning, he had picked up his rifle as he left his lodge. Several other men were already gathering to see who the women had spotted. The visitors were still too far away to identify, but Eagle Claw was relieved to see they were coming from the south. Snake and the two white men had ridden out to the north. Thoughts of the belligerent son of Jane Little Bird caused the chief to frown as he stood watching the two riders approach. He couldn't help but wonder if trouble was to befall his village twice before the sun had completed a single journey across the sky.

Two riders and three horses—one was definitely a white man; the other, hard to tell. Eagle Claw shielded his eyes with his hand and stared. Fording the creek, where it made a sharp bend toward the west, the riders topped the steep bank and headed straight for the chief's lodge. Eagle Claw's frown relaxed, transformed into a broad smile as he recognized the familiar form of his old friend Perley Gates. Even at this distance, the old trapper was easy to identify, slumped forward in the saddle, his bushy white whiskers resting on his chest. Shifting his gaze to the packhorse Perley led, Eagle Claw quickly concluded that Perley was not coming to trade, for the horse was carrying a light load.

Shifting his gaze then to the rider with Perley, Eagle Claw stared hard in an effort to recognize him. He had never seen this man before. Maybe he was a lawman. He sat straight in the saddle, riding a chestnut horse. Eagle Claw strode forward to meet his old friend, joined by the other men who had also been watching the visitors approach. Perley held up his hand and called out a greeting.

"Welcome, my friend," Eagle Claw returned the greeting as the two riders drew up before the rapidly growing welcome committee. Jordan remained in the saddle, quietly watching the cordial reunion. It appeared that everyone there knew Perley and counted him as a friend. The initial greetings completed, Perley stepped back and introduced his companion.

"This here's Jordan Gray," he said, as Jordan dismounted and stood next to him. "We're tryin' to catch up with four men that rode this way. I think one of 'em might be Thomas Kicking Horse—figured they mighta stopped here."

"They were here," Eagle Claw said, nodding to Jordan before turning his attention back to Perley. "I sent them away. They were trouble." Motioning with his head toward Jordan, he asked, "Lawman?"

"No," Perley answered and went on to explain why Jordan was trailing the four men.

Eagle Claw nodded, showing his compassion, as Perley related the sorrowful events that brought the young white man to the Choctaw village. "The four men you search for are now only three," he said. "Thomas Kicking Horse killed one of them right here in the village. I sent them away and told them never to return." He placed a consoling hand on Jordan's arm. "You must be careful. These are bad men." Jordan nodded. Eagle Claw continued to look into Jordan's face for a long moment before turning back to Perley. "He does not talk, this friend of yours."

"He don't much—that's a fact." Perley laughed. "But he damn sure listens."

Jordan's mind was busy, working on the information just acquired. One of the men was dead. He had confusing emotions upon learning this, almost disappointed that he had been robbed of his desire to take revenge on each of the four personally. Impatient to leave, especially when he learned that the outlaws were barely a half day ahead of them, he conveyed his sense of urgency to Perley. Perley explained that it would be impolite to refuse the invitation to eat with the chief. Considering the grave importance of his mission, Jordan could not understand Perley's concern for good manners. *To hell with manners*, he thought. *The sons of bitches are getting away!* He strongly considered riding on alone, but he realized he needed Perley's tracking skills, so he resigned himself to curb his impatience. Out of the corner of his eye, Perley watched his young friend, sensing the turmoil stirring in his brain. He was relieved to see Jordan finally relax his stern expression and step away from his horse.

It was late afternoon before Perley and Jordan thanked the Choctaws for the food and bade them farewell, Perley promising to return for a longer visit. Following the directions Eagle Claw gave him, Perley rode along the northwest creekbank until he picked up the tracks of the outlaws. Following a faint trail up a rocky bluff, they found a more obvious one that led across the grassy prairie. After a ride of roughly three miles, they spotted a line of trees that indicated the presence of a stream.

Within a couple hundred yards of the stream, Perley pulled up and paused to take a good look at the line of cottonwoods and willows. "Like ol' Eagle Claw said, these boys is bad. We don't wanna just go ridin' into them trees without we take a good look first."

After a moment, Jordan nudged the chestnut forward. "If they were in there," he said, "they would have shot at us by now." He made directly for the stream, following the trail left in the tall grass.

Perley held back a few moments longer before going after him. He had not lived to the ripe old age of fifty-eight by riding blindly into a perfect site for an ambush. "Keep your eyes peeled," he called after Jordan, who was already entering the trees at that point. When there was no sudden eruption of gunfire, Perley nudged his horse and loped along after his impatient companion. He found Jordan still sitting in the saddle, staring down at a corpse on the ground.

As Perley rode up, Jordan dismounted and turned the body over. "Johnny Spratte," he uttered softly.

"Dang," Perley commented. "Don't look like they spent much time on a funeral, does it?"

Jordan explained that this was the only one of the four he could identify. He stood, looking at the body for a long moment, his mind turning over the possible reasons for Johnny's new friends to turn on him. They had robbed him of the satisfaction of dealing with Johnny personally, but he decided it was just as well. Johnny had not joined the three outlaws until after they had killed Sarah and Jonah. In a way, he was relieved to have had fate take the decision from him. Even with the intense hatred he felt for those men, it might have been hard to kill someone he had known for a couple of years and might have considered a friend. His mind now rapidly returning to focus on the business at hand, he said, "Well, there's no sense wasting any more time here."

Perley, still seated in the saddle, looked all around him, then looked up at the sky. "Sun's gettin' pretty low. We might wanna think about makin' camp. If I recollect, there ain't no more water for maybe twelve or thirteen miles."

As Perley had done, Jordan looked up at the sun. Perley was right; it was settling close to the distant hills, but there were still a few hours of daylight left. Jordan was impatient to push on, even if it meant making a dry camp. Then it occurred to him that it might be more important to consider the horses. They needed water. "Maybe you're right," he conceded, although reluctantly. "We'd best camp here and start out early in the morning." He took another look at the stiffened features of the late Johnny Spratte, the eyes staring blindly beneath the one black bullet hole in his forehead and what appeared to be dried vomit streaking the scraggly new beard. He wondered then that he had even been able to recognize the man. He looked a far cry from the loud-talking, cocky young deputy who had led the posse on a wild-goose chase up through the hills north of Fort Smith. *Look at you now, Johnny*, he thought as he turned away to follow Perley.

The old trapper was already walking his horse toward the opposite side of the stream, anxious to get up wind from the corpse. His horse seemed to share the old man's thoughts. It snorted as if trying to rid its nostrils of the stench already emanating from the ripening body. The snorts turned into one long scream at the same time the crack of a rifle split the air and ripped into the horse's chest. The fatally wounded horse stumbled several more steps before reeling to the side and falling heavily in the middle of the stream. Perley was barely able to clear the saddle to avoid being pinned beneath the mass of dying horse.

"Dammit," Snake swore as he ejected the spent cartridge, and tried to quickly sight again. He thought he had the old man dead in his sights, but he had aimed too low, hitting the horse instead. It was too late to get off the second shot. The old man had managed to scramble down the bank of the stream to take cover behind a log. *You better run, you old fool*, Snake thought, angry that he had cost himself a perfectly good horse when he missed the old man. He had recognized the familiar slump of Perley Gates while the two riders were still trailing along the grassy slope leading down to the stream. He did not recognize the man riding with Perley, but he assumed he was a lawman since the two appeared to be following the trail Snake and his partners had left.

Moving to a new position several yards away, Snake tried to see where the stranger had managed to find cover. Thinking it might be a clump of willows near the bank, he fired several shots in rapid succession, sweeping the willows from left to right. There was no return fire or cry of pain, so he couldn't be sure if he hit anything or not. A movement on the other side of the stream caught his attention, and he jerked his rifle around, ready to fire. But it was just Perley's packhorse seeking safety. Shifting his gaze back to the stream, he kept his eyes on the log Perley had taken cover behind while he reloaded. He didn't know where the stranger was, but he considered the possibility that the man might be trying to circle around behind him. *I ain't gonna be here*, he thought, having already decided that he could cross the stream under cover of the trees and work around behind Perley. Then there would be only one man to deal with, and Snake was confident who the loser of that contest would be.

Jordan had come out of the saddle the instant he heard the shot and saw Perley's horse stumble. Snatching his rifle from the sling as his foot hit the ground, he wasted no time scrambling for cover. When he saw that Perley had found cover behind a log, he concentrated his attention on the thick stand of trees along the banks of the stream. He had no idea where the shot had come from, but it had most likely come from that direction. When a volley of several shots blistered a clump of willows off to his left, he realized their assailant wasn't sure where he was. This time, Jordan was able to get the general location from where the shots had come. He did not return fire because he was still not sure of a target. He had the feeling that one rifle had done all the shooting, but he had to assume that the other two outlaws were lying low, waiting for him or Perley to show themselves.

From his position, he could see Perley hugging the ground behind the log. The old man was pretty much pinned down. There was nothing but open sand on either end of the log. Perley would be forced to expose himself if he tried to move. A stab of guilt flashed through Jordan's mind when he thought about the danger he had created for Perley. He had wondered about it before, but could never understand why Perley had continued on with him after Bannerman's. *And now I've gotten him pinned down about to get his ass shot off*, he thought. *Well, I'm not going to let that happen!*

With total disregard for his own life, Jordan pushed up from his position behind a water oak and charged toward the thick willow stand by the water. Oblivious to the branches and willow switches that reached out to whip his face and arms, he ran headlong into the thicket, his rifle before him, searching for any target that presented itself. Forgetting Perley for the moment, he was now driven by his desperate need to avenge his family. He had been trailing the murderers for days, and now they were in reach. He would not be denied; he gave no thought to the possibility that they might kill him.

The harder he ran, the more the fury built up inside him, until he became possessed by one dominant thought: to destroy those who had taken his life away. Visions of Sarah's mud-spattered body and little Jonah's crushed skull flashed through his brain, providing fuel for his rage. Breaking through to the stream, he found no one there. He almost cried out in anguish. Looking all around him, searching for someone, he spied several spent cartridges on the ground. Farther back along the stream, he caught a glimpse of a single horse tied near the water. It registered briefly on his mind that there was only one man. *Perley!* he thought and immediately started running back to help the old man.

As he had feared, the old man was in mortal danger, still huddled behind the log, unaware of the rifle aimed at his back. Jordan would never forget the vivid image of the twisted face that sighted down the barrel of that rifle. It was a cruel face beneath cold black hair, woven in a single braid with an eagle feather dangling to one side. He was certain at that moment that he was looking into the face of evil itself. It took on a crooked smile as Snake savored the pleasure he derived from the taking of a life. At the instant he started to squeeze the trigger, however, he was distracted by the sudden emergence of Jordan, charging from the brush of the thicket no more than a few yards from him. He quickly turned and fired. The bullet shattered the stock of Jordan's rifle. The impact at such close range was sufficient to knock the weapon from Jordan's hands and cause him to stumble and fall. Seeing him go down, Snake thought he had killed him, and he hesitated for a moment before cocking his rifle. It cost him his life.

In one continuous motion, Jordan hit the ground and rolled, pulling his skinning knife as he regained his feet. Snake tried to sidestep the charging mass of fury, but he was not quick enough. The force of the impact, as Jordan drove his shoulder into Snake's midsection, was sufficient to carry both bodies several feet before they crashed to the ground. Snake tried desperately to claw his way out from under Jordan, but his desperation was no match for Jordan's rage. Freeing his knife hand, Jordan drove the blade to the hilt up under Snake's rib cage. Snake gasped a long guttural scream, and the hands reaching for Jordan's throat suddenly relaxed. Jordan withdrew the blade and quickly thrust it into Snake's body again, causing the mortally wounded half-breed to cry out helplessly. His conscious mind almost blinded by his rage, Jordan looked deeply into the terrified eyes, watching Snake die. There were no words spoken between victim and executioner, but somehow Snake sensed that this was the man whose wife and son he had murdered.

Stunned by the violent confrontation that had occurred right behind him, Perley failed to react quickly enough to be a factor. When he did realize how close he had come to meeting his Maker, it was too late. As quickly as he could, he turned over on his back and tried to get a clear shot at Snake. But he could not fire without risk of hitting Jordan. Helpless to do anything but watch, he at once realized that he was witness to the most violent attack of one man upon another that he had ever seen.

When it was over, and Snake's last dying convulsions were stilled, Jordan continued to stare into the lifeless eyes, his hand straining against the handle of his knife as if trying to force every spark of life from the half-breed's body. Perley found himself almost afraid to speak, for fear he might somehow turn Jordan's blind fury upon him. It was only after several minutes had passed with no motion from his young friend that Perley risked breaking through the trance that seemed to have captured him. "Jordan," he said softly, "it's all over. He's done for."

As if just then realizing Perley's presence, Jordan slowly turned to stare at the old man, his eyes still somewhat glazed. He continued to gaze at Perley for a few seconds before his face finally relaxed, and the fury drained from his features. "Perley," he asked, "are you all right?"

"Thanks to you, I reckon I am," Perley answered, relieved to see that Jordan seemed to have recovered.

Jordan looked again at the dead man, then withdrew his knife and got to his feet. Staring at the knife, he seemed surprised to see the blade covered with blood. After a moment, he cleaned it on the shirt tail of the late Thomas Kicking Horse and went in search of his rifle. "He was gettin' ready to shoot you," he said.

"I reckon," Perley replied, still much in awe of the transformation he had just witnessed, turning a quiet somber man into a savage killing machine. "I'm obliged to you. I just hope you don't ever get that mad at me."

"Was he the one they called Snake?"

"He was," Perley confirmed, "and he was meaner than any rattler you'd come across."

"Two to go," Jordan uttered softly, not really speaking to Perley. He reached down and picked up his father's Henry rifle, the stock smashed and splintered. Turning it over in his hands, he examined it carefully. "I reckon it saved my life today," he said.

"I'd say you was pretty lucky," Perley agreed. He wondered if Jordan really appreciated just how lucky he had been. Charging blindly like he had, and Snake firing at point-blank range, he should have been dead. Perley decided somebody upstairs must have taken a liking to his young friend.

Jordan didn't reply to Perley's comment. Continuing to stare at his broken rifle, he seemed to be lost in his thoughts. It wasn't necessary for the old man to ask what he was thinking. He could fairly well guess that Jordan had never killed a man before. And if a man had any shred of conscience in him, it could be a damn uncomfortable feeling to trespass in God's business— no matter how much the mean son of a bitch needed killing.

Perley knew the feeling. He had experienced it himself, years ago, when he was a young man, maybe younger than Jordan. He thought about it once in a while, and it always made him melancholy for a spell. And it seemed the mood lasted a little longer each time, now that he was closer to the final chapter of his own life. Had he sought to examine it, he might have guessed that it was because he would be called to stand in judgment one day soon. Barney Tatum had been his friend and partner. Back in forty—or was it thirty-nine?—the two friends had decided to journey out to the Big Horn country to try their hand at trapping. They did pretty well for a couple of greenhorns, but the inexperience of youth and the evil influence of whiskey proved to be Perley's downfall. At the last big rendezvous on the Green River, they traded a good portion of their plews for rotgut whiskey, and during a drunken fit, they quarreled over a young Crow maiden. The quarrel led to a fight, and Perley was getting the best of it until Barney pulled his knife. Perley managed to wrest it away from him and drive it deep into Barney's chest. It didn't even register with him in his drunken state that he had killed Barney. In the clear light of dawn, when he realized what he had done, he was devastated. In desperate need for redemption, he laid the blame entirely on demon whiskey and vowed never to imbibe again. At the end of that summer, he journeyed back to Oklahoma Territory. He never told anyone the true story, telling family and friends that Barney had been killed by Blackfoot Indians.

So Perley had a notion as to what Jordan was feeling, but at least Jordan's kill was justified. Over the years since that rendezvous, Perley had slipped on his vow more than a few times. But he usually took no more than one drink on most occasions, and never more than two.

Shadows lengthened as the sun settled closer upon the crests of the distant hills as Jordan helped Perley pull his saddle out from under his horse's carcass. "Damn, I hate losing that horse," Perley said, shaking his head sadly. "I reckon I'll be ridin' Sweet Pea now."

"His horse is tied a little way up the stream," Jordan said, nodding his head toward Snake's corpse.

Both men had forgotten about the half-breed's horse. Their first concern after Jordan had killed Snake was why he was alone. Where were his two partners? When there were no further attacks upon them, they decided the other two outlaws must have continued on, leaving Snake behind. After making sure they were indeed alone, Jordan led Perley back along the stream to the point where he had glimpsed the horse tied in the willows. When they approached the horse, they discovered that there was not one horse, but two. "Probably the other feller's horse we found dead back there," Perley said.

Chapter 8

After examining the two horses the confrontation with Snake had provided, Perley decided to throw his saddle on the one Snake had ridden. It was a ragged-looking paint, but it had good lines, with a broad chest. Perley thought it a better choice for a saddle horse than his own mottled gray. He wasn't sure Sweet Pea would cotton to having a rider on her back, anyway. "You need a packhorse," he told Jordan, so Jordan put a lead line on Johnny Spratte's horse, resisting an urge to shoot the animal for having belonged to the deputy. In addition to Snake's rifle, a Winchester 66, there was a sizable roll of cash money in his saddle-bags. Jordan was content to let Perley decide what to do with that. It had to be part of the money stolen from the bank in Fort Smith. "Maybe I'll just hang on to it for a spell," Perley said, a sheepish grin covering his face, "until the next time I'm in Fort Smith."

Leaving the horses hobbled, and walking in opposite directions, both men scouted a wide circle around the camp to make sure there was no sign of Snake's two partners. Afterward, fairly confident there was no one near the willow stand by the stream but the two of them and the two cold corpses, Perley built a fire, and they settled in for the night.

Morning brought a clear day, and Jordan was up with the sun. There was a question in his mind as to whether Perley might decide to turn back after the previous day's confrontation, and the close call he had with Snake. He didn't mention it to Perley when the old man rolled out of his blanket and moved closer to the fire Jordan was busy rekindling. Jordan figured he could track the two outlaws if they continued to leave a trail as plain as the one they had followed to that point. Perley settled the issue when he announced, "We'd best get a little grub in our bellies if we're gonna chase them two varmints across Kansas Territory."

"I reckon," Jordan replied with a faint smile. He was to have his tracker with him, after all.

Snake's paint pony had appeared to be indifferent to the change in masters the night before when Perley was looking him over. The morning seemed to have brought a change in disposition, however, for the beast rolled a wary eye in Perley's direction when the old man approached with a strange saddle. Perley sensed the change in attitude, and he, in turn, kept a sharp eye on the paint as he gently settled his saddle upon the horse's back. The paint did not protest, showing no more than a nervous quiver in his front legs. "Easy, son," Perley cooed as he placed a foot in the stirrup. The paint did not back away. "Atta boy," Perley muttered and stepped up in the stirrup. That was as far as he got. Before he could throw his other leg over and settle in the saddle, the paint humped his back and threw Perley head over heels. He landed squarely on his shoulder blades and did a complete reverse sum-mersault before coming to rest in the grass.

Alarmed, Jordan thought the old man might have broken his neck. He dropped the chestnut's reins and hurried to help him.

"Got-dam," the old trapper forced out, the only sound he could manage after having the wind knocked out of him. "Got-dam," he uttered again when Jordan helped him sit up.

"Are you all right?" Jordan asked when he saw Perley struggling to regain his breathing.

"Got-dam," Perley repeated, and nodded his head in answer to Jordan's question. He sat there on the ground for a few minutes until he could breathe easily. Then he cocked his head to look up at the paint, which was standing quietly, watching the old man.

"I don't think he likes the feel of your saddle," Jordan said with some amusement, now that it appeared Perley was not seriously injured.

"Maybe," Perley allowed, getting to his feet, "he just ain't got to know me yet. It ain't the first time I've been bucked off a horse." He walked over to the still-smoking remains of the fire and pulled the largest limb from the ashes. Approximately the size of a woman's arm, the stick of wood was still smoldering on one end. Without any calming words or sounds, he walked up to the paint, and with one sudden motion, he broke the limb across the horse's face. Jordan couldn't help but wince as the paint squealed in pain and jerked its head away. Perley, with a firm grip on the reins, held the startled animal fast. When the paint settled down again, Perley placed his foot in the stirrup once more. Jordan got set for more acrobatics, but the horse seemed to have sensed who was to be the boss of the new partnership— accepting Perley's weight in the saddle without further protest. "Let's go," Perley said to Jordan, and turned the paint's head north. The paint, a long sooty stripe across its face, started out obediently, Sweet Pea following behind. Jordan, riding the chestnut with Johnny Spratte's roan behind him, fell in line, being careful not to ride too close to Perley's packhorse.

Less than a day's ride ahead of Jordan and Perley, the two outlaws approached the bluffs along the Arkansas River. Late in the afternoon, on the day before, they had heard the faint report of a series of rifle shots in the distance behind them. Knowing that it was most probably Snake's Winchester, they had speculated on the cause. They knew that the unpredictable half-breed could have been nowhere near Eagle Claw's village.

"No tellin' what that damn crazy Injun is shootin' at," Leach had commented. They both paused to listen for more shots, but there was just the one.

"Mighta been a squirrel or somethin' he just didn't like the looks of," Roach speculated with a grin.

"Yeah, well, it might not be a bad idea to keep on ridin' till dark, in case he changes his mind about goin' back to that Choctaw camp."

Once having rid themselves of the dangerous half-breed, both men were anxious to put as much distance as possible between themselves and their former partner. At this point, they had no reason to believe anyone other than Snake would be coming after them, but they pushed on until it was nearly too dark to see before making camp. Now, with the Arkansas in sight, they were approaching the point where they intended to lose the half-breed for good.

"Now what do we do?" Roach asked, after the two made their way down through the trees to the water's edge. "I ain't about to try to swim that far," he announced, gazing at the far shore. "I got a natural dislike of water that wide and that deep."

Leach pulled up beside him and studied their predicament for a few moments. Then, noticing a narrow path along the river, he said, "We'll just follow this trail upriver till we come to a place to get across."

The trail showed evidence of more than a little traffic, as it wound its way through the trees, sometimes leading away from the riverbank, before turning back close to the water's edge again. They had followed it for the most part of an hour, riding in silence until Roach spoke out. "I wish to hell I knew where we're goin'."

"Why?" Leach shot back. "You got an appointment somewhere?"

"Hell, I'd just like to know where the hell I am. Maybe we shoulda turned back toward Skullyville to spend some of this money for somethin' to eat. I'm about out of coffee and bacon." They rode on in silence again for a spell until Roach called out again, this time with a measure of excitement in his voice. "What the hell . . . ?" He turned in the saddle to gawk over his shoulder. "Leach! Lookee yonder!"

Leach, his hand automatically falling on the handle of his pistol, turned to see what had caused Roach's excitement. Through the screen of poplar and oak, a dark and monstrous image had suddenly appeared. In unreal proportions, it threatened to overtake them, belching black plumes of smoke and sparks. In a few seconds, they heard the sound of its huge paddlewheel churning up the calm river water. "Well, I'll be damned," Leach uttered as the steamboat slowly moved up to parallel the two men on horses. Then, recognizing the opportunity, he yelled, "Come on!" and kicked his horse into a gallop.

Racing along the path, he galloped until it led along a clear stretch of riverbank. He pulled up then with Roach right behind him. Waiting until the boat again caught up to them, he stood up in the stirrups and waved his hat over his head. Realizing then what Leach had in mind, Roach followed suit, waving his arm back and forth and yelling out. With both men yelling, they finally attracted a deck hand's attention. He waved back.

"We need a ride!" Leach called out between cupped hands, but the deck hand couldn't understand what he was saying. "We can pay for it!" Leach yelled. The deck hand was still unable to understand. Their yelling had caught the attention of the pilot in the wheelhouse, and he waved at the two horsemen. Leach reached into his saddlebag and pulled out a wad of the stolen money. He waved it over his head. This served to bridge the gap of confusion between boat and riders. The pilot pointed upstream, and motioned. "Come on," Leach said to Roach. "There must be a landing up ahead."

The trail turned abruptly, leading back through the

trees, away from the water's edge, but Leach held his horse to a gallop, confident the path led to a landing of some sort. His confidence was justified when the two riders suddenly emerged from the forest to discover a wide clearing that led down to the river. Reining the horses back to a walk, they rode past piles of neatly stacked wood, tended by a couple of Cherokee Indians, who stared at the strangers openly. Ignoring their presence, Leach and Roach rode on down to a bluff that formed a natural levee. Within seconds, the paddlewheel appeared from around the bend, inching her way close into the bank.

"By God, she's a rough-lookin' old bitch," Roach commented with a wide grin. "She don't look much like them riverboats back in New Orleans, does she?"

Leach didn't answer, but watched with casual interest as the two Cherokees caught a couple of lines thrown to them and secured the boat to the levee. Roach's comment had been sadly accurate, for the *Pandora* had certainly seen better times. Her wooden hull, scarred and worn, the sternwheel packet plied a short route between Fort Smith and Fort Gibson, carrying freight and an occasional passenger. The heyday of riverboat traffic was long gone since the railroad had come to the territory. None of this mattered to the two outlaws. They saw the battered old boat as a welcome convenience to take them upriver.

"You boys lookin' for a ride to Fort Gibson?"

Leach glanced at Roach and grinned before answering the bulky, sandy-haired boat captain. Until that moment, he had no idea where the boat went. "I reckon we are," he replied, "if that's where you're goin'."

The captain extended his hand as he stepped ashore to greet the two outlaws. "My name's Harvey Tanner," he said. "I'm the captain of this vessel. I don't usually stop to take on wood until we start back from Fort Gibson, but I seen you fellers needed a ride." In truth, Tanner would have pulled the boat over for any occasion that might bring in a few dollars. At the moment, he was trying to evaluate his potential passengers to determine how much he could charge them. They were a surly-looking pair, dusty and unshaven. Their clothes were rough and worn. Yet one of them had waved what appeared to be a sizable roll of currency. Probably ill-gotten, he decided, but that was no concern of his. After studying the two for a few moments more, he decided to take a stab at it. "Passage for you and your horses to Fort Gibson will cost you fifty dollars"—when Leach showed no sign of protest, Tanner quickly added—"apiece."

This brought a reaction, although mild. A slow grin crept across Leach's face. He didn't know how far it was from this point to Fort Gibson, but he could recognize a fellow crook when he met one. Looking Tanner straight in the eye, he asked, "When will we get to Fort Gibson?"

"Before nightfall tomorrow," Tanner replied.

"It ain't that far then, is it?" Leach responded, stroking his chin whiskers thoughtfully. "I woulda figured me and my partner here coulda rode all the way down to Fort Smith and back again for fifty dollars apiece. I'll tell you what I'll do. Since it ain't gonna put you out none to give us a ride, I'll give you twenty dollars for your trouble."

"Damn, mister, that ain't hardly the goin' rate," Tanner complained.

Roach, quiet to that point while he watched the negotiations, spoke up then. "Hell, there ain't no goin' rate. The goin' rate is what me and Leach are willin' to give for a boat ride. That's the goin' rate." He favored the captain with a broad smile. "All the same to me, I'd just as soon ride my horse to Fort Gibson."

"You fellers drive a hard bargain, but I reckon I could do it this one time for twenty dollars gold."

Leach shook his head and grinned. "Gold? Do you see us leadin' any packhorses? Twenty Union dollars is what we'll pay."

"I don't know." Tanner hesitated, hoping Leach would up the offer. When Leach shrugged as if to turn away, the captain quickly agreed. "All right, then, but I ain't carrying no grain or nothin' for them horses."

Leach winked at Roach as he peeled off twenty dollars and handed them to Tanner. Roach nodded, confident that, if the opportunity presented itself, they would most likely regain the money when they got to Fort Gibson—plus any pocket money the captain might be carrying. They led their horses up the gangway and onto the deck of the *Pandora*, settling themselves near the twin boilers. "That damn half-breed will have a helluva time following us now," Leach said as they unsaddled the horses.

Roach laughed. "He's most likely on his way to Kansas City and lookin' hard for our trail." Both men would have found it hard to believe that their half-breed partner was more likely taking a boat ride himself—across the river Styx.

"Looks like they mighta met up with somebody," Jordan speculated as he knelt down to examine a trail of hoofprints that intercepted those of the two horses they had been tracking.

Perley moved up beside him to take a look for himself. After studying the tracks for only a few seconds, he spoke. "Nah, these horses come along after our boys passed over this little knoll." He raised his head, looking around in all directions, as if expecting to see someone before returning his attention to the scattering of hoofprints. "Most likely a Cherokee huntin' party," he said. "We're in their territory now." He traced the outline of one of the prints with a gnarled finger. "These tracks is fresh. See how the edges crumbles off when I touch 'em? Our boys passed here some time before these Injuns come along."

"How do you know they're Injuns?" Jordan asked.

Perley looked at him, as if answering a child's question, but he was patient in his reply. "'Cause these prints is smaller than the ones we've been following since mornin'—Injun ponies, I expect. They ain't shod—coulda been rode by white men, but seein' as how we're smack-dab in the middle of the Cherokee nation, I expect they was Injuns."

Jordan did not reply, but Perley could see that his new friend was listening with close attention—a quality that Perley found admirable. Jordan seemed to absorb any tidbit of information that Perley offered. He watched as Jordan traced the outline of the hoofprint with his finger, then traced the older track of one of the shod horses. *He didn't know buttermilk biscuits from moose shit when I first met him, but he damn sure learns fast*, Perley thought.

"They're still headin' straight northwest," Jordan said, getting to his feet.

Perley nodded. "Straight for the Arkansas River," he said.

It was late afternoon when Jordan and Perley reached the banks of the Arkansas and led the horses down to the river's edge to drink. The river was wide at this point, the water dark and deep. Standing in the shade of a large oak, Jordan might have found the scene idyllic had he been there under different circumstances. But he was thinking that Sarah would have loved to see this peaceful river—a thought that brought back the sadness that dominated his conscious mind. He immediately called his thoughts back to the business at hand. The tracks they had been following led back to the west, along a path that ran along the river's edge. He turned to Perley. "Have you ever been up this river before?"

Perley snorted in reply. "Oh, I've been up it all right—up it and down it. I've been up this river all the way to the Rockies, I expect. She looks calm and peaceful here, but I've been where she's cantankerous—white water and rapids—but that's a helluva ways from where we're standin'. I expect these polecats we're followin' are most likely headed for Fort Gibson. That's about two days' ride from here. They coulda took the road the army built between Fort Smith and

Fort Gibson—mighta been quicker than following this little path."

"I expect we'd better get goin' then," Jordan replied, and stepped up into the saddle.

Following the narrow path along the river, they rode for the better part of two hours before emerging from the trees into a wide clearing. "Firewood for the steamboats," Perley observed, pointing to the stacks of wood near the water's edge. There was no sign of anyone around. "The Cherokees pick up a little money, cuttin' firewood for the boilers. From the looks of it, this must be a regular stop for the boats."

There were many tracks in the clearing, too many to follow two particular horses, so they rode across to pick up the trail where the path continued on along the river. There were tracks along the path, but they were older, and they were unshod. It was apparent that Roach and Leach had not continued along the riverbank. "Looks like they went for a boat ride," Perley said, stating the obvious.

The journey to Fort Gibson took less than two days, due mainly to Jordan's growing impatience to finish his quest. As long as he and Perley had been able to track the remaining two of Sarah and Jonah's killers, he had felt confident that he held a hand on their destiny. Tracks he could see—he could reach down and touch them. He could tell from the smoldering ashes of their campfires that he was closing the distance between himself and the men who had ended his world. Now, no longer able to see their hoofprints, he and Perley had continued along the river trail, often at a lope, stopping only occasionally to rest the horses. Jordan fought hard within himself to maintain his patience, but without visual evidence of the outlaws' trail to assure him, he feared that he may have lost them for good.

Perley understood the urgency that ate away at his young friend's soul. There were few demons that could drive a man as relentlessly as the craving for vengeance. He found himself fearing for Jordan's life, however. Remembering the complete abandon Jordan had displayed when he charged headlong into Snake, Perley was afraid such reckless abandon might cause Jordan to sacrifice his life. He found that he had developed a strong liking for the quiet young man, and he would hate to see him throw his life away in a moment of crazed passion. There were other concerns as well. Perley was a sensible man, and he also had some concern that he might be caught in the hail of bullets that could very well result due to a sudden sighting of the two outlaws. Consequently, on the few occasions they stopped to rest the horses, he tried to counsel Jordan on the importance of caution when dealing with lawless men such as the two he sought. Jordan would listen, quietly absorbing Perley's words of advice, but the dark, deep-set eyes offered no clue as to whether or not he heeded them.

"Been a good while since I was last in this part of the territory," Perley announced upon reaching the Three Forks area. "It's shore changed a helluva lot." This observation was partly as a result of the homesteads and farms they had passed along the river. "Years ago, this place was busier than a beehive with trappers and traders. This used to be big country for beaver, but not no more."

Jordan listened patiently, but he was not really interested in the history of the region. His mind was occupied with the prospect of catching up with the two outlaws. In spite of this, he could not help but be impressed by the Three Forks area. Two rivers, the Verdigris and the Neosho, emptied their waters into the Arkansas within a half mile of each other. They still had three miles to go, however, before reaching Fort Gibson on the east bank of the Neosho, and the sun was sinking fast. Without responding to Perley's comments, he turned the chestnut's head and started out on the road to Fort Gibson, leaving Perley to follow.

In the fading dusk, the two riders headed for the lights of the town, bypassing the fort itself. The two outlaws they were searching for would hardly have any business with the military. Jordan was surprised to find the little town near the army post to be a fairly busy place with several buildings along a main street. Passing a saloon, he saw a couple of soldiers entering the wide swinging doors. Down toward the stables at the end of the street, he spotted a few individuals going and coming in the doors of the various business establishments. There was no evidence of two outlaws. He had to silently reprimand himself for being so naive as to think he would spot the two as soon as he reached the town. He didn't even know what they looked like.

"We can put the horses up at the stable," Perley said, "then get us a room at the hotel yonder." Not burdened with the heavy weight that constantly dominated Jordan's mind, he was looking forward to first-class accommodations while in Fort Gibson. Thinking of the roll of bank money in his saddlebags, he had already decided that the good citizens of Fort Smith would be happy to stand him and his young friend to a comfortable stay in Fort Gibson. His suggestion surprised Jordan, who naturally assumed they would find a place outside of town to camp. He started to express it, but Perley cut him off before he got the words out of his mouth. "I ain't ever been able to afford to stay in a real hotel, and this might be my last chance. We've got this stolen money. Ain't no sense in just carryin' it around in my saddlebags."

Jordan thought for a moment to protest and remind his gnarled old friend that the money wasn't theirs to spend. But on second thought, he realized that neither he nor Perley might ever set foot in Fort Smith again. Besides, he reminded himself, he had told Perley to do what he wanted with the money when they discovered it in Snake's saddlebags. The more he thought about it, the more he was convinced that Perley probably deserved to have a little money to spend. So Jordan held his tongue and continued down the rutted street toward the stables.

Pulling up before the stables, they were met by a young boy as they dismounted. "Evenin', gents," the boy greeted them, looking the two strangers over with unabashed curiosity. "Lookin' to put your horses up?"

"That's right, son," Perley replied enthusiastically. "We want 'em took care of, stall and feed."

"We ain't got no empty stalls right now. I'll have to put 'em in the corral."

"Reckon that'll do then," Perley said. "Ol' Sweet Pea might get nervous cooped up in a stall, anyway."

Noticing the blacksmith's forge next to the stable,

Jordan said, "I think my horse has a loose shoe. I'd like to get him shod. It's way past time."

"Yes, sir," the boy replied. "We can take care of him. Pa does the shoeing. Most likely he'll be able to do it first thing in the mornin'."

"Better look at my packhorse, too," Jordan said. He had no idea what condition the horse's shoes were in. He hadn't thought to look.

"Yes, sir," the boy said, standing back to watch while the two strangers took their saddlebags and rifles off the horses. "You fellers are new in town, ain'tcha?"

Jordan answered. "That's right. I guess you see a lot of strangers passin' through every day. Seen anybody else passin' through lately?"

"Well, not every day," the boy replied, scratching his head as if trying to recall. "A couple of fellers come in yesterday on Captain Tanner's steamboat. Pa put their horses in the corral."

Jordan felt the muscles in his arms tightening and a quickening of his heartbeat. He glanced at Perley, who was watching his reaction. Perley gave him a brief nod, then asked the boy, "Which horses is theirs?"

"That big bay and the dun yonder with the black stockin's," the boy answered, pointing to one and then the other. His curiosity aroused by the strangers' interest in the horses, he asked, "Are they friends of you'rn?"

"You might say that," Perley replied and smiled for the boy's benefit. His eyes focused on Jordan now, he watched his young friend carefully, almost afraid Jordan might suddenly shoot the horses that had carried his wife's killers. But there was no sign of the violent rage Perley had witnessed when Snake was executed.

Despite the steady calm Jordan exhibited in his un-blinking gaze at the two horses pointed out in the fading evening light, Perley knew the fire was building inside his friend. "Well, son," he said, seeking to diffuse the storm brewing inside Jordan's mind, "you take good care of our horses." Turning to Jordan, he said, "Let's you and me go find us some supper and a room."

Jordan didn't respond for a moment, his mind deep in thought. It was only when Perley gave him a tug on the shoulder that he realized what the old man had said. "All right," he then replied softly. Turning to the boy, he asked, "What did they look like—these two strangers?"

"I don't know," he answered, trying to recall some features that made Leach and Roach different from other strangers. "They looked about like everybody else. One of 'em was a big feller—I don't know. I think they took a room up at the hotel."

"Obliged," Jordan said after waiting for a moment to see if the boy remembered anything else. He then turned and followed Perley out of the stable.

As the old trapper and his partner walked away toward the Cherokee Hotel, a dark figure stepped from the deep shadows in the back corner of the stable near the tack room. "Dang!" young Tommy Irwin exclaimed, startled by the sudden appearance of Roach right before him. Jumping backward a step, he dropped the saddle he had just picked up to take to the tack room. "Dang, mister, you gave me a fright. I didn't know you was back there."

"Who the hell was them two?" Roach demanded in a gruff voice that did little to calm Tommy's frazzled nerves. "They was askin' a helluva lot of questions. What did you tell 'em?"

Still shaken by Roach's sudden appearance from the shadows, Tommy stammered his reply. "They was just askin' if I'd seen any other strangers in town—that's all. I think they were lookin' for some friends of theirs. I didn't tell 'em nothin'," he pleaded.

Roach considered the boy's answer and decided he was probably telling him the truth. Having earlier seen a couple of fair-looking ladies enter the saloon on the first floor of the hotel, he had returned to the stables to retrieve his razor from his saddlebags. Being a natural thief, he had been rummaging around in some of the other tack he found there when he heard the two riders approach the boy at the front of the stables. Remaining in the dark, he had tried to hear the conversation, but could only catch a word here and there—enough to determine there were questions about other strangers in town. This was sufficient to alert his suspicions. "All right, boy," he finally said in an effort to calm the still shaken stable hand. "No harm done, I reckon." He patted Tommy on the back, and walked out the front of the stable.

Too late for supper, Jordan and Perley settled for a plate of cold beans and cornbread from the hotel kitchen, provided for them by a cordial bartender and delivered to their table in the back corner of the saloon by a benevolent saloon girl. "Now this is what I call first-class service," Perley said, eyeing the lady as she placed the plates before them. He was hoping the atmosphere of the saloon might serve to lighten Jordan's

mood somewhat. So intense upon his quest, Jordan
was seated as taut as a steel spring, staring at every
man who walked in or out of the saloon. Perley was
apprehensive that his young friend might go off half-
cocked before he knew for sure who he was attacking.
"I swear, I believe that pretty young thing was eye-
ballin' you somethin' fierce," he said, making another
attempt to jar Jordan's mind from deep thoughts of
immediate revenge.

If Jordan heard him, he gave no indication. His mind
was focused on a tall, heavily bearded man standing at
the far end of the bar. Slowly nursing a glass of beer, the
man seemed to be watching the door of the saloon,
peering at everyone who entered, as if searching for
something or someone. The longer Jordan stared at the
man, the more suspicious he became. There was just
something about the look of the man that alerted something inside Jordan's gut. His hand dropped to rest on
his empty holster, just then remembering that he and
Perley had been required to leave their firearms at the
front desk before entering the saloon. Foiled for only
the moment, he slowly rose from his chair.

"Where you goin'?" Perley asked anxiously and
turned to follow the direction of Jordan's gaze. "What
the hell are you fixin' to do?" Perley demanded when
he saw the object of Jordan's concentration.

Jordan didn't answer, his passion for revenge having
already fanned the burning coals in his gut. He pushed
the chair back and started toward the bar. The tall,
bearded man paid him no mind, as he continued to stare
at the door. When Jordan was halfway across the room,
a short bald man pushed through the saloon doors, and

made for the bar. The tall man immediately moved to meet him. "Now, Pete, you know damn well you ain't supposed to come in here with that pistol," he said.

The bald man flushed slightly. "I plumb forgot I was wearin' it, Dan." He immediately started unbuckling his gun belt. "It ain't loaded, anyway."

The tall man grinned. "You ain't either, yet. I don't want you to get a snoot full and hurt yourself with that thing. Give it to me, and I'll take it out front."

Feeling like a fool, Jordan did an about-face and returned to the table, where he was met with an impatient look from Perley that could only be described as parental. "I was just aimin' to find out who he was," Jordan offered lamely.

"Well, I reckon now you know," Perley replied impatiently. He watched while Jordan took his chair again before continuing. "Hell, boy, you can't go around askin' ever'body you see if they killed your wife and son. You'll end up being locked up. We ain't gonna spot them two we're after just by their looks. Hell, half the men in this town look like outlaws. We'll go down to the stable early in the mornin'. We know which horses them two strangers rode in on, so we'll keep an eye on them horses."

Feeling even more like a fool, Jordan nodded his head to signify he agreed with what the old man said. Patience was a hard lesson to learn with a live fire smoldering inside, but he knew he was going to have to master it.

Upstairs in a room at the end of the hall, Leach was busy cautioning his partner to restrain his primal urges to find a woman. After hearing Roach's report regarding the two strangers at the stables, he was as suspicious as Roach had been. He and Roach had wasted little time in traveling from Fort Smith to this little western outpost. He would be surprised if a marshal was nipping at their heels in this short a time. Not as reckless as his partner, however, Leach deemed it always the best policy to proceed with caution whenever there was a possibility of a brush with the law. "What did they look like?" He asked Roach for the second time.

Roach shrugged. "I told you, one of 'em looked like an old man. I couldn't really see that good. It was dark in that stable. The other feller mighta been younger— hard to tell."

"You think he mighta been a lawman." It was not a question. Leach was speculating to himself.

"I didn't say he was a lawman. He mighta been. All I know is they sure seemed mighty interested in who was new in town."

Leach thought that over for a long moment. A suspicious nature had served to help him avoid the gallows more than a few times before. Maybe he was concerned over nothing, but he decided it best to find out just who these two strangers were. It could be mere coincidence that they arrived practically on the two outlaws' heels. But maybe it wasn't. "We'll go down to the stables in the morning and see what we can find out." He cocked his eye at Roach. "It wouldn't hurt you none to stay outta sight until we find out what's what around here. We're mighty close to that damn army post. We might have to skedaddle outta here in a hurry." Roach wasn't particularly happy with the suggestion, but he gave in as usual. Leach always called the shots.

"You boys is out mighty early," Sam Irwin said cheerfully when Roach and Leach walked in just as the sun peeped in the open end of the stables.

"That's a fact," Leach replied. "But you can't make no money layin' around in bed. Right?" He fashioned as friendly a smile as he could manage.

"I reckon that's so, all right," Sam agreed. "You want me to cut your horses out?"

"No," Leach quickly replied. "We was kinda expectin' a couple of our friends to show up, so we thought we'd just see if you mighta seen 'em. Roach here was talkin' to your son last evenin'. He said a couple of strangers came in last night."

"Yes, sir. Tommy told me he put up four more horses last night. They're in the corral with the rest of 'em. I was just fixin' to put out some feed when you come up."

"You ain't seen the two that brought 'em in?" Leach asked.

"No, sir. Tommy seen 'em."

"Where's Tommy?"

"He better be gettin' hisself ready for school."

Leach nodded. He could see that he wasn't going to find out much about the two men from Sam, and he didn't want to exhibit more than a casual interest. "Well, maybe they'll show up sooner or later," he said, and walked out to join Roach, who had gone out to the corral.

Roach turned to meet his partner when Leach approached, his face reflecting grave concern. But he said nothing until Leach was beside him. Then he turned his head back toward the horses. "Do you see what I'm lookin' at? If I ain't crazy as a coot, that's that scruffy lookin' nag of Snake's."

Leach was immediately alert. He stared at the horse Roach pointed out, looking it over thoroughly. "It's Snake's, all right." He quickly shifted his gaze back and forth across the corral before settling upon a blue roan near the far rail. "And that roan over yonder looks a helluva lot like the horse Johnny Spratte rode."

"Goddam," Roach exclaimed, "they musta got Snake."

Leach didn't reply at once, but his mind was already working hard, and the picture it created was not to his liking. There was no way to affix coincidence to this. They had to have a couple of lawmen on their trail, and the shooting they had heard a couple of days before must have meant those men had done Snake in. Perplexed at how quickly the law could have caught up to them, he nevertheless spent little thought on it. The important thing now was to shake the dust of Fort Gibson from their heels. His concentration was distracted for a moment when Sam Irwin came from the stable. Leach turned to question the man again. No longer concerned with maintaining a casual facade, he asked, "Did your boy say they was wearin' badges?"

"No, Tommy didn't say nothin' about no badges." He thought for a moment before adding, "He did say one of 'em was an old, gray-haired man wearin' buckskins." His description confirmed what Roach had seen in the half-light of the stable on the night before.

Leach turned abruptly to his partner. "What does that sound like to you, Roach?"

Roach nodded agreement. "Sounds like maybe one lawman with a guide."

Leach turned toward Sam again. "I changed my mind. We're gonna need our horses right away. We'll be back in a few minutes to get 'em."

There was no need to discuss it with Roach. Both men had been on the run from the law long enough to know when a town was no longer healthy for them. Keeping a cautious eye, they hurried back to the hotel to collect their belongings, wary of even the few early risers who were preparing to open their shops for the day. The only scrap of information they had was that one of the men was old and wearing buckskins. To their advantage, however, was the fact that the lawman had no way of knowing what they looked like, either.

Sleep had not come easily for Jordan Gray, and when it had, it was from sheer exhaustion from nerves stretched as tight as a bow string. Even then it had come in short intervals, with him waking again and again to the steady drone of Perley's snoring in the bed next to his. *Sarah's murderers were sleeping under the same roof!* He couldn't say this for a fact, but he felt in his heart that it was so, and the knowledge was enough to almost drive him crazy. Had it not been for Perley's calming influence, Jordan might have suddenly lost control of his emotions and stormed from room to room, battering in every door in the long hallway, until he had found the men.

He awoke with a start. The light through the window told him that he had slept past sunup. Angry with himself for oversleeping, he came out of the tangle of sheets and blanket still groggy from a night of fitful tossing and turning. As he pulled his pants on, he gazed at Perley in the other bed. Still dead to the world, the old man had at least turned on his side, so the snoring had ceased. *The picture of perfect peace*, Jordan thought. According to what Perley had told him, this was the first time the old man had slept in a bed for at least six or seven months. Gazing at his grizzled partner now, his white hair and beard almost the same color as the dingy pillow his face was buried in, Jordan decided to let him sleep while he answered nature's urgent call.

Disdainful of using the porcelain chamber pot provided by the hotel, Jordan preferred to go down the back stairs to the outhouse behind the building. The sun was already casting long shadows in the early-morning light when he started back to the hotel. He paused for just a second to consider what kind of day it was going to be. No more than a few wispy gray clouds etched the rapidly changing sky. Soon the sun would clear the hills to the east and start its climb. He had a feeling this was to be a fateful day in his life. Feeling the urgency to finish the business that had brought him to this little Western town, he hurried up the steps to get his rifle.

When he opened the door at the top of the stairs, he encountered Perley in the hallway. The old man was still in nothing but his long underwear. "There you are," Perley greeted him, a look of relief on his face. "I thought you'd gone off and left me."

"I was goin' to," Jordan replied, "if you were still . . ." He was interrupted when a door farther down the hallway opened suddenly and two men, carrying rifles and saddlebags, stepped out into the hall. One was a large man, a head taller than his companion. Tommy Irwin's comment that one of the strangers was a big man flashed through Jordan's mind. With Perley partially blocking his view, he craned his neck to look around the old man and reached for the pistol he had stuffed in his belt. "Hold on there, mister," he called out.

Although taken by surprise, Leach was lightning-fast. Turning at the sound of the voice behind him, his pistol already drawn as a natural reflex, he found himself confronted by two men. One of them held a gun in his hand, although it was not pointed at him. The other, an old, gray-haired man, had his back turned to him. In an instant, the description of the two men who had been asking questions impacted upon his mind's eye. It was no time for introductions. Leach seized the advantage, firing point-blank in the narrow hallway, he emptied his pistol. The first two shots were wild, ripping into the floor as he was still raising the weapon. The other four slammed into Perley's back, knocking the old man into Jordan's arms. Only a second or two slower than his partner, Roach fired his pistol, sending another bullet into the already lifeless body of the old trapper.

Taken by surprise and unable to get a clear shot when Perley's body fell into his arms, Jordan tried to shoot around the old man. Perley fell to the floor just as Jordan felt a stinging blow like a solid punch in his chest, followed immediately by a second. Knowing he had been hit, he managed to get off one shot before his head started spinning, and the light in the hallway became dimmer and dimmer until total darkness shrouded his brain. He was not aware of anything after that, not even when he slumped to the floor. The last vivid image that was seared into his brain before consciousness left him was the sneering faces of his two assailants.

Though it had seemed to be longer, the entire incident was over in seconds. Stepping past the crumpled bodies on the floor of the hallway, Leach and Roach quickly made their way out the back door and were already halfway down the steps by the time the startled hotel guests were aroused from their beds.

"By God," Leach crowed as they ran behind the buildings toward the stables at the end of the street, "I reckon that'll stop 'em from followin' us."

Even though confident that the two men behind them were dead, Roach wasn't ready to gloat. "We'd better do some hard ridin'. We're gonna have the army after us now."

"Hell," Leach panted as they slowed down to a walk so as not to rouse suspicion at the stable, "that don't bother me a'tall. All them soldiers will do is ride around the prairie like they was on parade. We'll give them the slip in two shakes."

When they walked around to the front of the stable, they met Sam Irwin standing out in the middle of the street, staring anxiously toward the hotel. "What was all the shootin'?" Sam asked upon seeing Leach and Roach.

"Some drunk fool," Leach was quick to explain, "shootin' off his pistol." He winked at Roach.

"Yeah," Roach said, "I expect it's all over now. Me and Leach figured we'd better get outta there before we got hit with a stray bullet."

"Well, I'll be!" Sam exclaimed. "Who was it?" He continued to stare up the street toward the hotel, where a few people could already be seen running toward the building. "Did anybody get hit?"

"Nah," Leach replied, impatient with Sam's questions and anxious to get out of town, "nobody got hit. We don't know who the drunk was. Now how much do we owe you? We've got to be on our way."

Distracted by the sight of money, Sam accepted payment for boarding the horses. "I saddled 'em up for you. You're ready to ride." He stood back while they threw their saddlebags on behind the saddles. "Where you fellers headed?"

"Fort Smith," Roach replied, stepping up in the saddle, and wheeled his horse to follow Leach, who was already under way.

"Much obliged," Sam called after them, as they loped away. Under his breath, he muttered, "But you'll play hell gettin' to Fort Smith thataway."

Chapter 9

The second floor hallway of the Cherokee Hotel was filled with alarmed and horrified residents in various states of undress. Rudely awakened by the sudden explosion of gunfire reverberating through the confines of the narrow passage, most were afraid to open their doors until a considerable period of quiet had passed. Then one, and then another, chanced to peek out into the hallway, until they were sure it was safe. Soon everyone emerged to gawk at the bodies lying before the back door. A couple of the bolder men stepped forward to examine the bodies.

"They're deader'n a stump," one said, kneeling beside Perley's body, the old man's underwear soaked crimson with blood.

"They're both dead," the other man said, staring down at Jordan and seeing no sign of life. "This one's got two bullet holes right through the chest—looks like he got grazed on the side of his head, too."

At that moment, Marvin Sawyer, the owner of the Cherokee Hotel, pushed his way through the crowd, which was growing by the minute as curious outsiders came to investigate. "Oh, my Lord," he exclaimed when he saw what had happened. As he looked around him at the people shouldering one another for a better look at the bodies, it was obvious that the shooter was not among them. "Does anybody know what happened?" he asked.

No one did, but one boarder who was in the room by the back door was certain he had heard someone running down the back steps right after the shots were fired. Marvin turned to peer at the faces of the folks crowded in the narrow hallway. The two strangers who had checked in the day before were missing. "Somebody better get the sheriff," he said.

"Better get the doctor, too," someone else said. "This one just moved."

The conscious mind lingered in darkness for a time undeterminable by the man lying on the hotel bed. In actuality, it was for a period of two days as Jordan drifted close to the surface of his coma, only to escape again into the security of unconsciousness, which seemed to beckon for him to linger. It would have been easy to let go, but the snarling faces of Leach and Roach had been permanently burned into his memory, and the power of it was enough to force him to defy the dark angels who beckoned him. Gradually the fog lifted, and snatches of conscious thought crossed his muddled brain in random flashes of memory. Finally he became aware of voices about him. Still he did not open his eyes, reluctant to let the day in.

"He's still alive," It was a man's voice. "He's got

one helluva constitution, but I don't think he's gonna make it. He's lost too much blood."

In defiance of the comment, Jordan opened his eyes to find himself gazing into the eyes of an angel. At least that was what he thought. The angel recoiled slightly, her eyes wide with excitement. "He's awake! See, Father, I told you he was going to make it."

Captain Stephen Beard was the post surgeon at Fort Gibson, but he was often called upon to administer to the citizens of the nearby town. In most cases, it was to treat a sick baby or to set a bone. Rarely was it to treat gunshot wounds. He had already advised his daughter, Kathleen, that in treating soldiers in the field, wounds of this nature usually proved fatal. But she insisted that this patient was going to recover. She often acted as her father's nurse when he saw civilian patients, and she had taken a special interest in this young man.

"Do you know where you are?" the doctor asked Jordan.

"No," Jordan struggled to speak, still gazing into Kathleen's eyes. "Heaven?"

"Hardly," Beard huffed, "but you were well on the way. What's your name, young fellow?"

He paused for only a moment before answering, "Jordan Gray." The effort it took to speak made him wince with pain, and he suddenly remembered that he was wounded.

"Please don't try to move," Kathleen implored.

Beard shook his head slowly. "Well, Jordan Gray, you've got yourself shot up pretty badly. There isn't much more I can do for you. I've wrapped you as well as I could to stop the bleeding. You've got a lead slug inside your chest somewhere, and I expect if I tried to go in to find it, I'd kill you for sure. There was another slug that went right through, came out under your shoulder." He glanced at his daughter before continuing. "My daughter here will look in on you to see how you're getting along. She was pretty sure you were gonna make it. Tell you the truth, I wasn't. But since you finally woke up, and there aren't any signs of internal bleeding, I reckon the rest is up to you."

Jordan didn't say anything for a long moment. "Perley? Is he all right?"

Captain Beard frowned. "Perley? Was that the old gentleman's name? Was he your father?"

"Friend," Jordan struggled to reply.

"I'm sorry, but your friend's dead."

Jordan closed his eyes, and the image of the old man's face returned to his mind, his eyes wide with shock as he fell into Jordan's arms. It would be hard to accept Perley's death. He had only known the old trapper for a short time, but he felt as if he had always known him. Now, because he had befriended him, Perley was dead, and Jordan would add that to the grief that already burdened him. His eyes open again, he asked, "What about the two that shot us?"

Beard shook his head again and shrugged. "Lieutenant McCoy was sent out with a patrol of fifteen men to try to find them, but they were unable to pick up their trail. I expect they'll send another patrol out for an extended search in the morning." He reached down and placed his hand on Jordan's forehead, most of which was covered by a bandage wrapping the raw welt on the side of his head. "Your fever's down. I expect you're about starved, too. I'll tell the folks downstairs to fix you up some broth, although, if you feel up to it, you could probably eat something solid." Standing erect again, he said, "That's about enough talking for now. Rest if you can. The folks here at the hotel said they'd take care of you till you got better or died. I guess now it's not going to be the latter. You're a lucky man, Jordan Gray. If those shots had been an inch or two to the left, we'd already be burying you."

The days that followed were like months to Jordan, the painful monotony broken only by the daily visits from Kathleen. She proved to be a cheerful nurse and was faithful in her promise to visit him daily. Though slight and fragile in appearance, she was stern enough if he disobeyed her father's orders. Her visits were like a ray of sunshine in an otherwise dreary day.

The townsfolk buried Perley in the community graveyard outside of town. It was all taken care of by Marvin Sawyer. The owner of the Cherokee Hotel had at first been distressed to learn that Jordan would require his room for some time in order for his wounds to heal—that is, until he made it his business to search through Jordan's and Perley's saddlebags to discover Jordan could well afford his care. After that, it seemed he could not do enough for the convalescing young man.

Burdened by fits of depression caused by the knowledge that Roach and Leach were getting away, Jordan agonized over the slowness of his recovery. A week went by before he was able to sit up for any length of time, but each day he tried to do a little more until Kathleen would scold him for doing too much. "It takes time," she admonished good naturedly. "Are you in such haste to leave my care?" He would manage a smile for her, unwilling to tell her that the image of two smirking faces that he had memorized was the force that drove him to recover.

"Who is Sarah?" Kathleen asked one afternoon. "You spoke her name several times when you were unconscious. Is she your wife?"

Jordan hesitated, reluctant to talk about the things he held sacred to his memory. But Kathleen had asked in such an innocent way, with genuine concern, and not simply out of curiosity. "Was," he finally answered. "Sarah was my wife. She's dead now, along with our son, Jonah."

Kathleen was quick to put the puzzle together. "Those men—you came here looking for them, didn't you?" He didn't answer. "That's why they shot you and your friend—because you had found them." She suddenly became very excited as she realized what the town had puzzled over. Jordan had offered no explanation for having been targeted by the two outlaws. She could not know that he had his reasons—the main one that it was his private affair. The second reason was the possibility that he was a wanted man in Fort Smith, and he was carrying a sizable amount of the bank's money.

"They killed your wife and son," she said softly. It was a statement, but also a question, one he did not answer. It was unnecessary, anyway, for she could read the truth in his eyes. Sensing that the pain in Jordan's heart was far greater than the healing gunshot wounds, she said, "I'll not say anything to anyone, if you prefer."

"I'm much obliged," he said softly.

Captain Beard stopped in several times to change his bandages during the first two days of Jordan's convalescence. He removed the one around Jordan's head since it was healing nicely. "Might leave a scar over your ear," he advised. "Looks like Mr. Sawyer's people are taking pretty good care of you." Jordan allowed that they were and expressed his appreciation for Kathleen's efforts especially. Beard only grunted in reply, but he was thinking that his daughter had been extremely diligent in her devotion to duty—more so than ordinary. He supposed it was not all that unusual. She had always had a soft spot for injured animals of all kinds.

"You smell, Jordan Gray." Hands on hips, Kathleen Beard stood by his bedside like a mother scolding her child. Ignoring the offended expression he displayed, she continued. "Do you think you can walk to the bathroom if I help you?" Before he could answer, she added, "Or am I going to have to strip you down and wash you right here in this bed?"

Alarmed by the determined look on her face, Jordan quickly replied, "I don't know if I can or not, but I'll damn sure give it a try."

"All right, then—let me help you sit up." When she had helped him sit up on the side of the bed, she left him with instructions to get out of his underwear while she went to the bath at the head of the hall and prepared a tub for him.

Feeling a little light-headed, he sat there for a moment until he managed to bring a spell of dizziness under control. There was a definite sense of being bullied by the slight young daughter of the post surgeon, but Jordan had to agree that it was time he took a bath. Painfully, he removed his underwear and stood up, using the bedpost for support. He took a blanket from the bed and wrapped it around him. Then, afraid that if he sat back down, he might not be able to get up again, he stood waiting for Kathleen to return.

After a few minutes, she was back. "They're bringing up some hot water from the kitchen to fill the tub. You can soak for a while. Then one of the boys can rinse you off. Don't worry about your bandages. Father said it wouldn't hurt to get them wet, and I'll put on clean ones after your bath." She wrinkled her nose as she glanced at the bed. "We'll change those sheets, too." She took his arm and placed it across her shoulders, then started walking him slowly toward the door. "I think we'll find your razor, too. It's about time we found out who's hiding behind those bushes on your face."

After assuring her that he could manage to get into the wooden tub by himself, he waited until she had closed the door behind her before cautiously stepping into the water. In order to sit down, he had to draw his knees up close to his chin, and once he was seated, he feared he would not be able to get up again without help. As soon as he let his body relax, however, he quit worrying about it, and let the warm water soak into his stiffened muscles. He took the yellow bar of soap from the edge of the tub and scrubbed himself as best he could, using a cloth that lay beneath the soap. The effort almost served to exhaust him, and when he had finished, he laid his head back against the wooden staves of the tub to rest.

He closed his eyes for a few moments. A smiling image of Kathleen's face flitted through his mind for a brief instant before being replaced by that of a stunned and disbelieving visage of Perley. Without conscious effort, the muscles of his body tensed, and he automatically drew the images of the two faces from his memory. He did not know their names, but he would never forget their faces. Thoughts of the two murderers wrenched his very soul, and he wanted to cry out in anguish for his body to mend. Only the appearance of Marvin Sawyer's twelve-year-old son laboring to carry two buckets of clean water kept him from roaring out his anger.

With help from the boy, Jordan managed to stand up. Then the boy stood on a stool and poured the rinse water over Jordan's shoulders. From the hall, he heard Kathleen say, "Just wrap the towel around him, Petey, till we get him back to bed. I'll have to remove those wet bandages." Unable to resist peeping through the crack of the slightly ajar door, she glimpsed the naked man standing in the tub of water. His back was toward her, and she could see dark stains of blood that had soaked the soggy bandages. *I'll have to clean those up*, she told herself, in an effort to distract her mind from the lean, muscled body.

With Kathleen and Petey steadying him, Jordan

managed to hold the towel wrapped around him as they made it down the hall to his room. After they had him seated on the side of the bed, Petey left to empty the tub, and Kathleen began to remove the old bandages. "They don't look bad at all," she said, upon uncovering the wounds. "They're not bleeding anymore. I think you'll start getting your strength back pretty soon." He made no reply, but the grim expression on his face told her that he was probably thinking of revenge and how soon he would be able to ride again. "You have to let your body heal," she cautioned him. "You've lost a lot of blood. It will take a little time to get your full strength back."

After she had applied fresh bandages, she brought a basin of water to the bedside table and proceeded to shave him. He had not taken a razor to his face since finding his wife and son murdered, so it was necessary for Kathleen to use her sewing scissors on his beard before applying the razor. She left his mustache until last. When the rest of his face was clean-shaven, she took a long look at the results, then decided to shave the mustache as well. "There, that's better." When she was finished, she set the basin aside and studied the face. "You know, Jordan Gray, you've been hiding a nice face behind that scraggly bush. You're not quite so desperate-looking." She continued to study his face. He could not really be considered a handsome man, but he was not unattractive either. There was a certain genuine quality conveyed in those piercing blue eyes that seemed magnetic to her, and she knew at that moment that she must be careful. She could not afford to become intrigued with those eyes. "All right," she announced cheerfully, and got up to leave. "I borrowed a nightshirt from Mrs. Sawyer. You can put that on. Your things will be washed and dried by tomorrow." Favoring him with a warm smile, she turned and left the room.

"Kathleen, thank you," he called after her, finally finding his tongue.

She peeked back in the door. "So you *can* talk," she said, laughing. "You're welcome."

For a few days after that, it seemed to him that he would never regain his strength. But once his wounds began to mend, the progress was rapid. With Kathleen's daily attention and Mrs. Sawyer's cooking, Jordan was soon ready to pronounce himself ready to ride. Using a hand mirror that Kathleen had provided, he examined the still-red healing wounds in his chest, two holes no more than a hand's width apart. He knew that every time he took off his shirt, he would be reminded of the two who had escaped, and there would be no peace in his soul until that ledger was brought to balance.

While Jordan lay recovering, the two men responsible for his wounds sat by a campfire on the banks of the Verdigris River. Impatient with a trail that seemingly led nowhere, across a monotonous landscape that never changed, Leach decided to head back south to strike the Arkansas again. Roach, easily persuaded as long as there was some promise of whiskey and women, was willing to go along with whatever his partner suggested. "We could follow the Arkansas up to Wichita," Leach suggested. "I ain't never been there, but I hear it's a right lively cattle town. Might be just the sorta place we need." The decision made, they started out toward the southwest the following morning.

As Leach had heard, Wichita *had* been a bustling cattle town. But like other cattle towns before, the local farmers had organized in opposition to the Texas herds that fed off the land, leaving it barren of good forage. Now, after a few years during which thousands of cattle had been shipped from the town, Wichita was primarily a farming community—the cattle business having been shifted to Dodge City. It was a quiet town that Leach and Roach rode into on a late summer evening.

"It don't look too damn lively to me," Roach commented as he and Leach rode past long empty holding pens close by the railroad tracks. Still, it was a town, and one fairly established, judging by the stores and saloons along the main street.

"It's lively enough," Leach said. "I'd just as soon have a little peace and quiet for a spell."

After leaving their horses at the stables, the two outlaws ambled up the dusty street to the hotel, where they took a room, after paying in advance. Boyd Fowler, the desk clerk, at first had his doubts about the two strangers. But upon seeing the roll of bills Leach produced to pay for the night's lodging, he decided to reserve his judgment. "You gentlemen plan on staying in Wichita for a while?" Boyd inquired as politely as possible.

Leach smiled. "We're just passin' through, but we might decide to stay over if it suits us. Where's the best place to get a drink and maybe find a game of poker—the saloon here in the hotel or one of them down the street?"

"There ain't no better place than right here if you're looking for a poker game," Boyd was quick to answer. Sure now that the two strangers were gamblers, he suggested that they might want to settle themselves in their room, then be down in the saloon at about half past six. "Jack McQueen'll be settin' at the back table, and there's always three or four lookin' for a game. I'm sure you'd be welcome."

"Who's Jack McQueen?" Roach wanted to know.

"He's the owner," Boyd replied.

At precisely half past six, Leach and Roach walked into the saloon. Roach, not being as fond of card games as his partner, went immediately to the bar, impatient to slake a thirst that only a few days of hard riding could generate. Leach made his way directly toward the back table, where a huge man sat, holding court with three of the saloon regulars. It had been a long time since Leach had an opportunity to play cards with a large bankroll to stake him, and his hands itched with anticipation.

McQueen looked up as Leach approached. "Well, now, boys, here comes a poker player." He nodded toward an empty chair, smiling warmly. "We saved a chair for you. Boyd said you might be lookin' for a game." He slid a bottle of whiskey toward him and called out to the bartender. "Harvey, bring this gentleman a glass. And bring us a new deck of cards." He then introduced the other players, and Leach gave each one a brief nod before settling himself in the vacant chair. McQueen took the new deck, holding it up so everyone could see that the seal had not been broken. The deck appeared tiny in his huge, meaty hands, as he fanned the cards and removed the jokers. "New deck, new game," he announced. "We usually play straight poker—that all right with you, Mr. Leach?"

Leach nodded. "Fine by me, just deal the cards." He was not taken in by McQueen's neighborly attitude. When it came to playing cards, Leach was suspicious of everyone, especially when he was the only stranger at the table.

McQueen laughed. "Mr. Leach came to play." He slid the cards over toward Leach. "We'll let you deal the first hand, since you're a guest here."

The man on Leach's left won the first two hands, but after that, lady luck seemed to play no favorites. It was not until the fifth hand, however, that Leach took the pot with two pairs, jacks and fours, and felt comfortable that the game was an honest one. Leach was not adverse to cheating at cards, but only if he was the one doing the cheating.

"Your friend there," McQueen asked, nodding toward Roach standing at the bar, "he ain't interested in cards?"

Leach glanced briefly in Roach's direction before answering. "Once in a while, when he ain't tryin' to pick up the scent of a woman."

McQueen laughed. "Well, Harvey can tell him where he can get that taken care of."

The man opposite Leach laughed knowingly. "He needs to go see ol' Possum Annie. She'll take some of the starch out of him." His comment caused the other two players to laugh.

"Annie runs the Wichita Social Club," McQueen said. "That's the local whorehouse. Your friend will do better takin' on one of the other girls. Annie's lively enough till she gets your money. Then she just kinda lays there like a possum playin' dead while you finish your business."

Leach grunted, thinking about Roach. Roach preferred a pinch of violence with his copulating. He was out for a tussle as well as biological release. Possum Annie was in for a rough time if she wound up under Roach. When Leach glanced back toward the bar, it was to see Roach toss back his drink and walk out the door. There was little doubt in Leach's mind that Harvey had directed him to Possum Annie's establishment. Anytime of the year was rutting season for Roach.

The game went on until after three in the morning, long after Harvey had closed the bar and gone home, leaving McQueen to lock up. At the end of the night, there were only three of them left, the other two having been cleaned out. When they finally decided to call it a night, Leach noted that McQueen was a slight winner. Leach, himself, was down about forty dollars, not enough to upset him.

"Well, Mr. Leach," Jack McQueen said, getting to his feet, "are you gonna be around for a while?"

"I reckon I will," Leach replied. He had already made up his mind. "Maybe I'll have a little better luck tomorrow."

"Maybe you will," McQueen replied with a wide grin.

When Leach returned to the room, Roach was sleeping the contented sleep of one who had known fulfillment. He didn't even stir when Leach carefully removed the pistol from beneath his pillow. Roach always slept with the weapon under his head, and Leach wasn't willing to risk having him awaken suddenly and shoot him while he was pulling off his boots. Gazing down at the big man, Leach thought, *This town might be a good spot to spend the winter, if you don't get into trouble.* He knew the odds were long on that. Roach always seemed to get into trouble, and Leach didn't like the prospect of spending the winter on the run.

A week passed, and a relatively quiet and peaceful routine seemed to have been established. The poker game became a nightly event for Leach, while Roach contented himself as a regular guest at Possum Annie's two-story frame house at the end of the street. But the criminal mind was far from being converted to a peace-loving organ. Although the two outlaws had come to Wichita well-heeled with stolen money, Leach was not making a living at the poker table—Jack McQueen being the main beneficiary of his losses. And Roach was squandering a good portion of his share on women and drink. So it was only natural for them to cast coveting eyes in the direction of the small bank a few doors down from the hotel. By the end of the second week, Leach began having second thoughts about hanging around until winter.

While Leach may have been contemplating a

change of scene, it was to be Roach who expedited the decision. There were three working women at Possum Annie's establishment in addition to the madam herself, and Roach sampled them all. Rough and just short of brutal, his idea of lovemaking was more akin to the mating of a grizzly bear, and the women were grateful that he spread his lust around, instead of picking a favorite. Because he was possessed of insatiable lust, it was only natural that the single-minded brute became obsessed with forbidden fruit. Possum Annie had a daughter of whom Roach had an occasional glimpse whenever he passed the kitchen on his way out to the outhouse. It was enough to set a spark aflame in the big man's mind. He was informed early on that Rose, a tender girl of fourteen, was not on the menu. This only served to make the young girl more desirable. Roach had never had a virgin before, and it was an experience he greatly desired.

"I'll give you fifty dollars for a turn with Rose," Roach offered one night as he sat drinking coffee after a lively session with Evelyn. He had been watching the young girl as she washed a pan full of dishes on a table by the pump. Her back was toward him, and he saw her stiffen when he said it.

Seated at the kitchen table across from him, Annie cocked one eyebrow and fixed him with a menacing scowl. "You ever even think about touching that girl, and I swear I'll carve your guts out."

"Fifty dollars," Roach repeated, ignoring the threat, an evil grin across his face. "How long would it take you to make that much at two dollars a tumble?"

"You sorry son of a bitch," Annie replied, not sure

now if the huge man was serious or if he was just trying to get her goat. She didn't doubt that he had the money. After all, he had been pretty loose with it ever since he had paid his first visit to her social club. He had even voluntarily paid Justine an extra five dollars after he had gotten a little rough with her. Annie had warned him that she would not tolerate any more rough stuff with her girls, and if it happened again, he would not be welcome in her establishment. Roach had been properly contrite and promised it would never happen again. True to his word, he had been on his best behavior since that night—still rough as a bull elk, but not mean. And now he came up with this outrageous proposition. It was enough to make Annie nervous. "You just get your mind off my baby," she said. "She ain't never gonna be in this business." Then, without taking her eyes off of Roach, she said, "Go on up to your room, Rose. You can finish them dishes later—wouldn't hurt to let 'em soak a while, anyway."

The young girl did as she was told immediately, her eyes never daring to look up as she hurried toward the door. Again ignoring the icy threat in Annie's eyes, Roach turned in his chair to leer at the slender form until Rose disappeared from view. Turning back to her mother, he marveled, "Dammit, Annie, was your ass ever that little?"

"None of your damn business," Annie replied in a huff. "I've had enough of your sass for one night. Go on back to the hotel now before I have to send for the sheriff to escort you."

Roach laughed delightedly. "All right, honey. I ain't

lookin' for no trouble. I'll see you tomorrow night." He got up to leave. "I might even ask for you tomorrow."

"Humph," she grunted contemptuously, "I might not be able to sleep tonight just thinking about it." She could still hear him laughing after she closed the door behind him.

"I ain't never had a streak of bad luck this long," Leach complained to Roach one afternoon as they sat at a table in the hotel dining room. "And I ain't never seen a man have such a long lucky streak as that son of a bitch," he said, referring to Jack McQueen. "He's cheatin'—has to be—but I can't catch him at it."

"I've had about a bellyful of this peace and quiet," Roach responded. Even to a man with Roach's insatiable appetite, the tired, lifeless whores at Possum Annie's had become a boring routine. "Why don't we just go ahead and knock off that little bank and get the hell outta here?"

Leach sat considering the idea for a minute before replying. "I reckon we might as well, but I wanna catch that bastard double-dealin' before I leave this town. When I do, I'm gonna put a bullet right between his cheatin' eyes."

Roach shrugged indifferently. He failed to see why Leach just didn't go ahead and shoot the son of a bitch. That would damn well end his lucky streak.

That night, Roach found himself thinking more about the bank than the prospect of another evening of chasing whores. He never thought he could ever be bored with that activity, but he had to admit he had lost his enthusiasm for Annie's stable of overridden mares. This was the mood he was in when he happened to catch a glimpse of Annie's young daughter through the kitchen window. *Sweet little Rose*, he thought, *now there's something to put the starch back in a man.*

He walked around to the window at the side of the kitchen to get a better look at the young girl. Dutifully going about her chores, cleaning up the supper dishes, she moved with an elegant grace that immediately stirred the juices in Roach's mind. *It's time you and me got acquainted*, he thought as she dried the last of the dishes and carried the pan to the door to throw the dirty water out.

Rose was humming softly to herself as she pushed the screen door open with the pan of dirty water before her. She was always pleased to have the dishes finished early so she could retreat to her room in back of the kitchen. There she would close the door, shutting out some of the noise from the parlor: the loud laughter of her mother's staff; the raucous bluster of the cowhands liquored up to boost their courage; the low, cautious voices of the town's gentlemen; and the incessant creaking of bedsprings overhead in the guest rooms. Her mind was not focused on those things at the moment, however. She had no thoughts beyond emptying the dishpan and sweeping the kitchen floor when a huge hand suddenly clamped around her arm, and she was jerked off the back step.

The dishpan was sent flying, its contents spraying a dark swath in the dust. Terrified, Rose screamed, but only for an instant before another hand clamped tight over her mouth, stifling the sound, and her body was locked in a powerful embrace. Helpless to struggle against the massive arms that enveloped her, she felt the terrified panic of a lamb in the jaws of a wolf. The strong stench of tobacco and stale sweat that filled her nostrils would only register in her frightened brain later when she would recall this night.

"Now there ain't no use you makin' such a fuss, darlin'," Roach said, his voice low, his lips close to her ear. "You're bound to get rode sometime. It might as well be me that does it." With her arms imprisoned by one of his, and another hand pressed tightly over her mouth, she could do nothing but kick her feet as the big man dragged her toward a shed behind the house. Once he reached the dark shadows behind the shed, he removed his hand from her mouth and attempted to kiss her. She immediately screamed out for help. A sharp rap across her face was enough to silence her. "You might as well make up your mind that you're gonna get rode. If you behave yourself, I won't get rough with you. But if you want it the other way, I'll beat the livin' hell outta you. Either way, we're gonna get it done."

Paralyzed by the thought of what was about to occur, Rose began to cry. "Please don't," she pleaded pitifully, helpless to save herself from the horror that was promised.

Her whimpering pleased him, bringing a wicked smile to his face. "You might as well enjoy it," he said, "just like your mama."

Helpless against his strength, she was easily wrestled to the ground, landing roughly upon her back. He was immediately on top of her, groping and fumbling

DEVIL'S KIN

with her skirt. She closed her eyes in an effort to hide from what was happening to her. She heard the solid clunk of oak against his skull, but had no idea what it was. Suddenly, he was no longer upon her. She opened her eyes to see her mother swinging a piece of stove wood at Roach.

"You son of a bitch," Annie screamed, flailing away in an attempt to make solid contact with Roach's skull again. But Roach backed away from her, warding off the blows with his arms. "Run to the house, Rose," Annie commanded. The girl did not have to be told a second time. Annie paused in her attack only long enough to see that her daughter was safely away; then she advanced upon the huge man again. "I warned you to leave her alone," she spit at him.

His head stinging from the broken skin on the back of his skull, Roach steadied himself to meet her assault. Enraged by her attack, he stood his ground and waited. Like an angry mama bear defending her cubs, she charged the big man again, the stick of wood raised to strike. He easily avoided it this time, and catching her wrist, he clamped down until she had to drop it. Still holding her by the wrist, he reached down and picked up the stick of stove wood. Then he methodically began to strike her, again and again, repeatedly bouncing the hard oak against her skull until she fell senseless at his feet. Even then, he did not stop until the stick finally broke over her crushed and bloody skull.

His anger still at a peak, he stood over her lifeless body for a long minute before sounds from inside the house began to register in his brain. He threw the broken stub of the piece of fire wood at her body. "That oughta learn you somethin'," he growled and quickly departed the scene.

Leach was just preparing to go downstairs when Roach burst into the room. "We've gotta get the hell outta here!" Roach exclaimed and immediately started getting his things together.

Dumbfounded at first, Leach stood there motionless for a few moments while his partner grabbed up his saddlebags and rifle. "Now what the hell?" he asked, already starting to get angry even before he heard the answer.

"I beat the hell outta that damn whore, and we better get outta here before they go get the sheriff."

Leach guessed there was more to it than that. "You beat up one of the whores? Which one?"

Roach continued to stuff articles of clothing into his saddlebags. "Annie," he replied. "Only she ain't gonna be givin' nobody no sass anymore."

"You killed her?"

"Deader'n hell." He paused for a second and looked up at Leach. "She had it comin'."

"Damn you, Roach," Leach complained. Realizing the seriousness of it then, he hurried to gather up his belongings from the room. He could not have cared less that Roach had killed Possum Annie. He was angry over the untimeliness of his huge partner's senseless act. "We coulda knocked over that little cracker-box bank and left town a helluva lot richer."

"It weren't my fault. She come at me with a stick of stove wood. Besides, we've still got plenty of money left. At least, I know I have—if you ain't lost all your share to Jack McQueen. Right now, I expect we'd best be ridin'. Them whores is bound to go to the sheriff."

Disgusted with the brainless blunder Roach had committed, Leach was tempted to tell him that he was on his own and let the sheriff come get him. He wanted to hit that bank, and he had a score to settle with Jack McQueen before he was ready to leave Wichita. *Damn fool*, he cursed Roach silently and picked up his gear. "Come on, then. Let's go down the back steps, so Boyd don't see us."

They wasted no time hoofing it down to the stables to saddle up. In a matter of minutes, they were ready to ride. The sheriff, accompanied with the hysterical ladies of Possum Annie's house of pleasure, was just coming through the front door of the hotel when two riders galloped off into the darkness. Like so many other towns, Wichita was left to grieve after a visit from Leach and Roach.

Chapter 10

"Mr. Sawyer tells me you've settled your account and you're getting ready to leave us."

Jordan turned to find Kathleen standing in the open door of his room. "I reckon it's time I got goin'," he replied. While she watched from the doorway, he strapped on his gun belt, then looked around the room to see if he had forgotten anything before picking up his rifle and saddlebags.

She took a couple of steps toward him, a slight frown upon her face as she offered mild admonishment. "You're still healing inside. It might not be such a good idea to be too anxious to leave. Maybe it would be best to let Father take another look at your wounds before you ride off to who knows where."

Had he been a little more perceptive, he might have noticed the thinly veiled irritation in her tone. Being of a single mind, however, he perceived nothing beyond the casual interest of a nurse for her patient. "Oh, I don't think I'll bother your father with it. I feel pretty sound—just a little stiff from layin' around for so long."

She could hold her patience no longer. "Dammit, Jordan, why do you insist on going after those men? You came within a hair of being killed. Next time, you might not be so lucky."

Somewhat stunned to hear the gentle young lady curse, he didn't know how to reply for a moment. From the look of embarrassment on her face, he could see that she had startled herself as well. Her outburst was a distinct departure from the playful scolding he had become accustomed to, and he was at a loss as to how he had managed to displease her. "I reckon I owe you some money for your time," he offered lamely. It was the wrong thing to say, particularly at that moment.

She just stood there for a few long seconds, doubled-up fists on hips, fuming, as she stared at the bumbling young man. "I don't want your money," she finally exclaimed. "Do you think I've been taking care of you every day for money?"

"Why, no, of course not," he mumbled, confused by her sudden anger. "I just thought—"

"That's just the problem," she interrupted. "All you can think about is going off to get yourself shot again. Well, I hope you can find someone to patch you up next time."

Surprised to find she had a temper, and completely baffled that he had managed to ignite it, Jordan was the picture of confusion. It appeared that he needed to apologize, but he was not sure why. "I'm sorry, Kathleen."

She just shook her head sadly. She had already exposed more of her innermost feelings than she had intended, and he either had no like feelings for her or he was too dumb to realize it—she wasn't sure which. It was a lost cause, she decided. "Take care of yourself, Jordan Gray," she finally said, her voice dropping to a softer tone. Then she stepped close, reached up, and kissed him on the cheek. Stepping quickly back, she turned and hurried from the room, leaving a totally confused young man to ponder over the deep emptiness that had suddenly overcome him.

Lieutenant Lance McCoy had set his morning report aside and emerged from his tent when he was informed that he had a visitor. "Well, Mr. Gray," he greeted Jordan, "I see you seem to have recovered from your wounds."

"Mornin', Lieutenant," Jordan said. "Yeah, I reckon I'm ready to get on my way now."

McCoy had a fair idea of the purpose of Jordan's visit. He only wished that he had more information to give him. "Looks like you're packed up and ready to go."

"That's a fact. I'm hopin' you can give me some idea of which way to start."

"North when they left here," McCoy said. "That's about the best I can tell you. They followed the river as far as Sawyer Creek, and that's where we lost them. I don't know if they rode up the creek, heading northeast, or crossed over the river and headed west. We scouted about a four-mile arc, from a mile below the creek—nothing. I truly wish I could help you, but not one of my Indian scouts could pick up a trail."

Jordan had given no consideration to a meeting with the town's sheriff, figuring it a waste of time. Ben Waldren held an office that was little more than political at best. The army was responsible for maintaining law and order in the territory, especially since being reposted to Fort Gibson in seventy-two. But the people of the settlement thought they should have a sheriff, so they appointed Ben Waldren to the job. He didn't bother anyone and primarily served as an innkeeper for the town drunks when they needed a place to sleep it off. Ben had come by to talk to Jordan on several occasions while he was convalescing. Jordan found the man to be pleasant, but a bit windy, sometimes tiring Jordan out before ending his visits. If Lieutenant McCoy could offer no more than a general direction to start, then there was little more to be gained from Ben Waldren.

It seemed a hopeless picture. Jordan was attempting to follow a trail that was a month old now, but he had hoped that the army patrol could have at least given him some idea beyond the general direction of flight. But Mr. Jones and Mr. Smith—the names Leach and Roach had registered under at the hotel—had been very successful in hiding their trail. According to McCoy, their tracks had become mixed in with countless others almost as soon as they had left the stables. His visit to the fort a waste of time, Jordan thanked the lieutenant and turned the chestnut's head north. Discouraged, but still determined, he refused to let his mind work on the hopelessness of his mission. Nothing else mattered but the reckoning due him.

He had settled his account with Sam Irwin for boarding the horses by swapping two of the four horses for payment of the bill. Having no desire to keep the horses formerly owned by murderers, he left the paint Perley had last ridden, and Johnny Spratte's roan with Sam. It was fitting that he take Perley's Sweet Pea as his packhorse—the mottled and shaggy gray would serve as a remembrance of the old man who was responsible for most of the knowledge about scouting he had learned. Sweet Pea had become fairly tolerant of the chestnut, but Jordan knew that she had already taken a nip out of one of Sam's horses in the time she had been corralled with them.

Sheriff Waldren glanced up when Jordan rode by the jail, leading his packhorse. The sheriff had just made a pot of coffee for himself and had unwrapped a cold biscuit that Mrs. Waldren had stuck in his pocket when he had left for his office at the jail. As was his custom, he took a sheet of paper from the stack of notices neatly piled on the corner of his desk for a place mat. His wife used a fair amount of lard in her biscuits, and it wouldn't do to let them stain the solid oak desk. Unnoticed by Ben, for he always turned the notices upside down, the paper he selected that morning was to tell him to be on the lookout for one Jordan Gray, a suspect in the bank robbery in Fort Smith. He might have stepped to the door to wish Jordan well, but he had just poured his cup of coffee, and he liked to drink it hot.

Following the Neosho River as it wound in a generally northern direction, Jordan had to admit that his search might take years. He did not know the country he was riding into, and he had no notion of where he was heading. Lieutenant McCoy's scouts had not had any success in picking up the trail when it was still fresh. Now, with the trail almost a month old, even Perley would have had trouble finding tracks left by the two outlaws. Jordan did not allow his mind to dwell upon the hopelessness of his quest, however. His only purpose for living—and the sole reason he had refused to die—was to seek out and kill the two whose hands were soiled with the blood of his family and his friend.

From Lance McCoy's description, Jordan recognized Sawyer Creek when he came upon the place where it joined the river. According to the lieutenant, a settler, John McIntyre, had a small place about a quarter of a mile up the creek, where he lived with his Indian wife. McCoy also said that McIntyre had been of little help as far as Roach and Leach were concerned. Jordan decided he would talk to the man, anyway, and guided the chestnut along the creekbank.

He had ridden less than a quarter of a mile when he spotted a crude abode of logs and sod close by the bank of the creek. Having spotted a visitor long seconds before Jordan spied the cabin, an Indian woman stood motionless near the door, watching him approach. At first, it appeared that there was no one else around, but a slight motion near a large cottonwood tree caught Jordan's eye, and he discovered a man partially hidden by the trunk. John McIntyre, like his wife, stood motionless, watching. A double-barreled shotgun stood ready, propped against the tree, close by the man's hand.

"Afternoon," Jordan called out and pulled his horse up at the edge of the yard, deciding it best to wait to be invited in before approaching the cabin.

"Afternoon," McIntyre returned, still evaluating the manner of man his visitor might be. Being naturally cautious, a necessary trait for a man living in Indian Territory, he kept his eyes glued upon Jordan's every move.

Aware that his reception was especially cool, Jordan asked, "Mind if I step down?"

"Reckon not" was McIntyre's cautious response. He relaxed his guard somewhat, however, when Jordan dismounted, leaving his rifle in the saddle sling. McIntyre took one step forward, still within easy reach of his shotgun, while he continued to scrutinize the young man's face for signs of mischief. Finding none, he decided Jordan was just a traveler passing through. "What brings you out this way?" he finally asked, breaking the cool silence. "We go half a year without seeing nobody. Then in one month's time we seed a passel of folks."

"I'm lookin' for a couple of fellows that might have come this way a few weeks back," Jordan said. "I was wonderin' if you had seen them."

"Most folks passin' through this part of the territory follow the river. They seldom come this far up the creek." He paused for emphasis. "That's the reason I didn't build my place on the river." He studied Jordan's face for a few seconds longer, then asked, "You a lawman?"

"No," Jordan replied, "I'm not a lawman." He went on to explain why he was looking for Leach and Roach.

When Jordan had finished, McIntyre's stony, expressionless face softened a bit. He nodded toward the Indian woman still standing by the door of the cabin. She turned and went inside. "Wife and child," he murmured, shaking his head slowly. "I thought them two was on the run from the law—knew it before them soldiers come lookin' fer 'em."

His response surprised Jordan. According to what Lieutenant McCoy had told him, McIntyre had seen no one. "You mean you *did* see them?" Jordan asked. "The lieutenant said you hadn't."

"I seen 'em, all right," he replied, "but they never saw me. I was down by the river when they come through." He glanced toward the cabin door, where his wife had been standing. "I reckon it was lucky fer me they didn't, from what you say."

"But you didn't tell Lieutenant McCoy you saw them?"

McIntyre's face turned stony again, but just for a second as he explained. "I didn't tell him I didn't, either. I just told him I hadn't seen nobody around here. He didn't ask me if I'd seen anybody down by the river. I don't know if I'da told him even if he had'da asked me—come gallopin' up here like they was gonna swarm all over us. Two of his dad-blamed troopers rode right over the edge of my garden. I had to chase 'em out. They was just settin' there, lettin' their horses graze on my bean vines." He paused to allow a second for that insult to sink in. Then his voice softened a shade, and he nodded toward the cabin. "My woman didn't want me to tell 'em nothin', anyway. She's Osage, and she naturally ain't got no love for them Cherokee scouts ridin' with the soldiers." He shrugged in his own defense. "Besides, I figured them two they was chasin' was probably deserters or somethin', and hell, I didn't care if the army caught 'em or not." He looked quickly into Jordan's eyes. "If I'da knowed what they'd done, I woulda told them soldiers what I could."

After promising that he would ride down to the

river with him and show him which way Roach and Leach had taken, McIntyre insisted that Jordan should stop long enough to have something to drink. Jordan would have preferred to decline the invitation, but he didn't want to seem ungrateful, so he led his horses over to stand in the shade of the large cottonwood, then followed McIntyre over to the cabin.

"Set yourself down on that bench there," McIntyre said, "and we'll have us a cup of cool plum wine." He turned his head toward the doorway and called out some instructions to his wife. He spoke in the Osage tongue, so Jordan had no idea what he was telling her. In a few minutes, the Indian woman appeared, carrying two cups. She nodded politely to Jordan as she handed him one of the cups. After giving the other to her husband, she went to the creekbank. Pulling her skirt up almost to her bottom, she waded out into the water to a spring box, anchored in the center of the current. With one hand holding her skirt, she reached down to fetch a quart-size jar.

"Thank you, ma'am," Jordan said as she filled his cup with a dark red liquid.

"You're welcome," she replied in English.

Surprised, Jordan remarked that she spoke American very well. McIntyre chuckled. "PJ don't know but a few words in American, but what she does know, she speaks pretty good. We talk about half American and half Osage. And half the time I ain't even sure what I've said, right after I said it."

"Well, thank you again . . . PJ?" He looked at McIntyre, wondering if he had pronounced her name correctly.

McIntyre laughed. "I don't know how to spell it, but it sounds like PJ to me, so that's what I call her—means some kinda bird or somethin'." PJ nodded, smiling.

Jordan sipped the wine, while McIntyre watched him intently, waiting for Jordan's compliment. The wine *was* good, though a bit cloudy. It was not as sweet as most homemade wine he had tasted, probably, he decided, because sugar was not in huge supply. But it was good, and Jordan gave McIntyre the approval he waited for.

Satisfied that his guest appreciated his wine, McIntyre extended an invitation to supper. "PJ ain't started supper yet, but you're welcome to stay and share it with us."

Jordan thanked him, but declined, explaining that he was already a month behind on a cold trail, and he was anxious to get under way. McIntyre understood Jordan's impatience, and as soon as they had finished the wine, he slipped a bridle on his mule, and he and Jordan rode back down the creek to the river.

"I was settin' right down yonder near that old log stickin' outta the water—had me a line in—thought I might catch somethin' besides a catfish for a change." He started to veer off into a standard complaint about the lack of good fishing in the river, but caught himself in time. "Anyway," he resumed, "I was about to call it a day, when I heard their horses above me on the bluff. My mule was tied to a willow tree not more than thirty yards back up the creek. She didn't make a sound when them two horses went by." He paused to allow Jordan to express amazement at that. "I crawled up the bank to have myself a look. I figured they was Cherokees, maybe huntin' or somethin'. When I saw it was two white men, I just laid low for a while till I had a chance to look 'em over. There's a lot of outlaws in this part of the territory, and I didn't want no trouble. Well, they crossed over to the other side of the river after they talked about it for a spell. I couldn't hear what they was sayin', but it looked like they was tryin' to make up their minds to keep followin' the river, or cross over and head west. I reckon they decided to head west."

Jordan stood gazing at the shallow ravine that led up from the river on the far side. It appeared to be a trail of some sort, though seldom used, judging from the brush that grew unhampered there. "Where does that trail lead?" he asked.

"West," McIntyre replied. "Nowhere." He shrugged. "I mean there ain't nuthin' between here and the Smoky Hill that I know of—maybe a stray band of Osage or Cheyenne. 'Course, I ain't ever been more'n fifteen or twenty miles in that direction—as far as the Verdigris. I've heard tell there's a settlement on the Smoky Hill due west of here—I couldn't say for sure— supposed to been a favorite campsite for a band of Cheyenne ten or twelve years ago. They mighta been headin' for that, but I don't think them fellers knew where they was goin'—they was just goin'."

It wasn't much to go on, but at least Jordan knew the general direction. That was more than Lieutenant McCoy had been able to supply. "I'm obliged to you," he said and guided the chestnut down the bank and into the dark water of the river. The mottled gray followed without protest after attempting to take a nip out of McIntyre's mule as she passed.

McIntyre stood and watched until rider and horses had reached the other side. Then he called out, "If you get back this way, stop in for a longer visit." Jordan answered with a wave of his hand, then turned to follow the ravine up from the river.

John McIntyre had not lied when he said there was nothing between his cabin and the Smoky Hill. Jordan had hoped to strike the Verdigris by nightfall, but he had to settle for a late camp by a tiny stream that struggled to provide enough water for him and his horses. That night, as he lay by his fire, he felt almost smothered by the shroud of hopelessness that descended upon him. His mind was clouded by a hailstorm of random thoughts swirling around in his head, thoughts of his wife and child—of the men he hunted—of Perley—and even thoughts of the slender young girl who had been his nurse. Looking up at a dark moonless sky, he couldn't help but think that his chances of finding Roach and Leach were about as good as if he were searching the black starry heavens above him. The notion that he could find two men in the vast wilderness that lay before him was absurd to a rational thinking man. He didn't know where he was, and he had not the faintest idea where the two were heading. As McIntyre had said, he doubted that Leach and Roach knew where they were going. There was no trail to follow. In spite of the hopelessness of it, he never considered turning back, for there was nothing to turn back to. He would press on, taking the easiest route he could determine that took him in a general northwest direction, following a gut feeling that the two he sought would have done the same.

Early the next morning, he struck the Verdigris at a gentle turn of the river, just as McIntyre had described. This was as far as McIntyre had ventured in this direction. From this point on, he might as well be searching the surface of the moon. His hopes were raised, however, by the discovery of the remains of a campfire close by the water's edge. He dismounted to examine it more closely, not really knowing what more it could tell him. After stirring the cold ashes with his finger, he stood up and gazed toward the other side of the river. *The easiest way to cross would be toward that sand spit by the bend*, he thought, *so that's the way I'll go*. If there had been tracks remaining after a month's time, he might have been able to determine that this was the point where Roach and Leach had almost decided to change direction, but headed for the Arkansas once again.

Leaving the Verdigris behind, he set his course for a distant line of hills on the far horizon. He had now left behind him the heavily forested hills around the two rivers, and the land took on a grassy rolling quality that appeared to be endless. Riding with an urgency that allowed for no wasted time, he was careful, however, not to push his horses too hard. He had no desire to be on foot in this empty land.

It took him an entire day to reach the hills he had guided on. Grateful to discover a little stream cutting through the center of the slopes, he made his camp. Then, on the hopes of having a stroke of luck, he scouted a wide area around his camp, looking for an old campfire to let him know that his instincts were accurate. But there was no sign of any recent camps.

As he had done the day before, he selected a distant range of hills to sight on. These looked taller than the hills he had ridden toward on the day just past, and were now behind him. Proceeding solely upon his opinion as to the best line of travel, and the easiest on the horses, he started out again. His rational mind told him that the farther he rode, the greater his chances that he was just hopelessly wandering. Leach and Roach could have gone in any direction. Even so, the alternative—to give up completely—was a choice he could not make. So he passed that day as he had the days before, pushing onward across a land that seemed devoid of any living things except himself, his horses, and occasional colonies of prairie dogs.

He soon discovered that he was not fond of prairie dog. There wasn't much meat on the little critters, and the flavor reminded him of squirrel that had gone bad. To conserve what provisions he had, however, he forced himself to add them to his diet, but only until he chanced upon more desirable game.

Early the next afternoon, he picked up an old trail that led him to a river. He had no clue he was near water until the horses sensed it. Topping a gentle rise in the prairie, he discovered a narrow, serpentine river, bordered by cottonwoods and willows. He pulled the chestnut up short, and the horse sidestepped to slide its rump away from Sweet Pea's muzzle. Jordan took a long look up and down the river as far as he could see. Was this the Smoky Hill? he wondered. There was no evidence of a settlement or an old Indian camp. He decided that it was not the river McIntyre had described. But it was a welcome sight. The late August afternoons were hot and dry. Horses and man could use a dip in the cool waters of the river, so he decided to make camp for the night. His decision to rest was also strongly influenced by his concern for his horse.

The chestnut had begun showing signs of fatigue. Unlike Perley's mottled gray, the horse was not accustomed to long, hard days that covered miles of rolling prairie. Also, unlike the gray, the chestnut did not fare well on a diet of prairie grass alone. After Jordan's supply of grain was exhausted, the horse began to look lean and weak. Now he feared the horse might falter if it were not allowed to rest. So the river could not have appeared at a better time.

Selecting a spot some fifty yards off the trail, he set up his camp under the sheltering arms of a large cottonwood and released the horses to romp in the dark water of the river. The refreshing respite restored a friskiness to the chestnut that Jordan had not seen for some days. Watching the horses play, Jordan could not resist stripping off his clothes and joining them. The dip in the river made him feel almost as frisky as the horses. It was the best he had felt since he could remember, and for a short while, his mind was free of the images of the two faces that constantly burned in his brain.

Leaving the water, he gathered up his clothes and got a bar of lye soap from his saddlebag. Then he waded back into the shallow water and gave his shirt, trousers, and underwear a good scrubbing. Afterward, with nothing on but his boots, he hung his clothes up on the lower branches of the tree to dry. With plenty of dry limbs for firewood, he soon had a fire going. Shortly after, his little gray metal coffeepot was working away over the flames. *I just wish to hell I had something to eat besides this last little slab of bacon*, he thought as he unwrapped the slightly rancid salt pork. He had no sooner had the thought when a slight movement on the other side of the narrow river caught his eye. He turned quickly to discover three antelope edging down to the water to drink. To him, it was like someone had heard his wish. Moving very slowly, and never taking his eye off the three animals, he eased his hand over until he felt the cold steel of his rifle. Without any sudden moves, he drew the rifle up against his bare shoulder and carefully sighted upon his target. Then, in one swift move, he cocked the rifle and fired. At the sound of the rifle cocking, all three antelope stopped in their tracks. The one closest to him raised its head to look at the naked man, just as Jordan's bullet struck it at the base of the neck.

Content that providence had provided for him just when he needed it, he butchered the antelope, roasting strips of the meat over the fire while he completed the job. Although his supply of salt pork was exhausted, he still had a large quantity of dried beans. He decided not to bother with them, however, and feasted solely upon antelope meat. With a full belly for a change, he slept soundly that night, wrapping himself in his blanket, close by the fire.

Dawn broke gray and chilly for that time of year. His clothes were still slightly damp, and he shivered when he pulled the cold shirt over his bare torso. But his mood was positive, lifted by the timely appearance of

the antelope just when he needed it. For the first time
since leaving Perley behind, he felt that luck might possibly be with him. The feeling was not to last long.

After a breakfast of more of the antelope, he saddled up and headed back to pick up the trail. It was
easy to see where it forded the shallow river, but Jordan decided to cross where a sand spit jutted out from
the bank. It looked to be a quicker crossing. Both
horses seemed fresh and willing as he guided the
chestnut down into the water. The rest had evidently
restored the horse's stamina, and Jordan made a mental note to try not to push the gentle animal beyond its
capability. Glancing back at Perley's shaggy gray packhorse, he wondered if the ornery beast had enough
sense to get tired. She never seemed to show it.

Jordan never saw them. Lying peacefully coiled
under the bank, the nest of water moccasins was suddenly alarmed by the intrusion of the chestnut's front
hoofs in their midst. Immediately on the attack, the
angry reptiles struck out at the intruder, one striking
the unsuspecting horse on a rear leg. Startled, the terrified chestnut, bolted for the sand spit, kicking up its
hind legs. Jordan, unprepared for the sudden bucking,
lost a stirrup and nearly came out of the saddle. Still
unaware of the cause of the horse's sudden panic, he
tried to rein him back, but the chestnut could still feel
the stinging bite of the snake, and tried to climb out of
harm's way. In his panic, the gentle gelding stepped in
a hole halfway up the bank. Jordan heard the sharp
crack of the bone as the horse tumbled head first,
throwing his rider from the saddle.

Landing on his back, Jordan rolled over and sat up.

DEVIL'S KIN

With no concern for himself, he looked back at his horse, foundering painfully in an attempt to get up. Jordan was struck with a sick feeling in his stomach as he realized what had happened, and he saw the right fetlock dangling uselessly from the chestnut's leg. At that moment, he paid no attention to the packhorse, but Sweet Pea had given the snakes a wide berth, and left the water a few yards upstream. Jordan's concern was all for his horse, and he quickly moved to the stricken animal's side. It took but a moment to see what must be done, and the thought sickened him. The leg was broken badly, and the horse was suffering. He had no choice. Reluctantly, he drew his pistol from the holster and held it against the chestnut's head. The horse rolled a pitiful eye toward his master, and Jordan hesitated, reluctant to pull the trigger. Telling himself that his horse was suffering, he finally squeezed the trigger, ending the chestnut's pain.

Feeling as if he had lost another family member, Jordan knelt there for a time until his sorrow turned to anger—anger at the nest of moccasins that had caused his loss. Rising to his feet, he stalked back to the water's edge, his pistol still in hand, his initial thought to empty the remaining bullets into the midst of the snakes. The reptiles were no longer there. He fumed helplessly for a few moments before finally holstering the weapon and returning to the business at hand. The poor chestnut had been killed by panic. The snake bite would not have been enough to put him down.

Sadly, Jordan went about the business of pulling his saddle off the carcass. The stirrups were free, but the cinch strap became entangled with a root under the

173

horse's belly, and he had to use the gray's strength to pull it free. Next came the uncertain task of saddling Sweet Pea. Perley, himself, had been reluctant to throw his saddle on the ornery horse, so Jordan expected the worst. But he had little choice in the matter. It was ride the mottled gray or walk, and Jordan had no intention of walking.

The scruffy-looking animal made no move to back away when Jordan approached, but she kept a wary eye on the man. Always alert for a possible nip from the horse's teeth, Jordan pulled the packs from Sweet Pea's back. Still unmoved, she lowered her head when he removed Perley's old bridle, and remained docile while he replaced it with his own. Her only reaction was to shake her head a couple of times as if adjusting to the difference. As a precaution, in case the horse decided to bolt, Jordan tied the reins to a willow branch while he picked up his saddle.

Eyeing him suspiciously, the horse nevertheless remained still when he approached with the saddle. Her only show of protest was to sidestep a couple of steps as he neared her flanks. "Easy now, girl," Jordan cooed as he laid the saddle blanket on her. She registered no objection, so he picked up the saddle again, expecting a violent explosion. But the mare never flinched when she felt the saddle settle upon her back. Genuinely surprised, he stepped back and patted her on her neck. "Good girl, Sweet Pea," he said.

It didn't take long to sort through the things that had been in the packs. The items he deemed unnecessary, were discarded in order to lighten Sweet Pea's load, even though Perley's words—*if you can load it, she can carry it*—came to mind. He decided to carry only essentials, but after going through the packs, he realized that there were but a few items to be left behind— mainly a spare set of horseshoes and the tools to set them. Sweet Pea was an Indian pony. She had never worn shoes. From the discarded packs, he fashioned a cross strap that served as another rifle sling to carry the Henry rifle with the shattered stock. The Winchester 66 that had belonged to the half-breed called Snake was now occupying his own saddle sling. His weapons and his meager food supply were really all he deemed necessary, anyway. With everything packed, he was ready to step up in the saddle.

With Perley's words ringing in his mind—*She don't cotton to nobody a-settin' on her back*—Jordan put a foot in the stirrup. He took a firm grip on the saddle horn and braced for the violent reaction he knew was to come when she felt the full weight of his body on the stirrup. Beyond disbelief, he paused there with only one foot in the stirrup, astonished by her lack of protest. Still expecting the explosion, he threw his other leg over and settled his behind in the saddle. The horse remained docile, turned at his bidding, and started toward the trail at a slow walk. Jordan couldn't help but believe Perley had not known the horse as well as he had thought. He reached forward and stroked her neck. "Good girl—we're gonna get along just fine." The words had barely cleared his lips when she decided to express her objection. Caught off-guard, he was bucked out of the saddle when she suddenly humped her back and threw her rump toward the sky.

With nothing to grab on to but air, Jordan hit the

ground hard. More angry than hurt, he scrambled to his feet. "You deceitful bitch!" he cursed the horse. His initial thought was to formally introduce himself to the horse with a good-sized limb across her face, as Perley had done with the half-breed's horse. Restraining that urge, he grabbed the mare's reins and pulled her head up close, so he could look her right in the eye. "You might as well get used to it. I damn sure ain't gonna carry you." He climbed back aboard. Sweet Pea proceeded to repeat the routine, only this time Jordan was braced for her reaction. As before, she gently walked for a few yards before suddenly deciding to rid herself of the burden on her back. Unable to catch the man by surprise this time, she was forced to buck and flail with added violence, almost twisting herself in two. He stayed with her for a long time before losing his grip and coming out of the saddle again.

The horse stood a few yards away, her head down, staring at the man seated in the dust of the trail. With the firm knowledge of who was going to win in the end, Jordan got to his feet and approached the horse. The routine was repeated several more times before Jordan became familiar with every one of the ornery mare's moves, and the horse finally conceded defeat. The issue of who was in charge settled, the team of man and horse set out for the Smoky Hill.

Chapter 11

Briscoe Greenwell untied the string on his last sack of cornmeal. Spreading the top of the sack, he peered into it, looking for signs of infestation. It was not as bad as he had expected. He dragged the heavy sack over to the wooden barrel at the end of the counter and propped it there while he went behind the counter to fetch his scoop and a wire sieve. Laying the sieve across the top of the barrel, he proceeded to empty the sack of cornmeal, scoop by scoop, into the barrel. By necessity, his sieve was coarse. It had to be to allow the cornmeal to pass through, but it still managed to catch a large percentage of the weevils that had taken residence in the sack. By his thinking, he was being very responsible to his customers. *I oughta leave the damn bugs in it and charge extra for the meat*, he said to himself, knowing that wouldn't be right, even if almost all of his customers were Indians.

The cornmeal wasn't the only item in his small storeroom that was getting low. It was time to make his late-summer trip to Fort Gibson to restock his stores. The thought caused him to pause and gaze at the bundles of hides and the small stack of buffalo robes in the corner of the storeroom. The robes, a rarity these days, would fetch a good price in Fort Gibson. The buffalo herds were long gone from these parts, had been for years. He didn't expect to see many more of the heavy robes. On this trip, he was determined to buy something nice for Sally, even if it meant shorting himself on some of the supplies. *Lord knows she deserves it—putting up with an old coot like me.*

He shook his head sadly as he remembered his younger days when he had first set up his little trading post on the Smoky Hill River. Trading was good then. The Indians had accepted him, after they learned he would be fair in his dealings with them. He had taken a wife, a young Cheyenne girl named Summer Moon, whom he called Sally. She and her mother had been survivors of the massacre on Sand Creek, when Colonel Chivington's regiment of Colorado volunteers jumped Black Kettle's peaceful village. Along with other survivors, they had escaped to a Cheyenne village on the Smoky Hill, not far from where Briscoe's store now stood. It had been a good marriage, in spite of the fact that Briscoe was some fifteen years older than his young wife. Sally seemed content and pleased that Briscoe had taken her mother in as well. *Ten . . . no, eleven years since that cold November night*, he thought, trying to remember exactly when Sally and her mother had trudged wearily into the Cheyenne camp. He had taken her for a wife less than six months after that. *God, she was a pretty little thing*, he remembered, *slender and bright-eyed, like a fox pup.* She was still a relatively young woman today, but he had to admit that he was slowing down. "Damn!" he swore at the thought. Before he had time to dwell upon it, his thoughts were interrupted by the sudden barking of the dogs.

He walked over and peered out the door. Two riders were approaching on the south trail—white men, he quickly ascertained. He squinted in an effort to see them more clearly. They did not even have a packhorse, so he knew they were not trappers or traders. And since his little store was not on the road to anywhere, the next logical assumption was that they were on the run from the law. As a precaution, he got his shotgun from the corner and placed it in plain sight at the end of the counter. Then he returned to stand in the doorway to watch the riders approach.

Leach and Roach stopped to water the horses before fording the river, both men staring at the log structure on the other bank with one lone tipi behind it. A thin ribbon of smoke wafted upward from behind the building.

"Looks like some kind of store," Leach speculated.

"I'm damn glad to see it," Roach said. "My ass is startin' to take root in this saddle. I ain't ever seen such scruffy-lookin' country. Maybe there's something to drink in that little shack."

The thought appealed to Leach. "Let's go see," he said, just then noticing Briscoe standing in the doorway. At that point, it was difficult for Leach to determine if he was looking at a white man or Indian.

"Howdy," Briscoe greeted the two strangers when they rode up to his store. "Don't see many white men travelin' this way."

"Reckon not," Leach returned, looking around him at the desolate terrain.

"You got anything in that little shack to drink?" Roach asked impatiently, not willing to wait for polite greetings.

"A dipper of water," Briscoe answered, knowing what Roach was really after.

"Damn!" Roach swore. "You mean you ain't even got no private stock you keep for yourself? We've got money, if that's what's worryin' you, and right now I'd give five dollars for a good drink of whiskey."

Briscoe shook his head from side to side. "Wish I could help you fellers, but I ain't got a drop of whiskey—never carry it—it don't bring nothin' but trouble."

Roach stared at Briscoe in disbelief. "Are you some kind of preacher or somethin'?"

"Nope, just don't keep whiskey around. The Injuns can't handle it, and I never had a need for it myself. Now, like I said, if you fellers are thirsty, there's a water barrel inside. You're welcome to help yourselves."

Leach listened to Roach's interrogation of the old man for as long as his patience permitted before interrupting. "Never mind the whiskey," he said. "Have you got anything to eat?" A slight breeze had kicked up, causing the smoke from the fire behind the store to drift past his nostrils.

"Depends on what you want," Briscoe replied. "If you're needin' staples, I've got cornmeal and coffee beans, some salt pork left, a few dried beans, some salt, and a little bit of sugar. That's about all that's left. I'm fixin' to go to Fort Gibson tomorrow to lay in supplies for the winter. Too bad you fellers didn't wait until a week or two from now."

"We'll be needin' supplies, all right," Leach said. "But what I mean is, have you got somethin' we could buy to eat right now? I've et salt pork till I'm startin' to feel like a hog."

Briscoe grinned. "Oh, you're wantin' to know if you can get some supper."

"That's right," Roach chimed in and pulled a wad of bills from his saddlebag. "We can pay for our supper."

"I reckon I can fix you boys up with somethin' to fill your bellies," Briscoe said. The sight of a sizable wad of money was enough to curb some of his caution. He didn't get many chances to buy supplies for his tiny store with real U.S. currency, and his trade goods were meager at best this season. He had little doubt that the two strangers were on the run from the law. They seemed to be carrying a great deal of money. How they came by it was no concern of his, he told himself. "You got here just before suppertime," he said. "My woman is cookin' up some antelope stew right now. She cooks it up with beans and onions till the meat is nice and tender." He watched their faces, satisfied that they were properly tempted. "I expect I could get her to fry up some pan bread, too. It won't be long. We could go ahead and take care of what supplies you'll need, and by that time, supper ought to be ready." After seeing nods of approval from both men, he called out, "Sally!"

In a few moments, a slender Indian woman appeared at the corner of the store. Having heard her husband talking to the two strangers, she glanced quickly at one, then at the other, before gazing at Briscoe. She was at once troubled by a sudden feeling of dread. Her instincts told her that these two white men were dangerous, and she was immediately concerned for her husband.

"Sally," Briscoe said, ignoring her frown, "these fellers is stayin' to supper. Reckon you could make some pan bread to go with that stew?" She nodded and turned obediently to do his bidding, hoping that her instincts were wrong.

Turning back to Roach and Leach, Briscoe said, "Since you fellers is plannin' to buy supplies, it wouldn't be polite to charge you for a little somethin' to eat."

Never far below the surface, Roach's lust for women was immediately stirred by the sight of the handsome Cheyenne woman. Intrigued by the fact that she didn't appear to be mixed blood, he wondered aloud, "Is that your daughter?"

"She's my wife," Briscoe stated flatly, his tone tightening a little.

Both men looked surprised. Like his partner, Leach had automatically assumed the woman was Briscoe's daughter. He took a longer look at Sally as she disappeared around the corner. He glanced at Roach, who was grinning broadly, his gaze still nailed to the corner of the store. Looking back at Briscoe then, he discovered a hostile spark in the older man's eye. Leach chuckled and gave him a knowing wink. "Nice goin', old man." Before Briscoe had time to reply, Leach forged ahead. "Now let's see what we can buy for supplies." He stepped past Briscoe and entered the store.

His mind now on the business of turning a profit,

Briscoe brought out what supplies he had left, including some cartridges for their rifles. Leach wasted no time, pointing out the items he wanted with no attempt to bargain for better prices. He had come by his ill-gotten finances easily enough. It wasn't in his nature to bargain. "This trail we come in on, if we stay on it, where does it lead?" he asked as Briscoe weighed out the coffee beans.

"Well, if you stay on the main trail, you'll strike the Platte in three or four days. Where are you fellers headed, anyway?" It was plain to see that the two had no idea where they were going.

Leach's face formed a thin smile. "Nowhere in particular, just tryin' to take a look at the country, see places we ain't ever seen before."

Briscoe had his own ideas as to why the two were traveling through Indian Territory, and he doubted if it was to see the country. But he kept his suspicions to himself and played along with the game. "Well, you ain't gonna see much worth lookin' at between here and the Platte. But if you're of a mind to, you can follow the Platte west to Fort Laramie." Roach and Leach nodded to each other as if that was worth considering. Further talk was interrupted by the appearance of Sally carrying two plates of stew and bread while keeping a wary eye on the strangers.

In the Cheyenne tongue, Briscoe instructed his wife. "Put the plates on the counter, and go back to the tipi. I want to be rid of these two quickly." She nodded her acknowledgment and did as she was told, relieved to find that her husband shared her caution toward them. To his two guests, he said, "Eat up, boys, and I'll help you tote your supplies out to your horses. There's still plenty of daylight left, and you're probably anxious to be on your way. If you don't tarry too long, you can make Antelope Crick. That's a dandy spot to camp— good water and plenty of firewood." When neither man gave any indication of urgency, he went on. "'Course, you'd be welcome to camp here if you want, but I wouldn't recommend it. There's a band of Cheyenne—Sally's people—supposed to get here this evening, and they ain't too friendly to white men. They tolerate me because of Sally." He paused to see if it was necessary to build on to the lie.

"I reckon we'll keep movin'," Leach replied. "Right, Roach? I ain't lookin' to meet up with no Cheyennes."

Roach, a wide grin plastered upon his face, nodded without taking his eyes off the Indian woman as she set the plates upon the counter before them. He had followed her every move from the time she appeared in the doorway, the never-rusty wheels of lust turning rapidly in his head as he formed an imaginary picture of what was beneath her long calico skirt.

"I'll be leavin' out of here myself in the mornin'— me and Sally. I'm already late in makin' the trip to Fort Gibson," Briscoe said. The statement was partially true. He *was* planning to leave in the morning, but Sally was going to remain behind with her uncle. She never accompanied him on his twice-a-year trips to the white settlement. He couldn't tell if they bought his story or not, but they made no comment. And when they had finished the supper Sally had brought, Leach pulled out a wad of money and paid up, much to Briscoe's relief. He had harbored more than a few

184

thoughts about whether the strangers really intended to pay for their supplies and if he was going to find it necessary to reach for his shotgun.

There was little more said as Roach and Leach climbed into the saddle again and turned their horses toward the north. Briscoe stood watching them as they rode away. "Much obliged," he called out after them. "Just stay on that trail. Antelope Crick—you'll recognize it when you get there." He had a feeling the two knew he was anxious to get rid of them, but it didn't matter. They were gone, and he felt he was lucky to be done with them. He remained there at the edge of the yard, watching until they disappeared from his sight. He had cash money in hand, and they had given no indication of causing him trouble. Maybe he had misjudged the pair, but he couldn't help feeling a sense of distrust. *Maybe I oughtn't to leave here tomorrow*, he thought, thinking it might be wise to wait another day or two in case they decided to come back. "Hell," he said aloud, "they're long gone. They've got no reason to hang around here. The law or somebody's probably chasin' 'em, anyway."

It was almost dark by the time Leach and Roach reached Antelope Creek. As Briscoe had predicted, they had no trouble recognizing it: a ribbon of dark water lined with cottonwoods and low brush. They set up their camp close by the water's edge. Leach kept a suspicious eye on his partner, who had been unusually quiet during the entire ride from the Smoky Hill. It wasn't like Roach to be so quiet. Something was eating at him, and Leach was pretty sure he knew what it was. "You're thinkin' about that damn little Injun woman, ain't you?" he finally asked.

"That old man ain't plannin' to take that woman with him to Fort Gibson," Roach replied, speaking out in the middle of a thought. "He just wants us to think he's takin' her." He paused to think about it. "I'll bet she's gonna be there all by herself. Think about that, Leach: pretty little thing just settin' there waitin'."

Leach recognized the faraway look in Roach's eyes. He had seen it many times before, and most of the time trouble followed as a result. He knew Roach was picturing the Indian woman alone and vulnerable. It was a picture that appealed to his crude desires as well, but he wasn't as big a fool about it as Roach. "I reckon you wanna go back there tomorrow to see if she's still there," he said.

"I'm thinkin' about it," Roach said with an evil grin.

On some days, usually when the mornings were cooler than normal, Jordan could feel the bullet lodged deep in his chest. There was no physical pain, just a cold reminder of its presence, and he would concentrate hard to enslave in his mind the image of the two faces he hunted. He accepted the fact that the odds of finding Roach and Leach were against him. It might take years of scouring every square mile of territory between there and Oregon, but he was resigned to the task. He had room for no other purpose for his life, and the images of the faces he endeavored to keep fresh in his mind were the only link between himself and his quest.

Lost deep in his thoughts of Sarah and the life that was theirs before that tragic day when his world was destroyed, he was suddenly surprised by the appearance of a wagon and a team of mules on the trail ahead. He pulled the gray up short to take a longer look. The wagon was still more than a mile away, and it was difficult for him to identify the driver, whether Indian or white man. Jordan remained stationary for a while, watching the wagon approach. He could soon see that there was just one man, and the wagon appeared to be loaded with hides. *Maybe this trail does lead somewhere*, he thought. He nudged the gray with his heels and moved to close the distance.

Briscoe pulled his pistol from its holster and laid it on the wagon seat beside him. He had spotted the lone traveler as soon as the mules topped a rise in the prairie some several hundred yards back. *Another damn stranger heading for my place*, he thought. *It's getting so you'd think you were on a street in St. Louis.* "Ha, Blue," he called out, encouraging the lead mule to pull harder as the trail dipped into a shallow draw. When he emerged from the draw, he was no more than a hundred yards from the lone rider. It was a white man for sure. He had rather it had been an Indian. White men alone in this territory often meant trouble, and his mind went immediately to the two he had left behind the day before. This one looked no better, with his flat-crowned hat pulled low against the afternoon sun and about a week's growth of dark beard covering his face. Like the two before him, this one carried no evidence of tools or packs to suggest an honest way of making a living. Briscoe decided to give him the benefit of the doubt, but he would keep his hand close to the handle of his pistol just in case.

"Howdy," Briscoe called out in greeting and pulled his mules up.

"Howdy," Jordan returned as he reined up alongside the wagon.

"Don't see many white men on this trail," Briscoe said, looking the stranger over thoroughly. Upon closer observation, he determined the rider to be a young man. Solidly built, he sat his saddle easily and looked Briscoe directly in the eye. Briscoe quickly took inventory of the stranger's gear: two heavily loaded saddle packs, two rifles, one with a busted stock. It was the look in his eyes that caused Briscoe to decide the man was a hunter, and not for four-legged game. "Where you bound for?" he asked.

"I'm lookin' for two men that mighta headed this way," Jordan replied.

"Friends of yours?"

"Hardly."

"Figured as much," Briscoe said, still looking Jordan over. Seeing no badge, he asked, "Are you a lawman?"

"No," Jordan replied impatiently. He couldn't help but wonder how many times he had been asked that question. "Have you seen two white men ridin' this way?"

"As a matter of fact, I have. Two strangers was at my store yesterday." He went on to explain that he had a small trading post on the Smoky Hill. Roach and Leach had showed up there the afternoon before, but pushed on north. "Ain't none of my business, but if they ain't friends of your'n, how come you're lookin' for 'em?"

Jordan was reluctant to discuss his reasons. "I just need to find 'em," he answered simply.

Briscoe wasn't satisfied with that explanation. His mind had been troubled by thoughts that he should have waited another day or two before starting for Fort Gibson to make sure Leach and Roach were not lingering. He had not been blind to the way both men gawked at Sally when she brought them food. With that in mind, he had told her uncle, Red Deer, to take her and her mother to his village until his return. Now he worried that he should have at least stayed until he saw them on their way to the Cheyenne camp. "Look here, young feller. I know it ain't polite to stick my nose into another man's business, but I left my wife back there with nobody but her mother and an old half-blind Cheyenne to look after her. I need to know if them two you're trailin' is somethin' to worry about."

"Mister," Jordan replied in no uncertain tone, "you'd better hope those two kept ridin'." Deciding Briscoe had a right to know, he went on to tell why he was after the two outlaws.

"Lord have mercy," Briscoe uttered softly, his eyes now wide with fear that his wife might be in danger. He immediately turned his team of mules around, yelling to Jordan as he cracked his whip over their rumps. "Please, mister, go on ahead to my place. You can make better time than I can. It ain't more'n seven or eight miles." With no need for comment, Jordan was off at a fast lope.

If there was ever a horse misnamed, it had to be

Sweet Pea. Jordan had never seen a more ornery horse. But he had to admire her strength and stamina. What she lacked in beauty, she more than compensated with a broad chest and a stout heart. As his partnership lengthened with the scruffy-looking gray mare, his appreciation for Perley Gates' appraisal of horseflesh grew. Though Perley had never seen fit to saddle his cantankerous packhorse, thinking the animal would not tolerate a man on her back, Jordan was certain the horse's antisocial behavior stemmed from a simple matter of jealousy. Ever since the chestnut had been removed from the scene, Sweet Pea had mysteriously acquired some manners. And after her initial protest to the strange sensation of a man on her back, she had evidently decided to accept her role, responding to her master's commands with a willing spirit, just as she was doing on this late August afternoon.

Jordan soon left Briscoe Greenwell and his wagon behind, a speck on the horizon, and then completely out of sight, as Sweet Pea steadily ate up the miles to the Smoky Hill River. There was still plenty of daylight left when he spotted the river and the simple log building on the far side. He reined the gray back to a slow walk as he looked the situation over. There was no sign of anyone about the cabin or the tipi behind. There was a horse in the small corral beyond the tipi, a smallish paint pony that pricked up its ears when it sensed Sweet Pea's presence. Jordan guided the gray into the water.

When he reached the bank on the other side, he pulled Sweet Pea to a halt and took another careful look around before proceeding. There were no horses around, other than the little paint in the corral. He might have assumed that the woman and her uncle had gone, as her husband had expected. But the little pony in the corral bothered him. Why would the woman leave it penned up in the corral if she was expecting to be gone for several days while her husband went to Fort Gibson? Although he felt sure he was the sole human around, he drew his rifle from the sling and cranked a round in the chamber.

Approaching the crude log structure, Jordan had an eerie feeling that he had lived this moment before, and his mind went back to the rainy afternoon when he had returned to his own cabin and the horrible scene that had left an ever-festering scar upon his heart. He rode slowly up to the cabin and dismounted, eyeing the partially open door warily. After another look around to make sure he was alone, he walked up to the door and pushed it open with his rifle barrel. There, on the floor, just inside the door, lay the body of Sally's uncle. A pool of blood had gathered under the old man's head from a ragged gash that ran almost from ear to ear, leaving his neck gaping in a macabre grin. One look and Jordan knew the old Indian had been dead for a good while. He was already starting to get stiff as Jordan turned him over, disturbing the swarm of flies that had been feeding in the bloody pool.

Jordan stood up and looked around him. Leach and Roach had obviously ransacked the cabin before leaving. Articles of clothing and trade goods lay scattered about on the floor. There was a deathly silence that filled the log building, with nothing but the whining of the flies to prevent its being a total vacuum. There was another door that Jordan assumed led to the store owner's private living quarters. *Unless he lives in the tipi behind the store,* he thought. That door was also partially open. Jordan wondered if he would find the man's wife in the other room. Moving as quietly as he could, although he felt certain there was no other living soul around, he pushed the door open wide and peered into the darkened room. What first appeared to be a body on the bed in the corner turned out to be a disheveled roll of blankets. He stared at the bed for a long moment, then shifted his attention to the rest of the room. Like the store, the floor was strewn with articles of clothing and personal items. But there was no sign of a woman. That could be good or bad news for the man following him in the wagon.

With his rifle still held ready for any surprises, he went back outside, and walked around the cabin to the tipi. He discovered the ashes of a cook fire a few paces from the back of the cabin. They were still warm. Fully expecting to find the bodies of the two women inside, he stuck his head inside the tipi. There was only one. The old woman's head had been bashed in, her body left in the center of the lodge. Realizing there was nothing he could do for the dead, he walked back around the store to wait for the man following in the wagon.

Cracking his whip over the backs of his mules, Briscoe pushed the lathered animals hard in an effort to demand more speed. His hands shook with anxiety as he guided the lead mule into the water. Seeing Jordan coming to meet him, he cried out in despair, already fearing the worst, "Sally?"

"Not here," Jordan replied. "But they've been

here—took your wife with them, it appears." He was not without sympathy for the stricken man, but he didn't know what to say to console him.

Briscoe scrambled down from the wagon seat and hurried past Jordan, heading for the door of his store. "Maybe Sally and her uncle were already gone," he uttered hopefully. "They was supposed to go to the Cheyenne camp."

"There's a dead man inside with his throat cut," Jordan said. "I expect it's her uncle. Her mother's inside the tipi. She's dead, too."

Briscoe's heart sank, his pain reflected vividly in his face. It was what he had feared when he first saw Sally's pony in the corral. He knew that she would not leave the paint behind, but he had desperately prayed that she had taken his horse for some reason. Jordan's statement stopped him in his tracks, and he stood hesitating before the door for a few moments before going inside. Jordan waited outside.

After a few minutes, Briscoe reappeared, his face drained of all color, his jaw set in grim determination. "It's Red Deer, all right. The poor old man didn't have much chance against the likes of those two." He stood there, trembling, not knowing what to do at the moment, desperately trying to keep his mind from painting a picture that he could not bear to envision.

Jordan knew the terrible pain the man was feeling, but he was aware of his own mission of vengeance, and he felt he was now closer to his quarry than ever before. He was anxious to get started after the two outlaws, but he felt he had to offer his help. "I'll help you bury the dead," he said, "but then I've got to be on my way." The plight of Briscoe's wife at the mercy of those two murderers was something he didn't like to think about. And every minute he wasted might mean the difference between her living and dying. "It might be that your wife's all right. I didn't see any sign of blood anywhere except around the bodies." He watched Briscoe carefully, waiting for his reply, but the man seemed stunned.

After a long moment, Briscoe appeared to come out of it, and his face took on a look of anger. Shifting his gaze to meet Jordan's, he spoke in quiet determination. "I reckon you got a partner, mister. I'm goin' with you."

Jordan didn't reply at once. He preferred working alone in the grim business of tracking Roach and Leach, but he couldn't expect a different reaction from any man. "All right," he said, after a moment. "But I don't have much time to waste." He glanced around him, thinking of the man's mules and possessions, and the possible delay while he took care of them.

Guessing what Jordan was thinking, Briscoe said, "I ain't gonna waste no time." He nodded toward his team of mules. "I'll unhitch the mules and let 'em loose. They can take care of theirselves. I'll have to worry about the dead later."

Briscoe wasted little time in packing what supplies he deemed necessary on his wife's pony while Jordan studied the tracks that led away from the river. When they were ready to ride, Briscoe paused for a moment and extended his hand. "Have you got a name, mister?"

"Jordan Gray," Jordan replied, taking the hand.

"Mine's Briscoe Greenwell. Let's ride."

Chapter 12

Bill Leach removed his hat and wiped the sweat from around the band with his bandanna. He squinted up at the midday sun. It was damn hot, considering that a few days ago the weather had begun to show signs of an early fall. Now the sun shone down mercilessly on the rolling grassland. "Gawdam crazy country," he muttered to himself. "We need to get movin'." He turned to glance back at his partner, who was far too busy with his carnal gratification to pay any attention to Leach.

Soaked with sweat, Roach grunted and strained, working hard to gain his sinful satisfaction. The slight Indian girl lay beneath him, her body broken and beaten, unable to resist further assaults upon her. Her face bloody and bruised, she closed her eyes, trying to close her mind as well to the horrible fate that had descended upon her. Slowly her mind drifted from reality. Like a cloud of fog ascending from a winter stream, it floated from her consciousness until there was no longer any feeling in her body.

"Come on, Roach," Leach complained. "Ain't you had enough?" He was anxious to ride, after having satisfied his own desires with a turn with the Indian woman. He absentmindedly touched the scratches on his cheek, still fresh enough to sting a little. The large bruise beside the woman's left eye was a result of his retaliation for those scratches.

Roach paid no attention to his partner's nagging. Unlike Leach, when it came to women, Roach's appetite was insatiable. Impatient to be on the move again, Leach walked up to the brow of the shallow ravine to take a look around. "Gawdam crazy country," he repeated. Glancing up at the sun to get his bearings, he turned to look toward the north. There appeared to be a line of hills some distance ahead. He would have preferred to reach them before stopping, and he would have, had it not been for Roach's overpowering lust—and the tiny trickle of water that crept along the bottom of the ravine. A slight movement to the west caught his eye, and he turned to stare in that direction. At first, he saw nothing, and then they topped a rise and came into view. He wasn't happy with what he saw. *Indians!* A small hunting party, he guessed. There looked to be about six or eight, and they were headed in his direction. He wasted no time scurrying back down the side of the ravine.

"Roach! Get your ass off her. We got to ride." When Roach still refused to be distracted, Leach aimed a boot at his ribs, knocking him over sideways. Immediately enraged, Roach bounced up, ready to fight.

"Injuns!" Leach exclaimed. "We got to get the hell outta here."

Roach snatched his trousers up from his boot tops.

Hearing Leach's warning, Sally tried to cry out for help, but was unable to summon much more than a loud moan.

"Shut her up," Leach ordered.

Fully alert to the situation now, Roach reached for his knife before remembering he had removed his belt to keep the weapon out of Sally's reach. Leach tossed his knife to him. Roach caught it and rolled over on top of the helpless woman. "It's been a real pleasure knowin' you, darlin'," he said, clapping a huge palm over her mouth to stifle her moans. Her only reaction to the sudden thrust of the knife was a stiffening of her entire body before sliding gratefully into eternal sleep.

"How many?" Roach asked as he buckled on his gun belt.

"Half a dozen or more," Leach said, "and they're comin' this way. Grab her horse's reins, and let's get outta here."

"Hell," Roach replied, "leave the damn horse. Maybe that'll keep 'em satisfied for a while."

"Suit yourself," Leach replied, already in the saddle. "I ain't waitin' around to see." Using the ravine for cover, he rode off along the bottom, following the tiny trickle of water. Roach was right on his heels.

Wounded Elk was the first to spot the two riders, some three-quarters of a mile away when they emerged from the head of a ravine and headed directly away from the Indians at a gallop. "There!" he exclaimed and pointed to the north.

Spotted Bull pulled up beside him, staring hard at

the two riders in full flight. Even at that distance, it was obvious that they were white men and had evidently spotted the Cheyenne hunting party. By their reactions, it was easy to assume the white men had been up to some evil. Spotted Bull's first thought was that they were probably slaughtering some animal for the hide only, leaving the meat to rot. "Let's go and see what mischief they have been up to," Spotted Bull said.

It was a grim scene the Cheyenne hunting party came upon at the bottom of the ravine. The woman's face was battered and swollen so badly that she was not recognizable at once, even though they knew her well. A few yards away, a buckskin stallion stood by a tiny stream, watching the warriors approach.

Wounded Elk knelt next to the body, which was still bleeding out its lifeblood. He jerked his head back, shocked when he realized who it was. "It's Summer Moon," he gasped, then quickly pressed his ear to her chest to see if she was alive. "She's dead," he announced to the others.

There was an immediate reaction of rage among the hunting party, and the cry went out to go after the two white men. "Wait!" one of the hunters near the rim of the ravine called out. "Two more are coming." Wounded Elk leaped upon his pony and rode up to see for himself.

They were white men, one leading a packhorse. They had apparently not spotted the Indian ponies waiting just below the lip of the ravine. Enraged by the scene they had just come upon, the warriors checked their weapons, preparing to attack the two riders.

"Wait," Wounded Elk said. "Let them get closer." Heeding his command, the warriors backed their horses below the brow of the ravine, watching the riders as they closed the distance between them.

"It's Greenwell," Spotted Bull said, recognizing the familiar form of the old man from the trading post by the Smoky Hill. He squinted hard against the brightness of the midday sun in an effort to identify the man with Briscoe. "The other one I have never seen before." He glanced back toward the bottom of the ravine, realizing what his white friend was about to discover. Seeking to spare him from the shock of seeing his wife's body without prior warning, Spotted Bull rode up from the ravine to prepare him. Sharing the same thoughts, Wounded Elk and the others followed him.

At the same time he saw the Indians emerge from the ravine ahead, Briscoe heard Jordan cock his rifle behind him. Taking but a moment to identify them, he called back to Jordan, "It's all right. It's some of Sally's people." He recognized Spotted Bull and Wounded Elk immediately. He held up his hand in greeting. "Maybe they've seen sign of the two we're after."

The news that greeted him struck Briscoe with devastating impact, even though he had prepared himself for the worst. Knowing what the likely outcome would be, he had still kept his hopes alive with thoughts that Sally was a captive. Jordan's heart went out to him, for he still felt the pain of his discovery of Sarah's body. Briscoe's loss only served to intensify Jordan's impatience to extract the vengeance he sought, however. And upon learning that Roach and Leach were only minutes ahead, he was anxious to ride. "Stay here with your wife," he said. "I'm goin' after them."

Sick with grief, Briscoe held the body of his Cheyenne wife close to his chest, gently rocking back and forth as if she were a baby. He looked up at Jordan with doleful eyes, silently asking why God above could permit one so innocent to be taken so brutally. After a moment, the pain in his eyes turned to anger, and he knew he could not turn back, not even to take Sally home, until she had been avenged.

Seeing the pain in the grieving man's eyes, Wounded Elk realized the indecision tearing at his white friend's heart. "One of my warriors can take Summer Moon back to the village," he said.

"There ain't nothin' I can do for her right now," Briscoe replied emphatically. His mind made up, he looked at Jordan. "I'm goin' with you. I'll come back for Sally." He quickly pulled his saddle off her pony and put it on his own horse. Then, with Wounded Elk's help, he lifted Sally's body onto the back of her pony. Wounded Elk then sent a younger warrior who owned no rifle back to his camp with Summer Moon's body.

"Damn! They're comin' after us, all right." From his position at the top of a low hill, Roach looked back over the open prairie they had just crossed. "Whaddaya think we oughta do, Leach, make a run for it or try to hide somewhere in these hills?"

Leach didn't answer for a moment while he looked the situation over. The small hunting party he had seen might not have but a couple of rifles. Just below where he and Roach now stood, there was a deep gully that cut across the side of the hill. "Two men with rifles could set in that gully and pick off half of that little party before they even got close to the trees. I expect it wouldn't take much to chase that bunch back to where they come from."

"Suits me," Roach said. "I'd just as soon put the fear of God in 'em right away."

With his rifle and a belt of extra cartridges, Roach positioned himself at the head of the gully where he had a full field of vision over the rolling prairie that led up to the hills. Leach led the horses out of harm's way around a crook in the gully near the other end. Once they were tied safely out of sight, he returned to take up a position at the curve of the gully some fifteen yards from Roach and waited for the Indians to come into range.

"There's a couple more with 'em," Roach called back to Leach, "at least it looks like there's more of 'em to me."

Leach craned his neck to see, but his view was not as sweeping as Roach's. The Indians were just coming into his field of vision. "Let 'em get a little bit closer," he called back. He was about to call out again, but Roach beat him to it.

"Hell, them other two are white men. It's that ol' man from back at the river, come lookin' for his little Injun wife, I reckon." Roach found humor in the thought. In the next second, the smile froze upon his face, for he recognized the man riding with Briscoe. His jaw dropped as if he had seen a ghost. "Leach! I swear I think it's the son of a bitch I killed back at Fort Gibson."

Leach stared hard at the approaching party. Roach could be right. He did resemble the man in the hotel hallway. "I reckon you didn't kill him enough 'cause that sure as hell looks like him ridin' with them Injuns."

The sight of a man he was certain he had killed unnerved Roach to the point where he could wait no longer. He raised his rifle and fired. The bullet kicked up dirt a few feet before Jordan's horse. "Dammit, Roach," Leach cursed. "I told you to wait till they got closer." What would have been like shooting ducks in a barrel had now developed into a gunfight, thanks to Roach's premature shot. In frustration, Leach fired at the scattering party as rapidly as he could in hopes of a lucky shot. In a matter of seconds, the warriors and their two white allies disappeared from his view behind a deep swale in the prairie.

"I don't know where that first shot came from," Briscoe said as he crawled up beside Jordan. "But them last shots came from the trees near the end of that gully." He pointed toward the lower end of a long gully that cut across the side of the hill. "If we charge straight at 'em, they're gonna pick us off one by one. Our best bet is to divide up and circle around that hill. If we're quick enough, we might be able to box 'em up in that gully." It made sense to Jordan, and Wounded Elk nodded his agreement with the plan. They split up then, one of the warriors going with the two white men, the others following Wounded Elk.

* * *

Back on the hillside, Leach craned his neck in an effort to see what was going on behind the swale. For a few moments, there was no sign of any movement, and he wondered if they were simply going to stay put. A few moments later, he saw four warriors race from the west end of the long swale, heading for the cover of the trees at the foot of the hill. Roach immediately opened fire, but at that distance to no avail. "Dammit!" Leach swore, quickly shifting his gaze to the eastern end of the swale. As he expected, the three remaining members of the party came galloping toward the trees on his left. It was fairly obvious what they had in mind. Although he knew it to be wasted ammunition, he fired off a couple shots, hoping for a lucky hit. Fully irritated now, he yelled at his partner, "Damn you, Roach, we coulda finished half of 'em if you'd waited like I told you. Now they're gonna try to come at us from both sides."

"Let 'em come," Roach called back, smarting properly in reply to Leach's chastising. "They'll play hell tryin' to root us outta this gully."

Still irritated, Leach looked above him toward the top of the hill. *If they get behind us, on the brow of that hill,* he thought, *they could make short work of us.* "Keep your eyes peeled," he warned Roach. "I'm gonna make sure the horses are all right."

Roach cast a quick glance toward his partner as Leach disappeared around the crook in the gully, then shifted his gaze back to the foot of the hill to his right. Seeking better cover now that the Indians would be coming from a different direction, he moved to position himself behind a sizable rock where he could cover a wider field of fire. He then laid his bullet belt on the ground beside him, where it would be handy, and placed his pistol beside it. Satisfied that he was ready, he watched for the first sign of movement in the pines below him. His wait was not to be lengthy. In a matter of minutes, a rifle ball split a limb above his head. It was followed by three more shots in quick succession, all whining harmlessly above him, and all seeming to come from one rifle. *They ain't got but one rifle among them*, he thought, straining to see where the shots had come from. In a moment, he thought he caught sight of a muzzle flash at the base of a large pine when a couple more shots were fired. He immediately responded with a series of shots, peppering the tree trunk and the ground beside it. *That'll give them something to think about*, he thought.

There followed a lull in the exchange of gunfire. The rifle at the base of the large pine seemed to have been silenced. Roach decided that he may have gotten a lucky hit—either that or they might have decided it was too risky to charge the gully. His speculation was answered in the next moment with a hail of rifle fire that caused him to bury his face in the dirt while a dozen bullets sang their deadly song over his head. "Damn!" He uttered as a slug ricocheted off the rock, throwing chips of stone on his neck. Staying flat to the ground, he pushed back to find cover behind a stunted pine. "Leach!" he called out. "They've got up the hill above us!"

Once again, a lull occurred in the barrage of gunfire, and Roach knew the other men were moving to find new positions. He crawled up as close to the edge of the gully as he dared to try to spot some movement that would give him a clear target. He caught a glimpse of something that he took to be an Indian, just as it disappeared behind a rock. "Damn," he uttered, knowing that he had missed a clean shot by moments. Another movement below the gully caught his eye, and he quickly turned his head in that direction, but he could see no one. *I don't like this worth a shit*, he thought, knowing that they would soon have him in a cross fire if he didn't get a clear target soon. In desperation, he leveled his rifle at the spot in the trees where he thought he had last seen some movement, and fired three times in rapid succession. His shots were immediately answered from below and above, causing him to scurry backward from the rim of the gully. "To hell with this!" he decided and scrambled back down to the bottom. "I'm comin' back with you," he yelled out to Leach.

Running, half stumbling, he made his way along the bottom of the deep defile to the point where it took a sharp turn. Rounding the crook in the gully, he was stopped in his tracks. *Leach was not there.* It took a moment for it to register in his confused brain. "You son of a bitch," he uttered when he realized that his partner had deserted him, leaving him to hold off the Indians while he made good his escape. "Leach! You son of a bitch!" This time he roared it out in anger. It occurred to him then that he had not heard Leach fire a shot during the time he was being dusted by rifle fire at the other end of the gully. *The bastard didn't wait around for the shooting to start*, he thought. Being of the same criminal mind as his partner, Roach also knew why Leach had taken his horse as well. Leach knew Roach would be coming after him if he escaped the assault—and with blood in his eye. By leaving Roach on foot, Leach also figured he would be forced to hold them off until his ammunition ran out. But Roach was not inclined to serve as Leach's sacrificial goat. He quickly evaluated his chances of survival, and he didn't like what he came up with. Digging in and holding them off was not an option as far as he was concerned. He decided his best bet was to climb up the hill, instead of running down through the pines. The party had split up to cover both ends of the gully. He figured there weren't enough of them to cover the entire length of it. Maybe he could catch one of them from behind and get a horse for himself.

His decision made, he retraced his steps to the crook in the gully, then climbed up the steep side to the rim, where he waited for a few moments before risking exposure of his body. The rifle fire at both ends of the defile was sporadic now, with only occasional shots searching for a lucky hit. They weren't sure he wasn't still there. He eased himself over the edge of the gully and crawled a few yards to take cover in a patch of low brush, where he again waited while he searched the trees above him. The gunfire was below him now. Satisfied that he had not been seen, he cautiously rose to his feet, and with his body bent low in a crouch, he started up through the trees toward the top of the hill.

As he climbed, making his way through the sparse covering of pines, he thought about his partner. Leach had gotten away, but he only had a thirty-minute start at best. *You ain't got away with it yet*, he thought, *not by a long shot*. The higher he climbed, the madder he got. He and Leach had double-crossed a few partners in the past, without conscience, but he never even considered the possibility that Leach would turn on *him*. His thoughts were interrupted by a sudden barrage of gunfire below him, and he knew that his attackers had stormed into the gully. *Shooting at an empty ditch*—the thought was almost enough to bring a smile to his face. Odds were better than even that he could work his way around them. He knew they had split up to attack the gully from both ends, so half of the party had to have left their horses somewhere back along the ridge. With that thought in mind, he stopped climbing and started out to traverse the ridge. *I need a horse*, he thought, *and then, by God, we'll see if the devil's got a grip on ol' Ernest Roach or not*.

He had taken no more than two or three steps when he caught something moving out of the corner of his eye. Immediately dropping to one knee, he scanned the trees above him, his rifle ready. Certain his eye had caught something or someone, he squinted hard in an effort to pick out a target. Seeing nothing at first, he was about to decide his eyes were playing tricks on him. Below him now, he could hear the excited voices of Indians as they searched the gully, looking for his route of escape. A sudden howl of triumph told him that they had found the trail he had left when he climbed out at the crook of the gully. They would be coming soon. He was suddenly aware of his heart pounding in his chest from the climb—or was he beginning to feel the panic of a trapped animal? He didn't want to admit that it might be the latter. He needed a horse if he had any chance at all. That much was certain, and there was little time left to find one.

With his nerves dancing along the length of his spine, he began to run when he was stopped abruptly once more. As if in answer to his prayers, he saw a horse standing quietly in the trees where he had first thought he had seen movement among the branches. *The devil looks after his kin*, he thought, but he didn't move toward the horse at once, cautious that his rider might be nearby. Knowing that he had little time to be overcautious, he quickly scanned the hillside around the horse, but he could see no sign of anyone. His gaze returned to the horse. It was a mangy-looking mottled gray, but it couldn't have been a more beautiful sight to him at that moment. It was even outfitted with a good saddle. The horse undoubtedly belonged to one of the white men. Even in these desperate moments, the thought brought a smug grin to Roach's face.

Still careful, Roach held his rifle in front of him, ready to fire if the horse's rider suddenly appeared, and then he approached the gray slowly. Watching the man approach, the horse snorted and backed away a couple of steps until stopped by the reins, which were tied to a stout branch. "Whoa there, boy, you ugly-lookin' son of a bitch," he cooed softly in an effort to calm the nervous animal. He untied the reins, slipped his rifle in the empty saddle sling, and prepared to mount.

"Her name was Sarah. The boy's name was Jonah."

Startled by the voice behind him, Roach froze for a second before he could think to react. There was no time to pull his rifle out of the sling. His hand dropped to grasp the handle of his pistol, and he spun around, drawing the weapon as he turned, only to be staggered by the impact of a rifle butt across his nose. Reeling from the blow, he tried to raise the pistol, but squeezed the trigger prematurely when the rifle smashed against the side of his head, knocking him to the ground. His pistol ball ripped harmlessly into the dirt. Roach was a big man, intimidating in every saloon brawl in which he had ever been involved, but he had never faced the fury that confronted him now. Dazed, almost senseless, he tried to raise his pistol again, but his wrist was firmly pinned by Jordan's boot. Another blow with the rifle rendered Roach unconscious.

Gradually, Roach's mind began to grasp reality once more as he emerged from the blackness that had descended upon him with such force. Still reeling from the hellish fury that had descended upon him so suddenly, he experienced the feeling of utter helplessness that he had so often administered to others. It was a sick, paralyzing sensation. He opened his eyes, and the forest seemed to be spinning slowly around him. The sound of voices calling out through the trees below registered in his brain, but he could place no meaning to them. In a few moments, the forest stopped spinning, and he raised his head to look around him. His gaze fell upon a man a few yards from him, squatting Indian-fashion, watching him, patiently waiting, a rifle cradled in his arms.

"Mister," Roach pleaded in an attempt to save his life, "you've got the wrong man. I swear I ain't never hurt nobody."

His pleas, though pitiful, made no impression upon the cold stony face of his executioner. He was a dead man from the very moment he had first spotted Jordan's horse on the hillside. The sole reason he had not already been dispatched to join Snake and Johnny Spratte in hell was because Jordan waited for him to regain consciousness. Certain now that Roach was fully aware of what was about to happen, Jordan got to his feet. In motions slow and deliberate, he took a step closer to the terrified man and aimed the rifle at Roach's head. Unable to look at the rifle barrel leveled at him, Roach closed his eyes moments before his life was snatched away by the roar of the Winchester, the sound of which he never heard.

Jordan stood over the body, staring but not really seeing. His mind was not yet at peace. There was still one left—one final reckoning before the debt was paid. The sound of excited voices approaching from below him on the hill failed to totally penetrate his concentration on the one remaining demon in his mind. Not until Briscoe's familiar twang rose above the Cheyenne war whoops did he turn away from the corpse.

"The other'un run," Briscoe announced apologetically as he walked up to look at the body. "You done for this'un right enough," he added when he saw Roach's battered head. He would have preferred to have had a hand in the execution, but he understood Jordan's prior claim for justice. "I reckon we'd best be goin' after the other'un."

"I reckon," Jordan replied, his voice without emotion as he ejected the spent shell from his rifle.

Chapter 13

Leach couldn't be certain, but he thought he could still hear the faint sound of distant gunfire as he pushed his horse to keep up a steady pace. *Ol' Roach must be giving them all they can handle*, he thought. There were no feelings of betrayal on his part for having left his partner to face the assault upon the gully. Leach never burdened himself with the baggage of guilt or concerns about honor. He and Roach had been partners for a long time, and he appreciated the fact that Roach was most likely sacrificing his neck so that he could escape—even though it was not by choice. In a way, the hotheaded fool deserved it. They might not have been in such a fix if Roach had held his fire when Leach told him to. It would have been handy to have the big brute along in case of future trouble. Another gun was always welcome. But Roach's share of the bank money was tucked away in the saddlebags of the horse Leach was leading. Together with his share, it represented a small fortune—certainly worth throwing Roach to the

Indians. Maybe Greenwell and the other white man with him would be satisfied to give up the chase now.

Briscoe stood silently watching as one of the Cheyenne warriors took Roach's scalp and held it up for the others to see. Puzzled when he offered it to Jordan and it was refused, the warrior then turned to Briscoe. Briscoe accepted the grisly trophy, and the warriors raised their voices in war whoops. Wounded Elk then picked up Roach's rifle and pistol and brought them to Jordan.

"You take them," Jordan said. Then realizing the Cheyenne didn't understand, he turned to Briscoe. "Tell him he can have them."

Briscoe did as Jordan directed. Wounded Elk seemed to be astonished and looked to be at a loss. Briscoe explained that a rifle and pistol were gifts of great magnitude, and Wounded Elk felt he should respond with a gift of his own. The problem was that the Cheyenne had nothing with him that he considered of equal value.

"Tell him it doesn't matter," Jordan said, already concerned that he was losing time standing there.

"It does to him," Briscoe stated flatly.

Briscoe's tone caused Jordan to pause. Realizing that it was a matter of the Cheyenne's pride, he nodded his head and said, "Then tell him I fancy that bone-handle knife he's wearin'."

Wounded Elk was still somewhat puzzled, but Briscoe explained that the carved bone handle was something that Jordan had expressed admiration for and had placed great value upon. Nodding his head and smiling,

Wounded Elk removed the knife and its antelope-hide case and gave them to Jordan. Jordan thanked the warrior and shoved the knife under his belt. The two white men then said farewell to the Cheyenne warriors as Wounded Elk led his hunters back to the southwest, leaving Jordan and Briscoe to continue the search alone.

"If it's all right with you," Briscoe said, "I'll go after Leach with you."

Jordan didn't answer at once, giving the matter serious thought. Thinking of Perley Gates, he said, "I ain't been very good luck for partners, but suit yourself. I reckon you'll be goin' after him either way, whether you're ridin' with me or not."

"I reckon," Briscoe replied.

"We'd best get started then. We're losing ground standin' here."

The afternoon sun, weary after a long journey across the plains, began to settle down upon the western horizon, anxious to call it a day. Intent upon using every bit of the light that remained, the lone rider whipped his mount mercilessly as he galloped up out of another grassy draw. He had covered his tracks well, crisscrossing a stream several times before reversing his direction and riding down the stream for almost half a mile before leaving the water at a rock ledge. Once he was out of the hills, he headed straight north with no thought of sparing the horses. It would be dark soon, he thought, the horses could rest then. But for now, the urgent need was distance from his pursuers. So he whipped his horse for more speed until the animal began to falter. Then he stopped and changed mounts, starting out again on Roach's horse and leading his own.

Bill Leach was a violent man, but his cunning was the asset that had allowed him to escape reparation for his evil deeds. A good portion of his adult life had been spent avoiding those who would punish him. On some occasions, it had been most expeditious to wait in ambush for his pursuer, usually a lawman, and bushwhack him, thus ending the chase. Other times—and this was one of them—his instincts told him that it might be best to run. There were too many chasing him. If he waited again in ambush, he might eliminate several of them, but in so doing, he would allow the rest of them to catch up to him. And he had no liking for the thought of several Indians surrounding him in the dark.

There was something else that triggered his instincts to run: the two white men. Even if he could have known that the Cheyenne hunting party had turned back, he might have rejected the idea of standing to fight. One of the men he identified. It was the storekeeper whose Indian wife Roach had killed. But who was the other man? Roach had thought it was the man he had shot in the hotel in Fort Gibson, but Roach might have just been seeing ghosts. Leach's gut feeling told him that this man was not a lawman, but one who had a score to settle, a relentless stalker who might have been after him since God knew when. So he decided to lose them on the plains. Then if he was not successful in that endeavor, he would have to kill them.

"Dammit," Briscoe blurted in total frustration, "he ain't makin' it easy, is he?"

Jordan didn't answer, but continued to scout along the stream, searching for tracks. The man he hunted—Briscoe said his name was Leach—had gone in and out of the water several times, changing directions at least once. He had been successful in delaying the pursuit, but a man riding a horse, and leading another, had to leave a trail somewhere, and Jordan would not give up before he found it. Using the skills that Perley had taught him, he scouted every inch along the streambank, knowing the sign was there. He just had to be patient. Darkness descended upon the little range of hills, forcing them to make camp and wait for daylight to continue.

At first light, Jordan was awake and impatient to resume his search. After a hurried breakfast, they followed the stream as it meandered in a general northeast direction. One on each side, the two men walked, leading their horses, scouring the grassy banks for any sign, no matter how slight. When their search offered up no clue that would even hint that a man on horseback leading another horse had passed that way, they stopped and reversed directions. Heading back downstream to the point where they had spent the night, they began the search again. Jordan was almost ready to believe that Leach's horses had wings when his eye caught a faint hoofprint in a broad area of short grass. "Here," he called out to Briscoe.

As Briscoe crossed the stream to join him, Jordan knelt down to examine the print, scanning the stubby grass carefully until he spotted another. Leach had done a creditable job in covering his intended line of flight. It would have been easy to miss the faint hoof marks. "He had better sense than to leave the stream in the tall grass," Briscoe commented. "This patch is so short it almost sprang back before we found them tracks."

Once they had found the point where Leach had left the stream, it was not difficult to pick up his trail beyond the border of trees and brush. He had headed straight north and, from the look of his tracks, had not spared his horses. Likewise, Jordan held his horse to a steady pace. The gray responded to the task willingly. It was Briscoe's horse that finally determined the necessity for a stop to rest.

"That damn horse of your'n must be part coyote," Briscoe commented as he watched his own horse drinking water from a tiny stream almost dried up by the August sun. He marveled at the endurance of the homely beast. "How'd you come by that horse—go down to the stable and pick out the ugliest horse in the lot?"

Jordan allowed a hint of a smile. It was the first comment Briscoe had made that even approached casual conversation. "She belonged to a friend of mine," he responded. Intent upon studying the tracks that showed where Leach had crossed the tiny stream, he made no other comment. Briscoe's remark brought back thoughts of Perley and the carefree swagger of the old trapper, however. Jordan had learned a great deal from Perley—things he might have taken a long time to learn for himself. Then the image of Perley's death mask flashed through his mind, and the heavy feeling of guilt followed. Jordan had been fortunate to have met Perley Gates. He regretted the fact that their meeting had not been so lucky for Perley. That thought caused him to turn and take a hard look at Briscoe. Was his acquaintance with Jordan Gray destined to seal his fate as well? Jordan wondered if he should insist on going on alone. He gave the matter no more than a few moments' thought before deciding that Briscoe would not consider turning back.

One day melted into the next as the search continued. The trail was easy enough to follow, but they never seemed to gain on Leach. They crossed a sizable river that Briscoe seemed to think might be the Republican. He changed his mind a day later when they struck a larger river, deciding that *it* was more than likely the Republican. Jordan didn't care which was which. His only concern was the tracks of two horses that never varied from a northern course as they crossed the lonely prairie. Leach, evidently figuring that he had disguised his trail sufficiently in the beginning, was no longer concerned with leaving tracks.

On the fifth day after leaving the Smoky Hill, they came to a faint trail left by the wagon wheels of some early settlers on their way to Oregon Territory. A short distance beyond, they spotted a long line of trees that stretched across the horizon, bordering the Platte River. Not far beyond the first faint wagon tracks, they crossed a well-worn trail close to the river, where hundreds of emigrant wagons had passed on their way west. This had to be the main trail that most of the emigrants had followed. It only made sense that Leach had probably followed that trail. East or west—those were the only reasonable choices. To continue north would lead to wild country inhabited by Indian tribes unfriendly to the white man.

"West to Fort Laramie is my guess," Briscoe offered after only a moment's consideration. Jordan agreed, but decided to cross over to scout the opposite side of the river in case Leach would do the unexpected.

Their supply of food was nearly exhausted, so the sight of vegetation and water was a relief to the two saddle-weary riders. Both horses needed rest now, as well as the men. Knowing that they had to take time to hunt for fresh meat, Jordan was still reluctant to pause from the chase. He was beginning to wonder what manner of man they tracked. Never once in almost a week had he seen any sign that told him they were gaining on Leach. It would seem that the man never stopped for more than a few hours at a time before pushing on. Jordan wondered if Leach sensed that he was being hunted. But his trail had been plain to see. This, however, was to change when they reached the banks of the Platte.

Guiding Sweet Pea into the trees near the water's edge, he discovered a wide expanse of shallow channels and countless tree covered islands as the river seemed to have spread over the prairie with no bluffs to contain it. With no option but to continue on the line that had led them to this point, Jordan nudged Sweet Pea into the water and headed toward the small island directly before them. As he had suspected, there were no tracks on the sandy spit of land.

"Damn!" Briscoe swore. There was no need to say more, as both men sat there for a long moment, looking around them at the maze of islands, knowing that if Leach had crossed, he could have gone in any direction.

With little choice in the matter, they continued across the wide expanse of river, moving from island to island until reaching the other side. Once across, they dismounted and set up camp among the cottonwoods. It was time to rest the horses and hunt for food. It was also time to decide where to go from there, since there was no longer a trail to follow. A short scout along the banks confirmed their original thinking: Leach had no doubt followed the Oregon Trail. The next morning they would follow it as well and head for Fort Laramie.

Chapter 14

John Durden was a stubborn man. Anyone who knew him would have confirmed that. He was also known to act on impulse. For that reason, none of his neighbors in Julesburg were oversurprised when John announced that he was pulling up stakes and leaving for the gold fields in the Black Hills. Those neighbors who were less compassionate might have even commented that it was just as well because Durden showed little aptitude for farming. Although he stubbornly worked the worthless piece of ground he and his wife, Mary, had homesteaded, his efforts failed to make the land produce. He stuck it out for three years before the discovery of gold in the Black Hills prompted him to forsake the plow and seek his and Mary's salvation in the sacred *Paha Sapa* of the Sioux. The fact that it was late in the season to start out for Dakota Territory did not influence his decision.

Abandoning his cabin, he loaded his wagon with everything of value he had left and struck out north, across the South Platte, to intercept the old emigrant trail at Ash Hollow. His plan was to follow the road to Fort Laramie to trade what he could to equip himself for mining gold. Never having been a forceful woman, Mary yielded to his authority as usual, never complaining, as was her custom.

"John, somebody's coming," Mary Durden called to her husband. She paused in her supper preparations to stand erect and stare at the lone rider approaching from the east.

Always alert to the possible appearance of unfriendly Indians, John crawled out from under the wagon, where he was mending a cracked board in his wagon bed. He pulled his shotgun from the wagon seat and moved up beside his wife to see for himself. "Looks like a white man," he said with some relief. He had been warned before he left Julesburg that there were increased reports of raids by Sioux and Cheyenne war parties against white settlements. So the appearance of a lone white man gave him no cause for alarm.

Leach looked the situation over carefully as he approached the wagon: one man and his wife, two mules grazing on the tender grass near the river, and the smell of frying bacon wafting by his nostrils. He could feel his stomach churn with the aroma. He had exhausted his provisions two days ago and had spotted no game during that same period. The option was his to delay his journey long enough to hunt for food. But his instincts had told him that he was still being hunted himself, so he had continued to push his horses hard, determined not to be caught on the open prairie. Once he reached the Platte and began to follow the road west, his concerns were lessened somewhat. He figured that the Cheyenne warriors would most likely give up the chase and return home. The two white men might continue on, but those were odds he felt he could deal with. *If they catch up with me now, it's their funeral*, he thought.

"Hallo the camp," Leach called out when within fifty yards or so.

"Howdy," John Durden returned. "Come on in." He watched the stranger approach: a man alone leading a saddled horse. Durden's curiosity was sufficiently aroused. When Leach pulled up before him, John couldn't help but comment, "Mister, you look plum wearied." He continued to gape at his guest.

Noticing Durden's questioning gaze at the empty saddle on Roach's horse, Leach offered an explanation. "Injuns . . . killed my partner . . . dern near got me."

"Lord have mercy," Mary gasped from behind her husband, at once alarmed.

"No need to worry yourself," Leach was quick to reassure. "I left 'em a long ways back."

"Me and the missus was about to set down for some supper. Why don't you step down and join us? You shore look like you could use somethin' to eat."

Leach smiled. "Much obliged. I ain't et in two days."

"Well, what we got is humble fare, some bacon and beans and a little corn bread, but you're welcome to share it," Durden said.

"Why, that's mighty Christian of you folks," Leach

said, and stepped down. Flashing his most neighborly smile, he extended his hand. "My name's Bill Leach."

"John Durden, and this is my missus," John responded.

Mary smiled politely and nodded. Then she went to the wagon to fetch another plate for their guest. The portions would have to be smaller now, but she would take only a little for herself and hope that Mr. Leach took no notice. It wouldn't do for him to see that his visit would cause her to do without. The fact that she sacrificed would go unnoticed by her husband—it always did.

"Where are you bound for, Mr. Leach?" Durden asked, still curious about their visitor.

"Fort Laramie," Leach answered. Then he quickly turned the point of conversation away from himself. "You folks look like you're haulin' everything you own in that wagon. Where are you headin'?"

Durden took the bait and related the reasons he had suddenly decided to pull up stakes and head for new horizons. Leach, while appearing to be an interested listener, was sizing up the fortunate opportunity that had presented itself in the person of John Durden. There he was, in desperate need of supplies, and fate, the devil, or whoever it was that took care of outlaws presented him with a wagon load. It occurred to him then that he could even take the wagon on in to Fort Laramie. A man driving a team of mules would hardly warrant a second look from any suspicious lawman. And he had to allow for the possibility that his description might have been telegraphed ahead to

Laramie. *I should have shot that other woman in the bank at Fort Smith*, he thought.

There was a brief pause in Durden's narration when Mary brought three plates of beans and bacon and placed them before the men. "The corn bread ain't quite done yet," she apologized and returned to the fire to watch the pan.

"What line of business are you in, Mr. Leach?" Durden asked around a mouthful of beans and bacon.

Leach smiled cordially, reached down and pulled his pistol from its holster. Holding it up for Durden to see, he answered, "Guns, Mr. Durden. Guns is my business."

Durden stopped chewing for a moment while he thought about that. Then nodding slowly as if he understood, he asked, "You sell 'em or make 'em?"

With his smile still in place, Leach answered. "I shoot 'em." Glancing back and forth at the astonished expressions on the faces of man and wife, he went on. "Robbin' and killin', I reckon you could say that was my business."

Having no reply for that statement, Durden let his mouth drop open; his face froze in disbelief. He noticed then that Leach's pistol had slowly dropped until it was pointed directly at him, and his expression turned instantly to one of terror. It was the expression that he would wear as a death mask, for that instant was his last.

Startled by the sudden report of Leach's pistol, Mary Durden almost lost her balance. Barely catching herself from falling into the fire with one hand on the ground, she turned to see her husband slump to the ground, his plate landing upside down on his chest. Shocked and unable to understand what was happening, she turned a terrified gaze toward her husband's executioner.

"No hard feelin's, ma'am, just business," Leach stated matter-of-factly. Then he shot her. The grisly deed done, he put his pistol away and finished his supper. When his plate was clean, he tossed it aside and went over to the fire to pull the pan of corn bread from the coals. Breaking the loaf of corn bread in half, he sat down to finish the small portion of beans and bacon that Mary had served for herself. When his hunger was satisfied, he got on his horse and rode up to the top of a bluff to take a look around, mindful of the feeling that he was still being followed. Seeing no sign of anyone else in any direction, he rode back down beside the river to finish his evil business.

After a brief search of the body to see if there was anything of value, he dragged John Durden's corpse over to the edge of the river and rolled it over the bank. He watched for a moment to see if it was going to sink before going back to pull Mary's body over and repeating the procedure. Although the water was not very deep near the bank, John's body sank to the bottom, leaving it to stare lifelessly at the surface. Mary's body did not sink right away, bobbing against the steep bank like a boat at anchor. Leach looked around him until he spotted a good-sized rock. Straining to lift it, he struggled to carry it over to the water and dropped it on the dead woman's stomach.

The bodies disposed of, Leach climbed up into the wagon to examine the cargo. Indiscriminately tossing household items out of the wagon as well as clothes and family keepsakes, he soon had it emptied of everything but food stores and grain for the animals. With plenty of space now, he threw his two saddles in the back of the wagon and hitched up the mules. There was still a good bit of daylight left, so he thought it best to put a little distance between himself and the business that took place at that campsite. As he drove the mules up from the bluffs to strike the main trail, he felt satisfied with his good fortune. The traveling would be a little slower, but it was only a short distance to Fort Laramie. If, as he suspected, someone was still trailing him, he felt he would reach the fort long before they could catch up.

As he drove the mules along the trail, he rethought his hastily formed plan. He felt sure a man driving a wagon would arouse no suspicion at Fort Laramie, but what if he decided he wanted to stay out the winter there? *Might be a little bit awkward for a peaceful mule driver to explain killing two men right under the army's nose*, he thought. A better plan would be to bushwhack them on the trail before he got to Fort Laramie. That way, there would be no one to ask questions. "I'll just set me up a little camp a few miles up the trail," he said aloud, "and wait for company to come a-callin'."

There were very few words passed between the two riders following the wide trail etched upon the floor of the prairie. Deep ruts formed over three decades by the wagon wheels of countless emigrants spoke of the great migration of settlers to the Oregon Territory. They reminded Jordan of thoughts he had considered when he and Sarah were wed. It had been in his mind to strike out for Oregon, but Sarah could not bear the thought of leaving her family so far behind. If he had not given in to her wishes, she and Jonah would still be alive, and he would not be on this forsaken trail. It occurred to him then that Sarah was no longer constantly in the forefront of his mind. Feeling a slight stab of guilt, he reached into his pocket to retrieve the small silver chain that was the only remaining link between him and his late wife. Found in the ashes of his burned-out cabin, it was the only physical remembrance of Sarah he had managed to keep. Back in the beginning of this death hunt, he used to hold it in his hand each night when he went to sleep. It made him feel closer to her. But the ritual was interrupted when he lay half-dead from gunshot wounds in Fort Gibson. Since then, he seldom removed it from his pocket. "I reckon we'd best rest the horses," Briscoe spoke from behind him, breaking into his thoughts.

"I expect so," Jordan replied. "We might as well set up camp in that grove of trees over there. We're about to run out of daylight." The prospect of a warm fire and a little coffee suddenly appealed to him. There was a chill in the early evening air that seemed to emphasize the stiffness in his saddle-weary body. It made him wonder. "It must be getting up into September," he mused aloud.

Surprised to hear a mundane comment from his typically silent companion, Briscoe paused to think about it. "Why, I expect it probably is," he replied. Jordan's comment caused him to think about his cabin by the Smoky Hill, and he began to wonder about the mules he had left to stray and his wagon and tools. The Indians wouldn't bother his things. His concerns were for the possibility of white strangers stumbling upon his little trading post. He suddenly realized that, unlike Jordan, he had roots back in Indian Territory. It would be lonely without Sally, but he was too old to start a new chapter in his life. When he had seen Sally's mutilated body, the rage inside him had driven out all thoughts of anything but vengeance and the death of the two men responsible. His desire for revenge was still a dominant force in his mind, but the long days on a seemingly endless trail were beginning to dull the passion that had first consumed him. He paused for a second to observe his partner in this manhunt. Going about the business of building a fire, the young man gathered wood, his face expressionless, and Briscoe ventured to speculate that there were never any thoughts in Jordan's mind beyond the day that Leach was dead. Briscoe was suddenly struck with a feeling of great compassion for the somber young man. It was a sad thing to have no place to call home he decided.

"I expect I'll be headin' back to the Smoky Hill after we get to Fort Laramie," Briscoe blurted.

Jordan paused to gaze in Briscoe's direction, but made no reply beyond nodding his head slowly to acknowledge hearing the older man's statement.

"I've got to turn the soil in my garden, and it's already gettin' a little late to make that trip to Fort Smith."

Again, Jordan nodded his understanding. He placed a few more dry limbs on the flames before rising to his feet. "You can start back in the mornin' if you want to. I'll get Leach. I promise you that."

"Oh, no," Briscoe was quick to reply. "I'll go on to Fort Laramie. I expect that's where we'll catch up with him. I'm just sayin' that Laramie is as far as I'm goin'."

Realizing that Briscoe was battling within himself to justify a decision to return home, even if he did not personally avenge his wife, Jordan sought to assure him. "You've got things to take care of. Maybe it's best to leave this business to me."

"No, like I said, I'll stay with it till Laramie. We'll get him, and then I'll go on back home."

"Suit yourself," Jordan said.

They awoke the next morning to discover a thin frost on the ground—way too early in the season according to Briscoe. It served to add a bit of quickening to the task of reviving the fire, and after a hasty breakfast, they were mounted and on their way. With the sun at his back, Jordan led out on Sweet Pea, following the rutted trail. The ridges of the old wagon tracks fairly sparkled as the sun's rays danced off the frost, giving the road a silvery sheen. The sight triggered a memory in Jordan's mind, and without consciously thinking about it, he reached into his pocket and pulled out the silver chain that had held Sarah's locket. Suddenly he felt a warmth that seemed to envelop his entire body. It was almost as if Sarah herself were near. He closed his fingers around the tiny chain and held it in his hand.

"Somebody's camped up ahead," Briscoe called out as they topped a rise.

Jordan didn't answer. He had already seen the wagon standing near a line of cottonwoods on the bluffs of the river. It was so near the main trail that he had at first thought it was abandoned. But as they came closer, he could see a brace of mules in harness standing in the trees.

"They didn't camp very far from the trail, did they?" Briscoe commented. Again, Jordan did not answer.

It was unlikely that someone would set up camp so close to the trail. It seemed more likely to Jordan that someone might be in trouble. There was no sign of anyone around the wagon or the mules tied in the cottonwoods. He thought of the kind of man he followed, and his instincts warned him to be careful as he and Briscoe approached the wagon. Still, there was no sign of the owner of the wagon. If there were anyone about, they should have called out to two strangers approaching their camp. Jordan suspected foul play, possibly another unfortunate victim of the cold-blooded outlaw he trailed. Glancing back at Briscoe, he said, "This don't smell right to me." Nodding toward the trees along the bluffs, he said, "Let's head for those cottonwoods and come up from behind that wagon."

Sharing Jordan's suspicions, Briscoe nodded quickly in agreement, and they turned their horses toward the trees. Suddenly aware then that he still held the silver chain in his hand, Jordan reached back to put it away. In doing so, his hand brushed the handle of his pistol, causing him to drop the chain. In instant reflex, he reached down in an effort to catch it. As he did, he heard the sharp snap of a rifle slug as it passed over him, exactly where his head had been a moment before. The angry bark of Leach's rifle reached his ears an instant later. Jordan rolled out of the saddle, using his horse for cover.

On the ground now, Jordan struggled to keep the skittish horse between him and the bluffs by the river, whence he thought the shot had come. He looked around for Briscoe. With no conscious thought necessary, Briscoe immediately kicked his heels in his horse's sides. Lying low on the animal's neck, he galloped for the cover of the trees. Jordan quickly retrieved the silver chain, and keeping Sweet Pea between him and the bluffs, he ran after Briscoe. Another shot from the rifle brought a yelp of pain from the old man, and Jordan knew Briscoe had been hit. The rifle spoke again, this time kicking up dust before his horse, and Jordan knew Leach was trying for his legs beneath the horse's belly. With no more than fifty yards to reach cover, he placed one foot in the stirrup, and holding on to the saddle horn, he clung to Sweet Pea's side. Requiring no encouragement at that point, Sweet Pea hightailed it toward the trees.

Safely reaching the cover of the cottonwoods, Jordan dropped off the stirrup and went immediately to Briscoe's side. The old man was sitting on the ground, staring at his shattered right arm, where the bullet had broken the bone just below his elbow. When Jordan dropped down beside him, he rolled his eyes toward his young friend and moaned. "Damn, ain't this a poor piece of luck?"

"You're bleedin' pretty bad," Jordan said. "We need to tie something around that arm." He took a quick look back toward the bluffs, but could see no sign of Leach. Then he untied the bandanna from around Briscoe's neck and tied it tightly above his elbow. "That's all I can do for now," he apologized. "First, I've gotta find out where those shots are comin' from."

Grimacing with pain between his words, Briscoe gasped, "Don't worry 'bout me. Just watch you don't get your ass shot off by that bastard." When Jordan shot a concerned look in his direction, he sought to reassure him. "I'll be all right." He took his pistol in his left hand and cocked it. "I'll just lay low while you try to smoke him out." Seeing Jordan's obvious indecision over leaving him, Briscoe insisted, "Go get the bastard."

Another brief look at Briscoe's shattered arm to make sure the bleeding was slowing down, and Jordan was off. With his rifle in hand, he slipped through the trees to the river's edge and began working his way toward the bluffs. There were not many places along the broad river that formed bluffs of any significant height, so Jordan was forced to move slowly from one patch of brush to the next for concealment. Several minutes had passed since the shots had sent them running for cover. There was no sound but the occasional snorting of one of the horses behind him—Sweet Pea, he guessed from the pitch. It was as if the river itself was holding its breath as Jordan stalked the last of the men who had destroyed his family.

"Damn the luck!" Leach swore. He had held Jordan squarely in his rifle sights, but for some reason, Jordan had ducked just at the instant Leach pulled the trigger.

He had no opportunity to get a clear shot at the younger man after that, but he was certain that he had put a bullet in the other one. *At least the odds are one to one*, he thought, feeling confident that at those odds, he always came out on top. Knowing that Jordan would be coming after him, he quickly surveyed the terrain. There was but one way Jordan could stalk him. The brush and willows along the river's edge offered the only concealment in an otherwise open expanse of prairie before the bluff. "You just come on," Leach muttered under his breath while his eyes remained fixed upon the bushes growing along the bank.

A slight rustle in the leaves of a service berry bush brought an immediate volley of several shots from Leach's rifle, sending bits of leaves and branches flying, as well as a meadowlark whose search for insects had triggered the barrage. "Damn!" Leach swore when he saw the bird fly. The man lying flat in the sand at the base of the bush remained still for a few moments before carefully crawling along the bank toward a rotting log.

His patience thinning, Leach decided to move to a new position, fearing his last burst of fire had given his present one away. Moving a few yards to his right, he took cover behind a large cottonwood, never taking his eyes off the brush by the water's edge. He waited. Minutes passed with no discernable movement in the sprawling brush that lined the river. Leach began to wonder if maybe one of his shots had found its mark after all. In all this time, there had been no return fire. Maybe he had gotten in a lucky shot. Suddenly, he caught a flicker of leaves out of the corner of his eye, and he quickly pumped a couple of shots into the offending clump of alder bushes before realizing it was only the wind. He cursed his jumpy reflexes for going off half cocked. Then he cursed the fresh breeze that ruffled the leaves all along the riverbank. Straining to make his focus sharper, he shifted his gaze back and forth along the bank, stopping momentarily to stare at a rotten log before moving on. *Maybe I'd better move again*, he thought as he reloaded his rifle. *If he ain't dead, he might have seen where those last two shots came from.*

While he lay there, debating whether or not to move, he realized that he had neither seen nor heard anything since his first shots had chased the two men into the trees. The possibility occurred to him that both men might still be hiding among the cottonwoods farther downstream. And he might have simply been wasting ammunition, shooting at birds and the wind. The thought irritated him—enough to make him decide to find out for sure. He rose to one knee, suddenly flinching when the sting of flying bark cut his cheek an instant before he heard the report of the rifle.

Without conscious thought, he flattened himself upon the ground and rolled away from the trunk of the tree. Rolling over and over, he then crawled quickly up to the brow of the bluff to return fire. Before he could locate the point from which the shots had come, two more slugs kicked up sand on either side of his face. The rifle had him pinpointed. In a panic, Leach pushed himself backward, below the brow of the bluff. Scrambling back down toward his horses, he searched frantically for a place to set up a new ambush. With not much time to think about it, he picked a shallow gully and positioned himself to cover the bluff he had just descended. With eyes riveted upon the slope above him, he held his rifle ready.

Long moments passed with no sign of pursuit, and the riverbank grew silent once more. *Come on, you bastard,* Leach thought, impatient to get a clean shot at the man stalking him. *Come on, damn you.* His pleas were suddenly answered by a rifle ball that ripped a groove in the sand before his face. The man had circled halfway around to his side! Knowing the next shot might not miss, Leach dived out of the gully. As quickly as he could manage, he gained his feet and, stumbling wildly, ran through the trees toward his horses, rifle slugs nipping at his heels. With no thoughts beyond saving his neck, he jumped on his horse and fled. There was no time to bother with Roach's horse. He left the animal tied there.

Forced to backtrack to avoid Jordan's rifle, Leach whipped his horse savagely, galloping back toward the point where Jordan and Briscoe had first taken cover. Seeking cover in the trees until he could put some distance between himself and Jordan, he rounded a clump of alder just in time to encounter Briscoe Greenwell standing in his way. With his right arm dangling uselessly at his side, Briscoe aimed his pistol at the galloping rider with his left hand. Leach pulled his pistol from his belt, and both men fired at the same time. Briscoe's shot missed wide to the right. Leach's shot struck Briscoe squarely in the chest. The old man sank to his knees, making no sound beyond the sharp sucking in of his breath as Leach's horse grazed him, knocking him over on the ground.

By the time Jordan reached Briscoe's side, Leach was out of rifle range and rapidly disappearing from view. Jordan raised the Winchester again and aimed, but did not pull the trigger. It would have been a waste of ammunition. Breathing hard, as a result of his sprint through the trees, he knelt down beside Briscoe, his emotions battling wildly within his brain. Leach was so close! To let him escape after getting so close would serve to drive Jordan to the limits of his frustration. He looked down at his partner, lying mortally wounded, his eyes reflecting the pain deep in his chest. Briscoe knew he was dying. "I had a chance to stop him," he struggled to gasp, trying to apologize for missing.

Not knowing what to say, Jordan nodded and tried to reassure the old man. "It's all right," he uttered. Feeling helpless to ease Briscoe's pain, he was at a loss, for he knew there was nothing he could do for him.

Seeing the indecision in his young partner's eyes, Briscoe strained to speak. "Go after him, Jordan."

Jordan turned to look at the rapidly diminishing form of his wife's murderer, almost out of sight beyond a rise in the prairie floor. He glanced at his horse waiting a dozen yards away in the cottonwoods. The homely looking mare seemed eager to chase Leach's roan. Jordan hesitated. The moment of opportunity he had traveled so many miles to find, the long days of hard riding, the loss of newfound friends, the pistol slug he still carried in his chest—all those things implored him to do as Briscoe insisted. The purpose of his entire life was to balance that ledger. He could not linger here while Leach was once again getting away. The driving urge was powerful, but in the end, he could not bring himself to desert Briscoe. "Don't worry," he finally said. "I'll get him, but right now we need to see if we can make you a little more comfortable."

Jordan's attempt to sound reassuring did not fool Briscoe. "Don't waste your time here," he muttered, every word painful. "I'm done for. Go after him."

"The hell you say," Jordan replied. "You've got a lot more kickin' to do before you're ready to cash in." He started to grasp the old man's shoulders in an effort to lift him to a more comfortable position.

Briscoe winced in pain with the slight shift of his body. "Leave me be!" he cried out angrily, then attempted a faint smile in instant apology. In a calmer voice, he said, "Just leave me be. I'll be all right." He closed his eyes, resting from the effort it had taken him to speak.

Jordan was helpless to do anything but sit by his partner of a few days and watch him die. After a few minutes, Briscoe seemed to be asleep, for his body appeared to relax. He was still breathing, his breaths coming in short, shallow drafts, and for a few moments Jordan thought he heard faint sounds like snoring. *Maybe*, he thought, *the old man's going to make it*. A few moments later, Briscoe opened his eyes and gazed into Jordan's. "You're a good man, Jordan Gray. You take care of yourself."

"I will," Jordan replied, smiling. But Briscoe didn't hear, his weak smile fixed permanently in place. Several minutes passed before Jordan realized that the old man was gone.

Jordan remained at Briscoe's side for a long moment. Their relationship had not lasted long enough for Jordan to really know the man, but he felt a deep responsibility for his death. Raw-boned and determined while on Leach's trail, Briscoe now seemed small and fragile in death. Jordan had encountered death more times over the past summer than most men saw in a lifetime. It bothered his mind that he was becoming accustomed to it, and he felt a sense of guilt for the lack of grief for Briscoe's death. His thoughts were already focused on the man who had once again eluded him. With an apologetic sigh, he reached down and gently closed Briscoe's eyelids. Then he got to his feet and said, "I reckon you'll understand I've got to go after him." He took a couple of steps backward and stopped to gaze at the body. Then he turned to look out over the prairie, where Leach had fled and was getting farther away by the second. "Dammit," he swore, "I'm just wastin' time." He knew that he didn't have the heart to leave Briscoe's body to the buzzards and wolves.

It was a shallow, hastily dug grave, but Jordan felt it would serve to keep scavengers away. Leach was long gone, but Jordan was secure in the knowledge that he would find him, no matter the length of time it took. The immediate sense of urgency that had pulled at him before had now given way to a feeling of patience. Almost as if he were death itself, he knew that he would eventually catch up with Leach—as death catches up with every man.

With Briscoe's body in the ground, Jordan stepped up into the saddle. Taking the reins of Briscoe's horse, he started out after Leach once again. He had not gone more than a hundred yards when he heard a horse whinny from among the trees near the river. Sweet Pea answered with an indifferent neigh, and the strange horse whinnied again. Jordan guessed that the horse was probably a stallion from the little snort on the end of the whinny, a characteristic of stallions. He turned Sweet Pea toward the sound, making his way through the cottonwoods until he came upon the horse Leach had left tied to a tree limb. He didn't need another horse and saddle at this point, but out of compassion for the horse, he took the time to unsaddle him and set him free. Then he set out again on Leach's trail. Roach's horse followed for over a mile before turning back toward the riverbank. It was the last Jordan saw of the animal.

Chapter 15

"Jeez-sus," Leach swore as he pulled his horse to an abrupt stop and backed him down below the brow of the hill. Pulling out his rifle, he quickly dismounted and crawled up to the edge again. This was the second Sioux hunting party he had seen since noon, and he had almost ridden blindly into the midst of this one before spotting the warriors. He watched for a few moments to make sure the hunters had not detected his presence on the hill above them. Then he turned his head to look back the way he had come. There was no sign of the man who hunted him. *To hell with this*, he silently declared. It was common knowledge that the Sioux and Cheyenne were raiding ranches and small settlements in the territory. To keep riding north would only result in the loss of his scalp. It was time to get the hell out of Indian country.

He had to admit that, for once, he had gotten himself in a bit of a fix. He was fairly confident that he had been successful in losing Jordan for the time being. But he had no food supplies, having left those recently gained in John Durden's wagon. And with the frequency of close encounters with Sioux parties, he was afraid to risk hunting for food, for fear the shots would be heard. He had his saddlebags filled with money, but he couldn't eat greenbacks. The only choice left to him was to buy the supplies he needed and strike out for Montana Territory, and the only place he knew of within a reasonable distance to do that was Fort Laramie. Maybe Montana would be far enough to rid him of the relentless pursuit of the man behind him. He felt confident that he had gained at least a day on Jordan, maybe two. And if his luck held, Jordan would most likely be running into one of the Sioux hunting parties roaming north of the Platte. *I can double back to Laramie, buy me a packhorse and supplies, and be on my way to Montana before the first snow.* Satisfied with the plan, he turned his horse's head west.

Jordan led his horses as he walked along the banks of a shallow stream, searching for signs that would tell him where Leach had left the water. It was the second stream he had crossed since setting out after the outlaw. And as with the first, he was again delayed when he found no tracks on the other side. He was beginning to lose his patience, so he paused to think things over for a moment. Starting out from the ambush by the Platte, Leach would have him believe he was striking out toward the great Sioux reservation, which didn't make a lot of sense. Briscoe had told him that the Sioux were not especially cordial to white men at the present. If Leach knew this, he would hardly want to continue riding north. Then, too, Leach was taking a lot of pains to cover his trail over the last ten miles. This told Jordan that he was most likely getting ready to make a big change in direction. It also lessened the fear of another ambush, since he wasn't leaving a trail plain enough to follow. "He left all his supplies in that wagon back there," he said aloud. "He's either gonna double back to get 'em, or he's gonna have to go somewhere to buy more." The more he considered the choices, the more he felt that Leach would choose the latter, and the only place he could get supplies was Fort Laramie. It was a gamble, but he felt the odds were in his favor. So he decided to break off the chase and strike out straight for Fort Laramie.

It was almost dark when Leach's weary horse walked slowly past the outer buildings of Fort Laramie. He had passed several small ranches on his way in, and he was hoping to find some semblance of a town near the army post. It appeared, however, that he was going to have to settle for the sutler's store for his supplies. The irony of it did not escape him. One of the last places he would have sought out was a military post.

The post trader had already closed his store by the time Leach found it, but a couple of soldiers standing outside the door told him where he might still find a bed and some supper. "Woman named Della owns the place," one of the soldiers informed him. "She calls it a boardinghouse, but it's a little more than that, if you know what I mean. But you can get some supper there and a room for the night if that's all you want."

"Sounds like just the place I'm lookin' for," Leach

said. Following their directions, he rode out the road past the cavalry barracks, beyond the stables, to a two-story frame house. As the soldiers had said, Della welcomed him and, after showing him where he could put his horse up, led him back to the kitchen. He paid her in advance for the room, but declined when she offered other services. He explained that he was not in the proper frame of mind at the moment, but he might sample her wares before he left the next day.

Captain Stephen Beard opened the door to the post adjutant's office and held it for his daughter to enter before him. The corporal on duty immediately jumped to his feet. "Good morning, sir," he greeted the captain while his gaze remained fixed on the surgeon's comely young daughter.

"Good morning," Beard returned. "Is Captain McGarity in?"

Hearing his friend in the outer office, Paul McGarity didn't wait to be summoned by the corporal. "Morning, Steve," he said cheerfully as he came from his office. "And how is our prettiest addition to this homely post this morning?" This he directed to Kathleen.

"Fine, thank you, sir," Kathleen returned sweetly. She had known Paul McGarity since she was a young girl and he and her father were stationed at Fort Lincoln in Dakota Territory. She had regarded him as an uncle, since he and her father were close friends. In fact, knowing that Paul McGarity was posted at Fort Laramie was the only bright aspect in her father's recent transfer to Fort Laramie. As for Kathleen, the orders that reassigned her father to the Ninth Infantry at the busy post meant having to say goodbye to friends she had made in Fort Gibson. But having been raised in the army, she was accustomed to periodically being uprooted from one place after another.

"Are your quarters satisfactory?" Paul inquired.

"Yes, quite," Beard replied. "Kathleen and I were on our way to the commissary to pick up a few things, so we thought we'd just stick our heads in to say hello."

While the two old friends talked, Kathleen walked over to the window and gazed out across the parade ground—partly out of boredom and partly to escape the openmouth gawking of the corporal. The post was busy at this hour with morning fatigue duties. She watched as a file of soldiers marched by on their way to a cultivated area north of the compound, shovels and hoes over their shoulders instead of rifles. She followed them with her gaze until her eye caught a solitary man at the corner of the parade ground. Riding a scruffy-looking horse and leading another, he passed the end of the infantry barracks and pulled up before the garden detail. Apparently asking for directions, the rider turned his head to follow the direction pointed out to him. Then he pulled his horse aside while the detail filed by. There was something about the man that held her gaze, and she moved closer to the window trying to get a better look. Then it struck her. "Jordan Gray," she announced, unaware that she had blurted it loud enough to interrupt the two officers' conversation.

Not sure he had heard her correctly, her father asked, "What is it, dear?"

"That man," she answered without turning from the window. "That man on the horse, it's Jordan Gray."

"Who?" Beard asked, failing to recall his onetime patient immediately. His curiosity aroused, he stepped to the window to have a look for himself. Jordan Gray—the name was familiar, but he didn't place it at once. Then it came to him. "Oh, Jordan Gray, the young man who got shot in the hotel at Fort Gibson." He squinted his eyes in an effort to see more clearly. "It could be, I suppose," he decided.

"It's him," Kathleen stated without hesitation. There was a slight quickening of her heartbeat as she recalled the last time she had seen him. She had excused the emptiness his departure had left inside her by telling herself it was merely a natural feeling of compassion for a wounded patient. Seeing him now, she had to admit that it had been more than that. She was resigned to the fact that it would remain a secret within her heart, for she had never expected to see the young man again. Jordan Gray was a lost cause at any rate, possessed by a vow of vengeance that left him immune to all other emotions.

Kathleen was not the only person intrigued by the mention of his name. *Jordan Gray*—the name sparked curiosity in Paul McGarity's mind as well. He wondered why the name sounded familiar; he didn't recall knowing anyone by that name. And then it struck him. He had not heard the name; he had read it. Feeling certain that was the case, he went immediately to his desk and picked up a small stack of bulletins received during the last month. He shuffled through them until finding a notice that warranted one, Jordan Gray, in connection with a bank robbery and murder in Fort Smith, Arkansas. Without a word, he returned to the outer office and handed the bulletin to the surgeon.

"Well, my God," Beard gasped, upon seeing the notice, "he sure didn't strike me as being of the sort to do this kind of thing."

Alarmed, Kathleen didn't wait for her father to offer her the bulletin. She took it from his hand and read it. Turning to McGarity, she insisted, "This is all wrong, Uncle Paul," unconsciously lapsing back to her childhood name for him. "Jordan had nothing to do with this. The men who did this were the same men who shot him."

McGarity glanced at Beard, looking for any collaboration of Kathleen's claims. The doctor shrugged, having no notion if the accusations were true or false. "If that's the man on this bulletin, I've got to take him into custody," McGarity said.

Beard gave his daughter an apologetic glance, then shrugged again as he turned back to his friend. "I don't see that you have much choice," he said.

"No, Papa," Kathleen pleaded. "It's a mistake. I tell you he didn't do it!"

But it was plain to see that her bias was not sufficient to detain the post adjutant from doing his duty. "I'm sorry, Kathleen, but I have to take him into custody. The courts will have to decide whether he's guilty or innocent."

For an army post, there were a great number of civilians with business in the various buildings that sprawled around the parade ground. This was the thought passing through Jordan's mind as he made his way across the open expanse of the parade ground toward the building pointed out to him. Walking Sweet Pea slowly, he carefully took note of each man he saw who was not wearing a uniform, searching for the face still branded upon his memory. When he reached the post trader's building, he dismounted and took another look around him before looping Sweet Pea's reins over the rail and entering the store.

Alton Broom was busy filling a cloth sack with cornmeal from a huge barrel in the back of the store when he heard Jordan come in. Accustomed to seeing many strangers come in and out of the sutler's store, he found nothing particularly unusual about this one. "Be with you in a minute, friend," he said as he tied off the string. When he finished, he pulled the sack over to rest against several others, then came to the counter. Smiling cordially, he said, "Don't believe I've seen you in here before."

"Never been here before," Jordan answered matter-of-factly.

"That might explain it," Alton shot back with a grin. "What can I do for you?"

"I'm gonna be needin' some things, but, first, I'm lookin' for somebody." He described Leach as best he could. "He shoulda rode in sometime in the last day or two. I figure he woulda come in here for supplies right away."

Alton scratched his head, trying to recall. "Last couple of days I don't recollect no faces I ain't seen before." Then he remembered. "One of the soldiers come in here earlier for some tobacco, said some feller rode in last night lookin' plumb wore-out, askin' about a place to sleep. I was already closed. Might be the feller you're lookin' for."

"Might be at that," Jordan replied. "Did he say where the fellow went?"

"Della's," Alton said. "You know where that is?" Jordan shook his head, so Alton told him how to find the boardinghouse. "You'll know it by the white gate posts out front. There ain't no fence around the place, just two white posts by the path."

"Much obliged," Jordan said, preparing to leave. "I'll be back later to buy what I need."

Leaving the darkened interior of the store, Jordan paused on the single step, squinting his eyes to adjust to the bright morning sunlight. A half dozen soldiers had gathered near the door. An officer leaned against the hitching post a few feet from his horse. Feeling he should warn the captain, he said, "Mind you don't stand too close to that horse. She'll take a nip outta you if you get too close."

The officer shot a quick glance at Sweet Pea before taking a step away just in case. He nodded his head in acknowledgment of Jordan's warning. Jordan moved toward his horse. He took hold of the saddle horn and prepared to mount. Before he could put a foot in the stirrup, the soldiers closed in around him and grabbed him by the arms. His natural reaction was to try to break free of their grasp, but he was held fast. "What the hell is this?" Jordan demanded.

Captain McGarity stepped up to confront him then. "Are you Jordan Gray?"

"Yeah, I'm Jordan Gray. Now what's this all about?"

"Well, Mr. Jordan Gray," McGarity stated, "I'm placing you under arrest."

"For what?" Jordan demanded.

McGarity looked surprised that his prisoner should have to ask. "Why, that little matter in Fort Smith for openers. They say you left two people dead back there in that bank. Lord knows what other devilry you've been up to."

"Captain," Jordan protested desperately, "you've got it all backward. I didn't have anything to do with that business at the bank. I've been chasin' the men who did."

"Is that a fact?" McGarity answered sarcastically. "Well, boys, looks like we've arrested another innocent man." His expression sober once again, he informed his prisoner, "No use wasting your breath, Mr. Gray. I'm not the one making the charges. I don't care whether you're innocent or not. My job is to detain you until a court decides that."

The wave of total frustration that swept over Jordan's entire body was sufficient to almost paralyze him. He wanted to cry out to the heavens in protest of the cruel twist of fate that crippled him when he was so close to the end of his vengeance. In helpless desperation, he tried to wrench his arms free of his captors, but he could not do so. Two burly soldiers on each arm held him securely. "You might as well behave yourself," the captain counseled patiently. "You can go peacefully, or I can have the sergeant here lay you out cold, and we'll carry you." Knowing he would be useless if unconscious, Jordan quit struggling.

The incident taking place before the door of the sutler's store attracted the attention of a few civilians and off-duty soldiers, who stopped to gawk. One who seemed especially interested and amused was a dark-bearded man sitting motionless on his horse near the corner of the cavalry barracks, some fifty yards or more away. Leach could not help but grin as he watched Jordan being marched across the parade ground toward the guardhouse. *Looks like the army took care of that little problem for me,* he thought, enjoying the irony of it. He was reminded of a favorite saying of his late partner, Ernest Roach, and he chuckled as he recited it: "The devil always takes care of his kin."

With a slight prod of his heels, he walked his horse slowly along the road toward the sutler's store, his eyes still on the prisoner now being escorted toward a plain two-story building. Waiting at the rail until the arresting detail disappeared inside the guardhouse, he dismounted and walked into the store. Alton Broom, who had been standing in the doorway watching Jordan's arrest, stepped back to allow Leach to enter.

"Looks like you've had a little ruckus," Leach said, flashing what he considered his warmest smile for Alton's benefit.

"Yeah," Alton replied. "Don't know exactly what it was about, but I heard Captain McGarity sayin' somethin' about a bank robbery and somebody gettin' killed." He paused a moment while he looked Leach over. "You just ride in?"

"Last night," Leach answered.

"That feller was just in here askin' about somebody he was lookin' for. Said he mighta got here yesterday or the day before. That wasn't you he was talkin' about, was it?"

"Nope. Don't believe that feller is anybody I know. I don't associate with many bank robbers."

"I didn't mean to say you did," Alton quickly replied, properly contrite. "What can I do for you?"

"Well, I'm gonna need a whole new outfit," Leach replied. He went around the store, selecting items as his gaze settled on them, pointing out basic staples as well as rifle cartridges and tobacco.

As Alton gathered the many things selected, he piled them together at the end of the counter. When the stack of supplies had grown quite large, he began to wonder if Leach had any idea of the bill he was running up. "Mister, I ain't sure you can put all this stuff on that horse you're ridin'. Have you got a pack-horse?"

"Matter of fact, I ain't," Leach said. "That's the next thing I was fixin' to ask you about. Where can I buy me a good packhorse?"

At this point, Alton began to have suspicions that he was being japed. He paused before picking up the last item Leach had pointed out, a sack of green coffee beans. "Why, there's a feller not far from here that trades horses. I expect you could get one from him if you've got the money."

Picking up on Alton's concern, Leach reached into his inside coat pocket and produced a sizable wad of bills. "Oh, I've got the money," he said.

Alton's face brightened at once. "Yes, sir. Is there somethin' else you might be needin'? A blanket? Some pots and pans maybe?" His customer was a hell of a lot wealthier than he had appeared when he first rode up. And Alton was anxious to help him part with as much of his money as possible. "Are you gonna be in Laramie for a while?"

Leach grinned, feeling extremely comfortable with the situation as it now stood. "I was gonna head out right away, but I might decide to lay over for a day or two." The only threat to him was safely locked away in the guardhouse. There was no longer any need to hurry. He might just as well avail himself of Miss Della's services before pushing off for the mountains. "Yes, sir, I just might rest up a spell before I leave." He started peeling off greenbacks. "Why don't we just pile my stuff over in a corner till I see that feller with the horses for sale?"

Chapter 16

Jordan stood in the middle of the room, waiting for his eyes to become accustomed to the dark interior of the building. Looking around him, he saw fifteen or sixteen prisoners, standing against the walls, or sitting on straw pallets, all watching him. There was a general odor of stale urine and unwashed bodies that pervaded the room, causing his eyes to burn with the irritation. There were two windows in the wall opposite the door, so he went directly to one of them. Grabbing the iron bars, he pulled himself up against them and took a series of deep breaths.

"You'll get used to the smell," a voice behind him said.

Jordan turned to face a tall, thin man wearing a corporal's stripes. "I ain't so sure," Jordan said.

"Hell, I've been in this hole so many times it feels like home to me. I heard the captain tell one of the guards that you was a bank robber and you killed some folks. Is that a fact?"

His insides churning with frustration, Jordan

thought at first to tell the corporal it was none of his business, but the man seemed guileless in his outright frankness, and he seemed to be trembling for some un-apparent reason. "No, it's not a fact. I wouldn't have come ridin' into an army post if it was a fact."

"You mean, you didn't even know you was wanted?"

"No. I mean, maybe I did, but I wasn't sure." He was becoming more and more anxious by the moment, and the corporal's questions were not helping his pa-tience. He began to look all around him, at the walls and the floor.

Guessing what was on his mind, the corporal said, "Might as well settle in. There ain't no way to get outta here until they open the door for you."

Jordan glanced up at the ceiling. "What's upstairs?"

"Guards' quarters," the corporal answered. "Can't go up, can't go down, can't go out the window. Only way out is through that door yonder."

Jordan turned to stare at the door for a moment. Then he turned back to the corporal. "What are you in here for?"

"Drunk and disorderly," the corporal replied, as if proud of the fact. "I never have been able to get the best of whiskey. By God, I've tried, but it always seems to get the best of me and whips me ever' time." He waved his hand around him at the sullen faces. "Most of the rest of us are in here for the same reason: whiskey. Only thing is, I got a cravin' for it that I can't lick. I'd give my eyeteeth for a drink right now. Barnes over there was the rankin' prisoner. He pulled a knife on the first sergeant and carved him up a little. I reckon you're the rankin' prisoner now, since you killed somebody." Jordan didn't think much of the honor, but he didn't waste time protesting it.

Jordan tried to sit down against the wall and relax, but he found it impossible to do. Most of the other prisoners kept their distance except the tall corporal. Jordan learned that his name was Corbin, and he didn't know any of the other inmates himself, having just recently been transferred to Fort Laramie. "I was in a cavalry regiment at Lincoln, spent too much time in the guardhouse, I reckon. So the old man transferred me out to the Ninth Infantry to get shed of me. Hell, I'm a drunk, and there ain't much I can do about it." He pulled his sleeve around on his arm to show Jordan. "I've been a sergeant three times, busted back to corporal ever' time." He leaned his head back against the wall. "God, I need a drink! I don't know if I can stand it till tomorrow mornin'."

"You're gettin' outta here in the morning?"

"If I don't die for want of a drink tonight," Corbin replied softly.

For such a gentle young girl, Kathleen Beard could sometimes perplex the most patient of men when she believed strongly enough in a cause. And she believed in Jordan Gray so much that Paul McGarity was beginning to wonder if he was going to have to have her escorted back to her quarters so he could get on with his duties. "Kathleen," he said, trying to maintain his patience, "I can't just let the man go on your say-so."

"But Uncle Paul," she pleaded, "why would he rob a bank with the men who killed his wife and child?

They even tried to kill him at Fort Gibson. I should know. I nursed him back to health."

The captain threw up his hands, his patience exhausted. "Kathleen, honey, who knows why outlaws try to kill one another? I expect it was over the money. You don't even know for sure that this man ever had a wife and child. That may have been just a story he made up to play on the sympathies of a young girl." Seeing that his last remark ruffled her feathers, he hastened to continue before she could protest. "In my line of work, I'm bound to look at the facts of a situation, facts that are provable. The deputy marshal in Fort Smith had your Mr. Jordan Gray in custody for the bank job, but he escaped. Now, from what I've been able to learn, he and other members of his gang met up at Fort Gibson and quarreled over something, resulting in one of them getting killed, and Gray nearly killed. Now over a month later, he shows up here with a sizable sum of money in his saddlebags. Doesn't that look the least bit suspicious to you?" He rose from his chair and moved around the desk to confront her. Taking her hands in his, he gently pulled her up from her chair. "Kathleen, the man made up a story for your sympathy. Now you go on back to your quarters and forget about him. I've got work to do."

"What's going to happen to him?" Kathleen asked as she was being led to the door.

"I don't know for sure. We'll hold him till I get word if we're going to try him here or if he's going to be escorted back to stand trial in Fort Smith."

She went unresisting to the door, with one last re-

mark as the captain held it open for her: "He's innocent, Uncle Paul."

McGarity sighed wearily. "If he is, it'll come out in
the trial."

"Hey, darlin', did you come to see me?" Jordan heard
the prisoner's question, but paid no attention to it until
he spoke again. "Jordan Gray? Wait a minute, honey, I'll
see." The soldier turned to look at Jordan. "Ain't your
name Jordan Gray?" Jordan nodded. "There's somebody here to see you."

Jordan went to the back window. "Kathleen?" he uttered, hardly believing his eyes. "What are you doing
here?"

"We were just transferred here," she answered, her
face a frown as she tried to search his face through the
iron bars of the window. "You look awful. Are you all
right?"

"Yeah, I'm okay. Just need to clean up a little."

Ignoring the gawking of the other inmates crowd-
ing at the other window, Kathleen moved closer to the
bars. "They say you were involved in that bank incident in Fort Smith."

"I know. It doesn't look too good for me right now,
does it?"

"But you're innocent," she stated, although there
was a plea for confirmation in her tone.

"I'm innocent," he assured her, "but I reckon the
only man who knows that for sure is right here in Fort
Laramie, and I kinda doubt that he'll step forward to
testify."

"I tried to tell Captain McGarity that you had nothing to do with that bank robbery, but he just won't believe me. I don't know what else to do." For a brief moment, her complete faith in him slipped just a fraction. "Jordan, they found a lot of money in your saddlebags."

"I know," he replied. "Most of it belongs to me— money I saved to buy some land. The rest is stolen money that I took off of that half-breed killer. I reckon it does belong to the bank. I was thinkin' about givin' it back when I was finished with this thing. I hadn't made up my mind. Now I guess I don't have to. The soldiers took it and my money, too."

"Oh, Jordan," Kathleen despaired, not knowing what else to say. "I'd like to bump into you sometime when you were not either wounded or in trouble." There followed a long moment during which neither could think of anything to say. Finally, Kathleen realized there was no point in prolonging the visit. "I'll try to talk my father into persuading Uncle Paul—Captain McGarity—to hear your side of the story. Is there anything I can get you or do for you?"

"I guess not," he replied softly. She formed a faint smile for him and turned to leave. A thought occurred to him. "Wait!" he said. "There is something." He leaned close to the bars to keep anyone from hearing. "If you could persuade that captain to telegraph the sheriff in Crooked Creek, Arkansas, he might vouch for me—if that would help."

"Oh, I know it would," she replied eagerly. "I'll go right away."

"There's one other favor," he said. "Can you bring me a bottle of whiskey?"

The request caused her to raise her eyebrows and

cast a curious glance at him. "You want whiskey?" It was not the kind of request she had expected.

"Yes, a full bottle. It's important."

"All right," she said, "if that's what you want, but I'll wait until after dark. I don't want to be seen walking around the post carrying a bottle of whiskey."

"That'll do just fine," he said. "I can't thank you enough."

"You're welcome," she sighed, shaking her head, astonished by such a frivolous request in the face of the serious conditions.

Shortly after the sun dropped below the hills directly to the west of the post, Jordan moved back to the window and waited. Glancing over at Corbin, he could see that the corporal was trying to go to sleep, but the demons that drove him to drink were evidently tormenting him. Even in the half-light of the room, Jordan could see the man's hands shaking. *Poor devil*, he thought and turned his attention back to the window.

The guardhouse sat with its back facing the Laramie River, so it was relatively easy for Kathleen to avoid contact with anyone as she quickly stepped into the shadows of the administration building. Captain McGarity's office was in the front part of the building. But she was not concerned, for she knew that *Uncle Paul* was at that moment in his quarters, where he and his wife were entertaining Kathleen's father. Kathleen herself had been there moments before, but excused herself to fetch some linen she had borrowed from the adjutant's wife. The linen draped casually over the bottle of scotch whiskey she held in her hand, Kathleen made her way along the rear part of the building, which served as a school for the post children. At the back corner, she stopped to make sure the guard walking his post before the guardhouse was out of sight. Then she hurried directly across to the rear window, where she had earlier spoken to Jordan.

"Jordan," she called out softly.

"I'm here," he immediately answered. "Did you get it?" He had experienced some concern during the afternoon, for fear that she might have had some difficulty acquiring a bottle of whiskey.

"Here," she replied, poking the neck of the bottle through the bars of the window.

He couldn't help but ask, "Where did you get it?"

"I took it from my father's footlocker. I just hope he isn't going to be looking for it anytime soon." There was a definite tone of impatience in her voice as she said, "I've got to get back now before they miss me."

"Kathleen," he implored, "I truly am grateful for this and sorry that I had to put you to the trouble."

"Oh, you're welcome," she replied with an added hint of disgust. "Enjoy your evening." She turned to leave, then paused. "I sent a wire to the sheriff's office in Crooked Creek." Then she was gone into the night.

"Thanks again," he called out in a whisper.

"What the hell have you got?"

Jordan turned to find Corbin at his elbow. The suffering man had been aroused from his half-sleep by the sound of Jordan talking at the window. "Oh, a little somethin' to ward off the chills," Jordan replied casually, while letting Corbin glimpse the bottle.

"Oh, sweet Lord in heaven!" Corbin exclaimed when he was sure he was not seeing a mirage. His prayers seemingly answered, he asked, "Where the hell did you get that?"

"One of the women down the road," Jordan lied.

"Della's?" Corbin didn't really care. His eyes glued to the bottle.

"Yeah, Della's," Jordan answered. "I just needed a little drink."

"Well, hell, man, pull the cork on her, and let's have a snort." Corbin's trembling hands had already become steady just from the sight of the bottle.

Jordan pulled the bottle away. "I'm afraid I can't do that. You're gettin' outta here in the morning. If they find you drunk, they won't let you go." In the dim light of the room, he could see Corbin's face droop. "Besides," Jordan went on, "when you get out in the morning, you can go get yourself a drink then."

"For God's sake, man, have some pity. I need a drink bad." He moved closer, but Jordan took a step away, holding the bottle away from the corporal's outstretched hand.

The conversation was overheard by some of the prisoners near Jordan and Corbin, and soon all the prisoners were aware of a bottle of whiskey in the room. "Hey," a voice called out, "I'd like a drink of that whiskey." A second voice answered with, "We'd all like a drink." Several of the men got up from their pallets and started to crowd around Jordan. It was a situation he had anticipated, but hoped to avoid.

"You might as well all go on back to sleep," he said. "This whiskey is for me alone. Nobody gets a drink."

"Maybe we just might decide to take it away from you," one man said to an echo of "Yeahs."

With his back to the wall, Jordan faced them, holding the bottle by the neck like a club. "The first one that tries is gonna get his head busted, and I'll bust the bottle before I give anybody a drink." There was a long pause in the crowded room, with a few grunts of protest, but no one seemed willing to lead a charge. Jordan presented a formidable adversary to anyone brave enough to risk getting his skull cracked. After a few tense moments passed, the mob settled down, returning to their straw pallets with a few scattered comments of "Bastard" and "Greedy son of a bitch."

The crisis passed, Jordan moved over beside Corbin and sat down. The corporal had turned on his side, his back to Jordan, trying to forget the bottle so close, but forbidden. He had started to tremble again. When he was certain all was quiet again, Jordan pulled the cork from the bottle and waved it close over Corbin's head. It took but a moment for the fumes to waft past Corbin's nostrils. In a moment, he rolled over to face Jordan. "For God's sake," he pleaded desperately.

Without replying at once, Jordan slowly lifted the bottle to his lips and took a drink. Watching the pain form in Corbin's face, he brought the bottle down and recorked it. "How bad do you want a drink?"

"Bad enough to kill you for it," Corbin replied simply.

"Bad enough to risk spending more time in here?"

"Bad enough not to give a shit," the corporal admitted.

Jordan nodded, satisfied with the man's desperation. "I'll tell you what I'll do. I'll make you a trade." Corbin immediately sat up, a ray of light penetrating his dark abyss. Jordan continued. "I'll trade you this whole bottle of scotch whiskey, plus my shirt, for your shirt and cap."

Corbin didn't understand. At first, he thought Jordan was toying with him again. When Jordan remained silent, waiting for an answer, Corbin asked cautiously, "What kinda crazy trade is that? This shirt ain't as good as the one you're wearing." He was certain there was a catch to Jordan's proposal.

"Never mind that," Jordan pressed. "You want the whiskey or not?" He plugged the cork back in the bottle and started to take it away.

"Hold on a minute!" Corbin blurted. There was no need for further negotiations. "It's a deal!" He reached out for the bottle.

Jordan pulled it away from him. "The shirt and cap," he demanded.

Corbin shucked his shirt in an instant, pulling it over his head without bothering with the buttons. Jordan removed his own shirt and handed it along with the bottle to the trembling corporal. When the thing he coveted most was safely in his hands, Corbin held it close to his breast and looked furtively around him to make sure no one else had overheard the trade taking place. He made himself comfortable, seated with his back against the wall, shielding the bottle protectively. When he was certain no one was paying him any attention, he took a long pull from the bottle. Content at last, Corbin settled himself for the night with his evil mistress.

Morning broke, chilly and gray. Jordan roused himself by the sound of the bugler blowing reveille. It had been a fitful night with short periods of sleep. Each time he had awakened, he looked over at Corbin. Each time, he had found the corporal still seated against the wall, secretly nursing from his bottle. This last time, he saw that his unwitting accomplish had keeled over on his side, passed out on the floor, the empty bottle beside him.

Due to the rank condition of Corbin's shirt, Jordan had chosen to sleep without it. Now, shivering with the cold, he snorted, disgusted by the foul-smelling garment as he pulled it on and tucked it in his trousers. At approximately thirty minutes after the first bugle, he heard another. "Stable and watering call," he heard someone grumble. Moments later, he heard the sergeant of the guard at the door, so he put Corbin's cap on and pulled it down low on his head.

"Corbin!" the sergeant called out when he opened the door. "Which one's Corbin?"

"Right here, Sergeant." Jordan stepped quickly up to the door.

"Your time's up. Get your sorry ass outta there and report back to your company."

Jordan wasted no time filing past the sergeant. He didn't look back at Corbin, who was dead to the world. His primary thought was to remove himself from the vicinity of the guardhouse before some suspicious soldier questioned his identity, so he walked briskly across the parade ground toward the opposite corner. With no weapons, nor even a coat against the morning chill, he was acutely aware of a sense of vulnerability. He had bluffed his way past the sergeant of the guard simply because Corbin hadn't been at Fort Laramie long enough for anyone to know him. Jordan feared that it would have been too great a risk to make an attempt to recover his rifle and saddlebags. He wasn't even sure where they were taken. He would worry about that later, he told himself. The thought uppermost in his mind at the moment was the stranger rooming at Della's.

After crossing the parade ground, Jordan fell in behind a large detail of soldiers heading for the cavalry stables. No one seemed to notice that he was out of uniform as he walked along at the end of the column. Once they reached the stables, the men fell out to take care of their individual mounts. Jordan walked along the rows of stalls, searching for Sweet Pea and his packhorse. About halfway the length of the stable, he encountered a grim-faced sergeant who stood watching him approach.

"Soldier," the sergeant demanded, "who the hell are you?"

"Corporal Corbin," Jordan replied.

The sergeant knew the man was not assigned to his company. "What the hell kind of uniform do you call that?"

Remembering what Corbin had told him, Jordan replied, "I just got transferred in from Fort Lincoln, and my gear got lost." It was all he could think of at the moment, and he hoped the sergeant wouldn't ask how he could have lost his uniforms.

"What are you doin' here with my company?" the sergeant wanted to know. "Are you on stable duty?"

"Yes, sir," Jordan quickly replied. "Stable duty, I'm supposed to take care of a couple of horses that belong to a prisoner in the guardhouse."

"You must be lookin' for that mangy-looking beast out in the corral." The sergeant snorted a chuckle. "I wouldn't waste much time tryin' to groom that horse. She looks half-coyote."

"I'm just doin' what I'm told," Jordan replied and took his leave.

As the sergeant had said, both horses were running loose in the corral among a group of twenty or more. Jordan almost grinned when Sweet Pea took a nip out of the side of a roan stallion, causing the injured horse to kick at her. The ornery mare spotted Jordan as soon as he entered the corral and much to his surprise came immediately to meet him. Out of habit, Briscoe's horse followed her.

Jordan glanced around him to see if anyone was watching, but all the soldiers seemed intent only upon finishing their chores before the bugler blew mess call. Finding that his horses' bridles had been conveniently left on, he took the reins and led them out of the back gate. Once outside the corral, he stopped to again make sure no one had paid any attention to his movements. Then he looped the reins over the top rail and headed for the tack room. As he had hoped, he found his saddle and Briscoe's there. His saddlebags and weapons were missing, however.

Electing not to take the time to bother with Briscoe's saddle, he picked up his saddle and blanket and went

out the back door of the tack room. In a matter of minutes, he was ready to ride. Taking a final look around,
he stepped up in the saddle and filed slowly past the
rear of the corral. The sergeant in charge of the groom-
ing detail took notice of the man riding away from the
stables, but cared not enough to concern himself.

Chapter 17

"You son of a bitch," Della spat, flicks of blood from her swollen lip leaving a fine pattern on the torn tail of her nightgown.

Leach grinned at the bloody and bruised woman staring up at him from the floor beside the bed. "Now ain't that a nice way to talk to a good customer like me?" he said.

"You've done your dirty work, you bastard. Now why don't you get on outta here and leave me alone?" She started to get up from the floor, but her battered and exhausted body resisted, and she sank back again. "My help will be here soon. I've got friends. If you know what's good for you, you'd better be gone when they get here."

He knew she was bluffing. "Is that so?" he taunted. "Well, maybe me and you better have one more go at it before they git here."

She cringed as he approached her again. "Keep your dirty hands off'a me!" she shouted, trying to shield herself with her arms.

Grabbing one of her arms, he jerked her up from the floor and shoved her over on the bed. She tried to roll over away from him, but he backhanded her hard across the face. "Damn you!" she cursed. He lifted her gown and forced his way between her legs. She struggled to make his conquest as difficult as possible. He repeatedly tried to enter her body, but was unsuccessful in his attempts, at first due to her struggling, then because of his waning ability to perform. When she realized that he was no longer able to complete his intended assault, she taunted him. "You ain't got the starch you thought you had, you pathetic piece of shit. Now get your filthy body off'a me."

"Shut your mouth, you used-up old whore," he spat. Angered that she dared to mock him, he clamped one huge hand around her throat and slowly began to tighten his grip. "Now let's hear what you got to say," he growled.

She struggled for breath as he clamped down harder and harder. Feeling her windpipe crunch within her throat, she flailed with her arms, trying to fight him as the life was being squeezed from her body. Ignoring the fingernails that tore at his face and neck, he grinned down at her as he watched her die.

When at last the battered woman relaxed in death's embrace, Leach released her and let her body drop back on the bed. He backed away a couple of steps, then stood there a few moments gazing at the lifeless body. Reflecting on the hours just past, he muttered, "It just ain't your day, is it, bitch?"

The evening had begun peacefully enough. It had been Della's misfortune that he was the only guest staying the night. He had felt like celebrating the ironic twist of fate that had eliminated any concern for the man stalking him. So he had drunk more than he normally would have, and the more he drank, the meaner he got. It hadn't helped matters when he had at first tried to satisfy his carnal cravings with Della. He had been too drunk to perform, and Della laughed at his fumbling attempts. That was a mistake, and the ultimate consequence she paid for it was her own fault, as far as Leach was concerned. *I'll not be laughed at by any old flabby-thighed, saddle-weary whore*, he thought. He reflected that he had been stud horse enough when he had awakened in the predawn hours and gone downstairs to her room. He had been brutal in his assault, but she had earned it. "You ain't so sassy-mouthed now, are you?" He glared at the corpse.

How long he had been standing there, he couldn't say. When he turned away from the body, tying up his trousers, he was jolted by the sight of an Indian girl standing wide-eyed in the doorway. The two were frozen for a brief moment, shocked by the unexpected encounter. The girl recovered first and started to back slowly away. "Com'eer!" Leach roared and started toward her. She slammed the door between them and ran out through the kitchen. Wrenching the door open, he went after her, but soon gave up the chase. His clumsy feet were no match for those of the swift Indian girl. "Damn!" he swore for not having his pistol on him as he watched her disappear around the front corner of the house.

Well, that sure as hell changes things, he told himself. There was no telling how much time he had before the girl had an army patrol on his tail. He wasted no time getting his things together and heading for the barn. "Dammit!" he swore again as he threw his saddle on his horse, for he was again about to start out with no supplies. "I shoulda got them goods I paid for yesterday."

Jordan Gray leaned low over Sweet Pea's neck as the mottled gray mare stretched out in a full gallop, eating up the dusty road past the cavalry stables and away from the post. Rounding a bend, his horse almost collided with an Indian girl running as if fleeing the devil himself. He yanked back on the reins, bringing Sweet Pea and his packhorse to a sliding stop amid a cloud of dust. The frightened girl gasped for breath as she hysterically tried to tell him about the murder of her mistress. In her panic, however, she babbled in her native tongue, and Jordan spoke no Osage. Though he could not understand what she was trying to tell him, he had a fair idea who could cause such a state of fright. Not waiting for his response, she started running again. "Here!" Jordan yelled, wheeling his horse around her and dropping the reins to Briscoe's horse. It was unnecessary to say more. She immediately scrambled up on the horse's back and galloped away toward the fort.

Knowing that Della's couldn't be far, he gave Sweet Pea his heels, and she responded willingly. With no weapons but his two hands, Jordan gave no thought toward caution. He knew that nothing would keep him from fulfilling his vow of vengeance. Spotting the two white gate posts, he bent low on Sweet Pea's neck again, guiding her directly toward the house.

Hunter and hunted saw each other at the same time. Coming out of the barn, Leach was startled by the sudden appearance of a galloping horse rounding the corner of the house. Jordan charged straight for him. Out of the corner of his eye, he spotted an ax embedded in the top of a chopping block. In one swift motion, he reached down and grabbed it as he sped by. With no more than an instant to react, Leach reached for the pistol in his belt. In a wild panic, he squeezed the trigger twice. With no time to aim, he missed with both shots. Twice was all he had time for before the two horses collided. Sweet Pea, having an ingrained dislike for most other horses, was intent upon charging right through Leach's mount. The impact sent horses and riders sprawling. Frantic to recover, both men scrambled to retrieve the weapons that had been lost in the collision. On hands and knees, Leach recovered his pistol in time to turn just as Jordan reached him. He managed to get off one shot that grazed Jordan's shoulder. In his rage, Jordan ignored the wound and struck with the ax. The blow landed squarely on Leach's chest and sent him sprawling again. Jordan was immediately upon him, swinging the ax with the fury that had grown to a blinding rage. Leach tried to shoot, but could not aim the weapon while desperately trying to avoid the flailing ax. The moment came when Leach realized the full meaning of terror. He felt the sting of the blade as it thudded into his side, knocking him back against the wall of the barn. His eyes wild with fear, he looked in horror, paralyzed by the pain, and unable to resist as Jordan withdrew the ax. In one last desperate attempt, Leach raised the pistol to fire. Jordan swung the ax again, catching Leach's wrist, and pinning it firmly against the barn wall, the blade biting through the wrist and firmly imbedded in the wood. Leach screamed. Rendered almost helpless by the shock, he tried to free his wrist, but the blade had almost severed his hand. The pistol dropped harmlessly to the ground.

"Do you know why you're going to die?" Jordan demanded, his face close to Leach's. "My wife, my son—you killed them. Now you can join the other two that murdered my family. They're waitin' for you in hell." Then, wanting to be done with it, he picked up Leach's pistol. Grabbing a handful of the mortally wounded man's hair, he yanked his head back hard. When Leach opened his mouth to cry out, Jordan thrust the barrel of the pistol in it and pulled the trigger.

It was done. Jordan stepped back and stood transfixed for a long moment while he stared at the bloody corpse sitting against the barn, held in that position by the ax pinning one arm to the wall. He had imagined that he would feel a sense of peace and gratification at this moment. It didn't come. Instead of a feeling of exultation, he was, in fact, overwhelmed by a woeful sense of hopelessness. Though young in years, he had lived a lifetime in the few months just passed. Vengeance had been served, yet he was still alone. For months, he had harbored no thoughts of the future beyond this moment. There was nothing for him to go back to, and he had no idea of the trail ahead.

Subconsciously, he reached for his inside pocket to

retrieve the tiny silver chain he kept there, only to realize that he had left it in the shirt he had traded to Corbin. There was a fleeting moment of despair before he decided it didn't really matter. The chain was nothing more than a symbol. He had never found the heart-shaped locket it had once held. Now they were both gone, like Sarah and Jonah, but he knew he didn't need a silver chain to hold them in his heart.

Suddenly aware of a stinging sensation in his shoulder, he looked at the blood-soaked sleeve of the corporal's shirt, remembering only then that he had been grazed by one of Leach's shots. It didn't concern him. Already the blood was coagulating around the wound. He would tend to it in time. At the moment, he had a decision to make. Should he take Leach's weapons and run, or should he return to Fort Laramie and attempt to clear his name?

The former choice appealed to him. He had always held a fascination for the high mountains that lay to the west. But in this moment of sober thought, he was practical enough to realize the hardship that awaited a man striking out at this time of year, without the most fundamental of supplies other than a rifle and ammunition. There was no lack of confidence in his mind that he could make it in the wilderness—if any man could—with nothing more than that. But there was also a stubborn streak in Jordan Gray and a reluctance to part with property that was rightfully his. He had a horse and two damn good rifles back at Fort Laramie, plus the money he had saved. Besides these material possessions, there were more important issues. If he ran now, he might be running all his life. Turning away from the grim scene by the barn, he gathered up his horse's reins and stepped up in the saddle. "Come on, Sweet Pea, we're goin' back."

Paul McGarity stood silently contemplating the grisly scene before him. The corpse was a stranger to him, sitting upright against the barn, one arm extended and pinned to the wall by an ax. He had seen mutilated corpses before, the handiwork of Indian war parties. But this one was especially macabre in the way the dead man stared vacantly at him as if the eyes were looking right through him. "Get him off of there," he ordered one of the men with him and turned to go back to the house.

They had found Della's body first. It was in the bedroom as Janie White Feather had said. Della's Indian maid had not known about the body by the barn. Jordan Gray had told him about Leach. He had volunteered the fact that he had killed him.

Paul would have to decide what to do about Jordan Gray. The man's story was a wild one. Paul's friend, Stephen Beard, tended to believe Gray was innocent, and Kathleen was certain of it. McGarity had to explain to them that this was not enough for him to release a man on a wanted poster. In the end, he felt he had no choice but to turn Jordan over to civil authorities in Fort Smith and Judge Isaac Parker's federal court.

"Sooner or later," Deputy Marshal Jed Ramey gloated, "they all end up dead or back here in my jail."

Jordan made no reply and offered no resistance as

he was led into the crowded jail underneath the court-house. He had made a mistake in voluntarily return-ing to Fort Laramie. Standing here now in an open room with twenty or more other prisoners, waiting while Ramey removed his shackles, he knew he should have taken his chances in the mountains. Look-ing around him, he ignored the curious glances of the other inmates, his thoughts concentrated instead on the possibility of escape. Prospects were not encourag-ing.

There were no individual cells in the dank enclo-sure. Walls were solid masonry with flagstone floors. What little light and ventilation there was came from windows that were shielded by wide porches above them. Consequently, the air in the jail was foul and heavy with the smell of urine. The smell was so offen-sive that the urine tubs had been set in the unused fire-places in the vain hope that the fumes would go up the chimney. *I've got no one to blame but myself,* he thought. *I was a damn fool to think that captain would believe me.*

During the next couple of days, Jordan tried to re-sign himself to accepting the prison routine, promising himself that his chance to escape would come when he was taken upstairs to stand trial. And he was certain he would escape this hellhole or die trying. He was told by some of the other inmates that if they didn't hang him, he would most likely be sent to the federal prison in Little Rock. He made a solemn vow that if, in fact, he made the trip to Little Rock, it would be in a pine box.

On the third day, a man whom one of the other pris-oners identified as John Barrett arrived at the jail with two other men. Jordan was told that Barrett was a prosecuting attorney and most likely the man who would present the court's case against him. Barrett said nothing directly to Jordan, instead asking the guard to summon him to the door, where he and the other two men simply stared at him. A day later, the routine was repeated, only this time, instead of the two men, Barrett had a young woman with him. Again, Jordan was offered no explanation.

Judge Isaac Parker sat behind his desk, listening to the two barristers sitting across from him. Ben Farmer, the court-appointed defense attorney, was petitioning the judge to throw the trial out due to insufficient evidence against the accused. Barrett still wanted to prosecute, despite the fact that he had to agree that his case was less than compelling. "Hell, Judge, there ain't nobody who can say for sure that Gray wasn't a member of the gang that robbed the bank. And he sure as hell had a fair share of money on him when they arrested him."

Farmer shook his head as if perplexed by his opponent's stand. "John, you've already paraded the only three witnesses to the crime by Jordan Gray, and all three say they've never seen the man before."

"Maybe so," Barrett replied. "But two of them, Crowder and Spooner—two drunks—hell, they don't remember what they had for breakfast this morning."

"Hell, John, you're already discrediting your own witnesses. What about Polly Price? She's not a drunk, and she's the only witness who got a close look at all of them—and she's never seen the man before."

Farmer turned to Judge Parker. "I've got several character witnesses from Crooked Creek, including the
sheriff, who'll testify that Jordan Gray was a member
of the posse that chased the outlaws. And they'll also
confirm the fact that Gray's wife and child were murdered by them. As for the money, most of the cash was
found on that man, Leach's, horse. The amount found
on Gray could very well have been saved up by him,
just like he claims." He threw his hands up in desperation. "God! What more do you need to know you're
holding an innocent man?"

Judge Parker had heard enough. "All right," he
said, ending the discussion. "I'll think on it." With
that, the attorneys were dismissed.

A light snow covered the wagon ruts leading up to
the bridge across the Laramie River. It was an early
snow, but not unusual for this part of the plains. A lone
rider, his collar turned up against the cold wind
sweeping across the open prairie, made his way
leisurely past the outbuildings of the fort, heading directly toward the post adjutant's office.

"Captain McGarity, sir, there's a man here wants to
see you."

Paul McGarity glanced up from his desk. When he
saw the man behind his clerk, he immediately got to
his feet and walked around the desk to greet him. "Jordan Gray—come in, man. I got a wire from Fort Smith.
I guess I owe you an apology. I didn't have much
choice in sending you to—"

"No need to apologize," Jordan interrupted. He had
spent little time begrudging the circumstances that

had sent him to jail. He was content to be free. "I brought you some papers they said I should give you. They said they would give you the authority to give me back my horse and my other property."

"Of course," McGarity quickly responded. Then, in an effort to lighten the serious demeanor Jordan presented, he went on. "Your possessions are here in my office. I think the boys down at the stables will be more than happy to give you your horse. I don't think there's a horse down there that hasn't had a chunk bit out of him by that horse of yours. Maybe you can afford to buy yourself one that isn't part coyote."

Jordan couldn't help but smile at the thought of the homely nag. "Looks don't mean everything," he said. "I don't know if there's enough money to buy that horse from me."

After leaving the post adjutant's office, he threw his recovered possessions on the back of the blue roan he had bought in Fort Smith with reward money Ben Farmer had been shrewd enough to claim for him. Jordan could not help but appreciate the irony of collecting money offered for Leach's gang, and he, in turn, split it with Farmer. With release papers in hand from Captain McGarity, he headed for the stables to spring Sweet Pea.

The private on duty suspected something was up when the scruffy-looking nag cocked her ears up, threw her head up in the air, and snorted. Sensing trouble, the other horses in the corral backed away, giving the ill-tempered beast plenty of room. As a precaution, the private quickly slipped through the gate to watch from the other side of the rails. A few moments later, Jordan walked up, leading the roan. He handed the release papers to the private and stood waiting while the soldier read them.

"Well, there she is," the private said, handing the papers back to Jordan. "I'd offer to fetch her for you, but I ain't had a cravin' today to have my ass kicked over that fence."

"How about my saddle?" Jordan asked. The soldier turned and led him to the tack room, where he pointed out Jordan's gear. Then he helped carry it out to the corral. Jordan threw the saddle on the top rail and, with just the bridle in hand, stepped inside the corral. The other horses parted as the man approached. Sweet Pea stood watching him moving directly toward her, her eye watching his every move. Behind Jordan, the private, a wide grin on his face, climbed up on the fence to enjoy the show. His grin faded to a genuine look of astonishment when the ornery horse suddenly dropped her head and moved to meet Jordan, much like a puppy to its master. The bewildered soldier almost fell off the rail when Sweet Pea gently brushed Jordan's chest with her muzzle.

"I've missed you, too," Jordan cooed softly, rubbing her ears. He slipped the bridle over her head and led her out. She stood obediently while he saddled her. That done, he faced the private again. "I've got a pack-horse here."

The soldier nodded, remembering then. "I'll get that one for you."

Jordan waited while the soldier caught Briscoe's horse and led him out of the corral. "I'm tradin' this roan I rode in for my packhorse. I'd appreciate it if you'd see that the Indian girl who spoke up for me gets the roan."

"She wasn't the only girl who spoke up for you." Startled, both men turned to discover Kathleen Beard walking quietly up behind them. "Were you just planning to ride out again without even saying hello, goodbye?" She laughed then. "Or even asking me to steal some of my father's whiskey?"

"Kathleen," he stammered. In truth, he had not given the young girl much thought during the preceding days. Seeing her now, her face aglow in the chilly fall air, he was suddenly struck speechless. "I don't know," he finally managed. "I guess I was gonna come by to thank you for your help. I didn't know if your pa would like the idea of me showing up on your doorstep."

"You *guess* you were gonna come by?" She kept her face serious until she could no longer manage a stern expression. "Come on. You can at least walk me back to my quarters."

It was a long walk from the stables to the officers' quarters and the residence of Kathleen and her father. When Jordan commented as much, Kathleen replied, "I wanted to see that you were all right." She gave him a stern look again as she walked along beside him. "You would probably have just ridden off across the prairie somewhere without a word to anyone."

He could not argue the point because he knew that was probably what he would have done. Now, as they walked past the bachelor officers' quarters, he realized that he was extremely uncomfortable in the young girl's presence. And he was afraid the pretty sky blue eyes that gazed so earnestly up at him were going to embed themselves in his mind. He did not want that to happen. With Sarah and Jonah so recently gone, he could not allow himself to think of anyone else. They walked on in silence for a few moments.

"This is where I live," she said, breaking the silence. She turned to face him. "Papa says winter is a harsh time to head up into the mountains."

"Everybody keeps tellin' me that."

"Maybe you should just wait until spring."

"I'm thinkin' about it."

She smiled sweetly, then turned and walked up the steps, leaving a confused Jordan Gray to grapple with his thoughts. When the door closed behind her, he turned to step up in the saddle. The girl troubled him, and he wasn't quite sure why. Maybe it was because she reminded him so much of Sarah. That thought caused him to close his eyes in order to form the vision of his late wife's face in his mind. She seemed to be smiling.